DRAGONS of KINGS

Upon Dragon's Breath Trilogy
Book Two

Ava Richardson

BLURB

The battle for Torvald begins.

As the young heir of a noble house fallen into decay, Bower has reluctantly shouldered the mantle he was born with—that of Torvald's rightful king. It is his destiny to throw off the shackles of King Enric and lead his people to freedom, or so he's been told.

With the help of the wild and untamed Dragon Rider Saffron, he hopes to unite his downtrodden people. It will take an uneasy alliance with a rogue band of Dragon Riders and their charismatic leader, Ryland, to challenge the Dark Mage king, but distrust threatens to tear apart the force that he's risked everything to build.

Now, on the eve of battle, Bower will have to fulfill a mystical prophecy and become the leader he was born to be, or risk his future kingdom falling apart. Surrounded on all sides by deadly foes, he must face not only the evil king, but his deep doubts about himself.

Thank you for purchasing 'Dragons of Kings'

(Upon Dragon's Breath Trilogy Book Two)

If you would like to hear more about what I am up to, or continue to follow the stories set in this world with these characters—then please sign up for my mailing list at

http://www.subscribepage.com/b7o3i0

You can also find me on me on

Facebook: www.facebook.com/AvaRichardsonBooks/

Homepage: www.AvaRichardsonBooks.com

TABLE OF CONTENTS

PROLOGUE

THE STOLEN CHILD

The Salamander Prophecy:

"Old and young will unite to rule the land from above. From the dragon's breath comes the return of the True King. It will be his to rebuild the glory of Torvald"

(date and author unknown)

"What do you want for your birthday, Bower?"

I look up at my father, Nev, and tell him at once, "A dragon."

He laughs. "Dear Bower, one day you might see one, if you are lucky. A dragon back in Torvald. Now that would be a sight." He glances over his shoulder as if afraid someone will hear.

I am not yet of age, but I am old enough to know not to speak of dragons in front of anyone other than my father.

Seeing no one in the study with us, my father goes to his desk and pulls out a book. He brings it to me and hands me the heavy, leather-bound volume. "You must read this only when and where no one can see you."

I run a hand over the book's binding and open it. The page seems bright with color—a red dragon. My father touches the drawing and says, "That is a Crimson Red. Once the dragon of the kings of Torvald—the Flamma-Torvalds rode such a dragon."

I touch the dragon—but it is a flat image with no life, no warmth, no hard scales. Looking up at my father, I ask, "Do you think, one day, I will ride such a dragon?"

He puts a hand on my shoulder. "That would be my wish. But for now…" Taking the book from me, he hides it in the room behind what seems a shelf of dull books on farming and architecture. "For now, we will hide your book. But when you cannot sleep, come into the hidden room and read. Learn about dragons."

We start down the stairs to the main rooms, and I have to ask, "But, Father, the king says—everyone says—dragons aren't real."

He smiles, but his eyes still seem dark and sad. "Oh, they were real. And that is a secret you must keep. Our family has many secrets, as does House Daris. One day, perhaps I will be able to tell you all of them. But if I cannot, I hope that you will understand."

"Why wouldn't you be able to tell me?"

My father shakes his head. We stop in the great hall, the entrance to House Daris. My father puts his hands on my shoulders. "Bower, my child, throughout your life I have told you things that perhaps I should not—in the eyes of our king, they are lies. But, know this, I have tried to teach you as much as I can about a forbidden past. You need to know the truth just as one day you will need to know all of the skills and learning that I have tried to instill in you. There is a reason I have you reading the banned books as well as the forbidden stories of long ago. There is a reason I wish you to study strategy, tactics, administration, geography and so much more."

I stare up at him—I don't understand.

Before I can ask, the door shakes with a pounding fist. My father's face pales. He waits and a servant answers the door—he is also pale and shaking.

At once the hall fills with the Iron Guard, and then with a captain who strides in, glances at me and then faces my father. "In the name of King Enric, charges have been placed against you, Nev of House Daris, that you spread lies about how our king's illustrious ancestor Hacon Maddox did not free Torvald, but stole the throne and how you read the banned books. What say you to these charges, Nev of House Daris?"

My father steps forward so that I am behind him now. Glancing around it seems the Iron Guard surround us. But Cook comes up from the kitchen stairs and puts her hand on my shoulders.

My father smiles a little and waves a hand. "Look if you will. You will find no banned books."

It seems a dangerous gamble to me, but my father has hidden rooms throughout all of House Daris. Our family is an old one, one of the few original noble houses. I know House Daris was never as grand as House Flamma or House Torvald, the royal houses. Or they were once royal.

Now they are banned names—just as the stories of Torvald's history are banned.

The Iron Guard march through our house, their metal boots clanking. I try to be brave, not to shake, to stand tall like my father. But it is hard—the Iron Guard is terrifying. I know, too, the stories about them.

But they come back to the hall with empty hands.

The captain faces my father, his eyes narrow and hard. "And what say you to the charges that you spread lies about your king?"

My father shakes his head. "I, Nev of House Daris, do claim I speak nothing but true accounts."

The captain's mouth twitches down. "And do you associate with those rebel troublemakers, the Salamanders?"

Now I frown—why is the captain asking about a kind of lizard. I don't understand this, but Cook does for her hands tighten on my shoulders and she gives a small gasp.

My father glances at me, then at Cook. He gives a small nod as if telling her something, and then looks at me and says, "Bower, I believe this captain will demand I go before the king to pledge and prove my loyalty. It may be…some time before I return. This means you are Bower of House Daris."

The captain waves and the Iron Guard grabs my father's arms. He shakes his head. "That is unnecessary. I will go with you. But who will care for my son if I do not return?"

It is my turn to gasp and I pull away from Cook and stand next to my father. "I will go with you."

Looking down at me, he shakes his head. He smiles again, but his eyes are even darker and sadder. "You carry my hopes, Bower. Never forget that. You must remain."

Stepping forward, the captain says, "The king looks after his loyal subjects. Your son will become his ward, and will be raised by the court."

My father glances at the captain and shakes his head. "The truth is my son is grown enough, and my staff will care for him." He starts to walk out the front door.

I call out to him. "Father?"

He pauses in the doorway. The Iron Guard surrounds him now. I want to beat at their metal skins. I want to pick up a sword to defend him. But he only shakes his head and says, "Remember, Bower, the fairy tales about dragon's breath and what it can do. Never doubt your mother—rest her spirit—loved you. As do I. And whatever you choose to do with your life, know that it is imperative that you survive. If you ever have need, others will come to your aid. Remember Torvald is your home, Bower, to be cared for and looked after."

He turns away and the Iron Guard closes in. I try to run to his side, but Cook holds me by my shoulders and our steward shuts the door. I can only cry out, "Father!"

My skin chills, my heart thuds heavy…and I know I will never see my father again. He is gone—as my mother was taken by sickness, one that came sudden and took her too quickly. Now my father is gone. I am all that is left of House Daris.

But what is the secret my father mentioned?

Will I find it in his library?

Will it help me find him?

Pulling away from Cook, I run upstairs to head onto the roof to try for one last glimpse of my father. But all I am left with is a book about dragons. And dreams of one day seeing dragons in the sky above Torvald.

PART 1

LEARNING TO FLY

CHAPTER 1

UNCONVINCED

And you are sure? I asked Jaydra, my dragon-sister. "*Bower really is supposed to be the king?* I sent the thoughts to Jaydra, but I was looking at Bower—still skinny and not much different than when we first met. But then I had to rethink that. He was different. We had both been through much of late.

Jaydra gave a snort and her consciousness brushed up against mine. It always made me feel safer, as if between us an invisible forest existed which she was forever roaming inside and all I had to do was ruffle the leaves of thoughts and there she would be. I had once tried to explain this relationship to Bower, but he hadn't really understood.

And now he was supposed to be King of Torvald.

Of course, Jaydra had managed to speak to Bower back in the city, when Bower had been imprisoned by King Enric. A man related to me. I still wasn't really sure I liked being a Maddox, but I had no choice in that blood tie. I did with my dragon-kin.

Do not worry, den-sister. Bower will grow and learn. He will become King of Dragon Mountain. Jaydra's thoughts seemed fixed with unflinching certainty. Waves of reassurance and calm reached me. I couldn't feel such optimism.

I had seen how the magic of my blood—the same magic King Enric had—was something to fear. I had found some control over it, but I had as much to learn as Bower.

Thanks, Jaydra. I sent the thoughts back to her, but I knew she could sense my unease.

Ahead of us on the wide river path, Bower tripped over a gnarled root and went sprawling. His hands vanished into the muddy river bank. He pulled himself out, his fingers dripping the thick, black sludge. We were heading back from our latest training, and I'd selected the river path through the dense island jungle as one of the few places where Jaydra could accompany us on land. We could have flown back to the clutch on Jaydra's back, but Bower needed to build more muscle. And he still was more of a city dweller than anything.

He gave a low growl of frustration, strode over to the nearest patch of greenery, and reached for the leaves to brush off the worst of the mud.

"Not that," I called out. Too late. He grabbed the Biting Reed and rubbed is over his hands. A moment later he gave a shout.

"That's Biting Reed." Coming up to him, I waved at the plant. "You can tell from the tiny leaves and the long stems. Now shove your hands back in the mud. It's the only thing that will cool the itching."

He shot me a sideways look as if I was to blame for his pain, but he did as I asked, turning back to the river and plunging his hands into the cool, fast flowing river water and the mud.

"Is everything out to kill me?" Bower muttered.

Jaydra splashed into the deep river as if it was a good idea to swim—or look for fish.

Are you certain he is supposed to be the king? I had to ask of her again.

Zenema is certain, Jaydra thought back to me, and closed her mind as quickly as if she had shut a door between us.

"I guess what Zenema says should be good enough for me, too," I muttered. Jaydra dipped into the river and resurfaced with a burst of hot dragon-breath, showering water over Bower. He yelled and then laughed.

I imagined presenting this mud-stained, laughing, accident-prone king to world. But he wasn't all bad. He knew more about books and learning and history than anyone I'd ever met. He had even saved my life when we had to escape Torvald. And he was in this fight with me to defeat King Enric and his Iron Guard. If we could.

Saffron. The voice of Zenema hit my skull like a knife blade against a rock. As one of the oldest of dragons, Zenema could summon all to her side with just a thought. Jaydra lifted her snout

out of the water and regarded me with her golden eyes. She'd heard Zenema's call, too.

Glancing up at the sky, I saw the sun was beginning to set. It hovered over the western horizon, burning the sky into rich oranges and deeper reds.

Straightening, Bower glanced around us. "Who called you?" He kept looking around as if expecting to see Zenema perched on a nearby branch like a bird. It surprised me that Bower could be so receptive to Zenema's voice. But then again Zenema was an ancient and powerful dragon.

"Zenema. I need to hurry back," I told Bower. And then turned to Jaydra. "Will you guide Bower? This time without a flurry from your clutch-brothers." The younger dragons tended to treat Bower like a toy that might amuse them, rolling him around on the den floor.

Jaydra gave bird-like chirrups in a tone that gave away how she thought this funny.

I shot her an annoyed look. *But she only thought back to me, Bower will one day be king so he must become accustomed to some dragons wanting to eat him.*

Only Jaydra's youngest clutch-brother wanted to eat him. Now, enough. I must go.

When the den-mother called, you ran.

I scrambled up the rocks that hovered over one side of the river, leaving Jaydra and Bower to find their way back to the den. Being smaller sometimes helped for I could climb where few others could. Of course, Jaydra might fly Bower back to the den, but that was her choice.

We had travelled far today, following the river that led from the center of the island and Den Mountain where all the dragons of the Western Isles dwelled. These cliffs would take me straight up to the mountain.

There were actually few land routes up the sides of the mountain for the dragons could fly and didn't need to walk. Those few that did exist were just shelves of rock that jutted from the mountain, big enough to accommodate the wide body of a dragon. Occasional waterfalls fell from the sides of the mountain and lush plants grew on the slopes. For a human, such as myself, I had to climb from one wide spot to the next, coming at last to the far western shoulder of the Den Mountain, to where I already knew that Zenema was waiting at the perch.

From this spire of rock, which formed a wide arrowhead that jutted out from the shoulder of Den Mountain, I could see the ocean, now streaked with gold from the setting sun. Zenema sat here, her silver-white back to me as she regarded the deepening red sky.

Did Jaydra ever tell you what dragons call a red sunset like this? Zenema spoke to me with her mind, as clear and as resounding as any voice spoken aloud. As a queen dragon, Zenema commanded all who lived upon this island. Power resonated from every line and curve of her body, from every gesture of head or eye flick. She was a perfect balance of strength, grace and beauty. Now that I could compare her to the humans and the sorcerer-king I had met, I found her even more awe-inspiring.

No, den-mother, I answered. Sitting down next to her, I dangled my feet over the ledge of rock and sat facing the sunset. The air smelled of salt water and a little of Zenema's warm dragon breath.

The Breath of the Mother, that is this sky. If you see the Breath of the Mother, it means next day will be clear and perfect for flying. It is a blessing.

A little confused why our den-mother would tell me this, I glanced at her. She had often taught me and Jaydra separate from the other hatchlings, because of my human-sized mind I had thought. But didn't we have more important things to worry us right now? Like how Bower would ever be ready to become king? Or what Enric, the usurper of the throne, was planning next? Or if the Iron Guard was still hunting us on the mainland.

Zenema gave a deep sigh and thought to me, *A mixed blessing, perhaps, for legend has it that the great Dragon Mother of us all breathes out the sun in the morning, and burns the sky to blackness at night when the seasons are about to change.*

Ah. I could see what Zenema really meant. Our lives were mixed blessings right now—we had survived one encounter with Enric and his magic, but that had been due in part to luck. "Bower is not yet ready." I used my human voice, finding it easier to make myself heard against the overpowering strength of Zenema's mind.

He must be ready. Bower is the True King of Dragon Mountain. Zenema's thoughts left no room for doubt.

Anger flamed inside me, burning hot and chewing at my stomach. Anger at Bower for not trying harder in these past few weeks to become more skilled at dragon riding and at other skills he needed. And, yes, even a touch of anger at Zenema for insisting that Bower's natural kingship must surface. But I had to also admit the truth—some part of the snarl inside me came from my not being able to teach Bower all he needed to know to survive. I stood. The wind had changed and now wrapped around the mountain as a chill breeze from the east.

Folding my arms, I rubbed the bare skin. I'd worn only a light, skin tunic and my skin trousers, and had no boots or cloak. Glancing at Zenema, I told her, "Have you seen him? He's no

15

natural flier. The other dragons in the clutch don't respect him, and he is still the worst fighter I've ever seen. How is he going to lead dragons back to their rightful place on the mainland? How is he to defeat Enric? All the world fears dragons because of Enric and the lies he and his father and his father's father have spread."

Zenema turned her head to look at me with her glowing eyes that swirled bright colors. *Do you think Zenema must be mistaken? That old Zenema's aging mind no longer can see the truth?*

Fear washed over me, chilling me even more than the wind. She would never hurt me, but it was still intimidating to have such a huge and old dragon looking at me with annoyance. "No, of course not—it's just..." I waved my hand.

Zenema nudged me with her nose. The rock below me slid from the cliff, and I struggled to keep my balance.

Reaching out, Zenema grabbed my tunic with one claw and pulled me back onto the perch as if I were any other hatchling and unable to look after myself. She raised her neck and looked down on me. *Even Saffron falls sometimes. That is why Saffron has dragon-kin to look after you. Saffron is now Bower's kin, so Jaydra is Bower's kin as well. We look after Bower, and Bower will be ready when he must be. His fate is in his blood, just as magic is in yours.*

Biting my lower lip, I wanted to deny the truth of that. I didn't know if Enric had been left mad because of his magic, or if he was mad before that. He had seemed so…so fair and good at first. I thought I'd found my family. But it had all been a sham. His mind and his body were as rotting and foul as his intentions. I shuddered. Would magic leave me like that, too?

What if the things we carried inside us ended hurting the ones we loved?

Zenema folded a wing around me and pulled me closer to her side. Her warmth held off the evening's cooling air, and her voice inside my mind seemed just as warm and encouraging, full of understanding. *Some dragons are born big. Others are born fast like Jaydra. Some dragons are gold and others have long tails. They are all dragons. What some of the Maddox clan did with their magic might be evil. But your mother and father brought you away for safekeeping. That shows good in them. So… magic is just that—it is magic in the blood. The same is true for Bower. He has the blood of Dragon Kings within him, but it is up to Bower to show if he will be a good and wise king or a weak one. And it up to us, and what we teach him.*

"Yes, den-mother," I said and curled up closer to her side. It felt better to know she believed we could teach Bower, but how long was all this going to take?

*   *   *

After our chat on the perch, I left Zenema to the evening sky and clambered up to the tunnel into Den Mountain. Hundreds of dragons over thousands of years had lived here in the Western Isles, so the mountain was riddled with tunnels and den-caves dug out by all the den-mothers for their clutches. Many of the tunnels opened to the sky, and inside the tunnels wove together into a maze. I knew it only because I had grown up here, looked over by Zenema and raised by her after my parents had left me in a cave on the beach.

It was nice to be surrounded by the cool gray and yellow rock of the tunnels again. Contrary to what the island villagers thought, dragons were actually hygienic creatures who kept their dens clean. The tunnels smelled faintly of ash and minerals, but no dung was allowed in the tunnels, as every young dragon learned as soon as it hatched. I didn't even need a light, as I knew most of the routes by touch alone, and moonlight spilled into the entrances, glinting off the crystals in the walls, helping me see the walls that had been carved into smooth curves by hot dragon breath and polished by dragon scales.

Stopping, I lifted my face for I smelled something odd— something like smoke, but sweeter. Holding still, I wondered if the island villagers had lost control of a fire and set the jungle ablaze.

It had happened once before, when I was very young. The island villagers had been celebrating something, and their fires

18

had gone wild and free, burning into the jungle with roaring, orange flames that had lit the entire island. It had been a night of terror and loud noises as dragons swooped and shrieked and flew around Den Mountain. Zenema's fierce roar had stopped the confusion and she'd organized the dragons to catch up water in their mouths and drop it onto the flames. The island villagers had never thanked the dragons, and the fire had ended up destroying most of their huts. They had never done anything so stupid again. They also learned to keep far from Den Mountain and the dragons they had angered.

Saffron? Jaydra's thoughts tickled my mind. I could sense her raising her head from where she had tucked it under her wing. She snuffed at the air and started to unfold her wings and legs.

Are we under attack? I asked her with my thoughts.

I could see nothing but the dark cavern—no fires seemed to be burning around Den Mountain. I heard nothing but my rapid heartbeat in my ears and my quick, shallow breaths. No crackle of flames carried to me on the breeze. There was just that faint smell of sweet smoke—it almost smelled like cherries.

Heading back to the tunnel entrance, I tried to follow the aroma. *Come, Jaydra, but do not warn the others, yet.* I sent the thought to Jaydra, and she sent me back a terse agreement. She also started to worm her way through the tunnels, heading toward me.

The smell of smoke became fainter as I headed out of the tunnel, so I turned and started back inside Den Mountain again. The smell became stronger and I followed it down a narrow, smaller tunnel that seemed too small for any dragon. Rocks littered the ground and I realized the tunnel must be one where the roof had fallen in, which happened sometimes. I glanced up at the roof and kicked one of the rocks. It rolled and echoed, but the tunnel seemed safe. Slipping past some of the boulders, I headed into the dark tunnel.

Saffron? You have gone where Jaydra cannot follow. Jaydra's frustration came through to me clearly. She couldn't get down this narrow tunnel. I asked her to stay calm and wait and kept following the smoke.

The smoke was wafting up from deep inside Den Mountain. I crept forward, my eyes stinging now. The tunnel twisted and turned and led out onto a narrow ledge that overlooked the jungle below. For a moment I could see nothing, but then I glimpsed a small glow, as if from a pipe. The faint glow lit a man's face and a long, white beard.

It had to be the Hermit.

The Lonesome One! Jaydra said in my mind, confirming my thoughts.

The Hermit lived not far from Den Mountain, in an old stone ruin right on the shore. Normally, he never went anywhere and had little to do with the dragons or even with the villagers. But then again, the Hermit was always doing strange things, like sailing around the island once in a boat he had built from skins and wood.

Jaydra's shadow passed over me as she glided overhead, having gone out of the den through one of the other tunnels. *Chase him?*

I shook my head. "No. Leave him alone."

It was from the Hermit that I'd learned to read and write. The Hermit had a few books, and Zenema had some kind of bond with the Hermit—at least enough that he allowed me to see the books and taught me a few things. I looked up at the perch, but I could no longer see Zenema's form blotting out the stars.

When I glanced down again, I could no longer see the orange glow of what had to have been the Hermit's pipe. He must have gone back to his tower already and taken his cherry-scented smoke with him.

Had the Hermit heard my talk with Zenema? Could he hear dragons in the way Bower almost could?

The Hermit was supposed to be the most knowledgeable human on the island, a friend to Zenema at least. Maybe he knew more than I'd ever thought about magic, my mother, and even the Maddox clan?

More importantly, maybe he knew how to teach a king to lead.

Saffron, ask Zenema first if you are going to do what you are thinking, Jaydra warned.

I gave a rude snort, but Jaydra only soared higher in the sky.

However, my heart was beating fast now. I had a plan. Now I just had to find Bower and take him with me to visit the Hermit of the Western Isles.

CHAPTER 2

INTRUDERS & CHERRY-SMOKE

Jaydra let me fly back to the den on her back, and from the way she had nudged me up onto her back and winked at me, I knew she did not want me telling Saffron I'd flown on Jaydra. Sometimes, Saffron seemed to think Jaydra was just her friend and wasn't mine. It was annoying.

Flying on a dragon's back was always a little frightening. I clung to Jaydra's scales with hands and legs and concentrated on staring at the horizon and not looking down. The sea seemed to stretch out forever around us with the islands dots of green amid the blue. Wind tugged at my hair. I could almost feel a sense of joy and freedom from Jaydra, but maybe I was imagining that. I could almost wish Jaydra would fly far away with me. But I knew there was no escaping my fate—I had to do something to save my city and my kingdom from Enric's harsh rule. But with the Iron Guard at his command, I had no idea how I was going to do that.

Jaydra spiraled down from the clouds to land on one of the wide ledges of the mountain. I climbed from her back and we both headed inside the den. It was dark in the sandy cavern, but not black. Shafts of light from the setting sun speared down through the tunnel entrances, splashing gold on the walls and pulling colors from crystals embedded in the rock. The sight reminded me of the colored drawings I had seen in my books, and a pang for the loss of my library twisted inside me. But this, in a way, was better—this place had very live dragons. The gentle breath of the dragons warmed the caverns.

Surprisingly, the dragons went to bed early, almost as soon as the sun set. Cold-blooded beings, they needed the heat of the sun and the heat of the earth. Even though I'd now lived here for a few weeks, every night still filled me with the same sense of awe. Only the exhaustion of training allowed me to sleep through the night. I still couldn't believe that I was here, living with not just one dragon, but a whole nest of them. I lived with legends—with dragons that I'd been taught were just creatures of myth used to scare children.

I'd found instead they could be cranky, noisy, gentle—they were all very much individuals. And the young dragons for some reason thought of me more like a toy to be knocked around. At least they were asleep now, deep in Den Mountain.

Heading to my bed, which was little more than an alcove not far from the tiny nook where Saffron slept, I tugged off my belt, pulled off my boots and stretched out on the leaves Saffron had gathered for me. In turn, I had shown her how to use oil pressed from the leaves and some of the nuts that grew here, and a crystalline rock to make a simple lamp. I didn't bother to light my lamp now—I still failed more often with the steel and flint I had to use to make a fire.

It was warm enough in the cavern that I'd no need for extra warmth—not even for a blanket. Heat from within Den Mountain warmed the rock under the leaves that I lay on, and it felt good against muscles that ached from the day. And flying here on Jaydra had let the wind dry my clothes. They were becoming tattered, and I'd soon need to trade for new ones or switch to skins such as Saffron wore.

A king in rags—that was what I was.

It was a depressing thought, so I rolled over and stared out into the dark tunnels and thought of the dragons instead.

I'd been trying to keep a journal on dragons, but it was hard to write down everything.

These dragons seemed to all be predominantly an iridescent sea-green color, shifting at times from a bright turquoise to an almost forest green. A few boasted white, shimmering scales—like Zenema. And I'd spotted two young ones who had deep, orange scales. I still didn't know if color meant anything. Was Zenema so large because she was a white dragon, or was that a sign of age? And were these dragons refugees from Dragon Mountain near Torvald—the dragons of old stories and tales? Perhaps they had fled here to the Western Isles after Hacon Maddox—Enric's ancestor—and his Iron Guard had betrayed the True King and seized power? Or were these dragons of a kind that had never been ridden by humans?

Did even Zenema, the den-mother and the oldest dragon here as far as I could tell, know the answers?

The way she looks at me sometimes...

I shivered and turned onto my back again, my muscles sore and my joints aching. It seemed at times that she could see into my mind. I knew Zenema—and the other dragons—could send thoughts to each other, and even to people. I had heard Jaydra at times...or I thought I did. It was difficult to really know if I was just imagining such things, and I had no idea how to become better at talking to a dragon.

Saffron seemed intent more on making me learn the physical side of how to survive and fight. She had me learning to tie vines together and how to reach up and grab Jaydra's claws. She had me walking along the highest branches of the tallest trees, and jumping from the tops of rocky waterfalls to dive into the river below. My life had become climbing, running and then sparring against Saffron using long staffs or wooden swords. She'd taught me how to light a fire, find food in the jungle and even to read the elements around me.

But I kept forgetting everything, it seemed.

"You have to feel the wind," she had said to me just today, which sounded like nonsense. "Feel how it moves. Is a storm coming? Is it a warm breeze from the desert? What will it bring to you?"

Sighing, I tucked my hands under my head.

Did the Dragon Riders of old have to learn all this? Or was Saffron just afraid I was going to get myself killed by taking a stroll through the woods?

A sudden pang of misery rose up inside my, almost choking me. How I could use my library right now. I thought of all of the banned books I had collected—ancient scrolls said to be written during the time of old King Torvald and even from when the Dragon Monastery had first been founded. They might have told me what a dragon rider really needed to learn.

And I'd had the writings of Strategicus, the ancient philosopher and tactician, as well as Instructor Mordecai, the alchemist. I'd scribbled a few things I'd remembered into my journal, but I had so little paper and so much to learn.

Including how to raise an army.

I had dragons—or rather I lived with dragons. But I needed riders—and enough strength to overcome Enric's Iron Guard, those seemingly mindless mechanical soldiers who obeyed Enric's every order. Saffron and I had saved Torvald from Enric's plan to wipe it clean—but now Enric hunted us. Even in the Western Isles we had heard that news.

And Saffron seemed to think that all I had to be was a strong enough warrior, know how to ride a dragon, and the rest magically happened. As if my showing up on a dragon and twirling a sword would inspire trust and awe. I wasn't so sure. Those on the mainland had been taught to think dragons fearful beasts that existed in old stories—seeing one might well send them running and not to my side.

What I needed was an army and maps and scouts and—

A hissing from the dark cut off my thoughts and had me sitting upright. Saffron, a slim shadow in the moonlight, crept up to my side, her red-gold hair glinting in the faint light.

"What is it?" I rubbed at my sore shoulders.

"Follow me. We're going on a new exercise tonight," she whispered. She turned and headed down the tunnel.

I let out another long breath. It wasn't enough she tortured me all day, now she had to do so at night as well.

But I grabbed my belt with my knife and rope and pulled on my boots. As I followed Saffron's light steps, I swear I saw a flash of white, but when I turned I saw nothing. Was Zenema watching? Did some dragons sleep with their eyes open?

"Don't wake the others," Saffron hissed at me. Turning to her, I hurried out into the night.

I was fast enough to bump into her back, and she glanced back. Thankfully, it was too dark to see her expression, but I could practically feel her annoyance. The moon hung in the sky, half full and offering some light, but leaving the world no color. As always, Saffron had no difficulties navigating her way down the side of Den Mountain, climbing more like a mountain goat than a person. I followed more slowly, picking my path carefully, testing each rock to make certain it would not slip out from my boot.

Once we reached the jungle floor, Saffron seemed to disappear into the trees.

Was this a test to see if I could follow?

I lifted my face and thought about what she'd said about the wind, and sure enough a thrash of leaves came to me on the breeze—that was Saffron.

I followed her. Saffron seemed much more intent on speed than silence. Beside her hurried steps, I picked out the cries of nocturnal birds, frogs croaking near the river, the buzzing of insects, and other animals moving through the dense jungle leaves. It seemed the island was even more alive at night—and probably everything would be trying to kill or eat me.

Sometimes I really missed Torvald and a soft bed and the comfortable chair in my library.

Glancing back at me, Saffron muttered, "Not far now." She clambered down a path that sloped to the river.

"Just where are we going?"

She pointed down the river and to a rise, a place where the trees thinned. I smelled a change in the air, too. It seemed brisk, bringing with it the salt tang of the ocean.

"We're near the shore?" I said.

Saffron nodded. Her teeth flashed white in a fast smile. "You're finally learning to read the wind." Her smile faded and she glanced around us. The way she was frowning—the expression barely visible in the moonlight—left me certain this was not just a simple night of training.

"Why are we here?" I asked, uneasy now. I followed Saffron as she moved up the hill and away from the cover of the jungle trees. She halted on one of the larger boulders and stood so still she could almost be mistaken for a statue—or one of the Iron Guard.

Stopping beside her, I glanced around. Below us, the surf hit against jagged rocks with a rumbling and then sloshed away again. The spray blasted up into the air, bringing the tang of ocean and kelp. Saffron's caution was infecting me. I kept looking around us, certain someone was watching, but I could see nothing other than the rough cliffs that led up to Den Mountain and the spill of moonlight on the ocean.

Saffron nodded and pointed just ahead of us.

Following her gesture, I spotted a squat tower. Or, to be more precise, what remained of a ruined tower on a spit of rock. The tower stood out, unmistakable against the dark water and darker gray boulders, its smooth walls rounded and the top long ago shattered and left a jagged edge. Just beyond it, I glimpsed a small beach and the white froth of the tidewater washing up on the sand.

"It's an old lighthouse," I said. That much seemed obvious, seeing how the place marked the ocean side of the island and made the rocky shore stand out.

"A what?" Saffron glanced at me, her head tipped to one side. She tossed her one long braid back over her shoulder and shook her head. "It's the Hermit's tower."

"You never said a hermit lived on the island. Right next to the dragons. He's probably the lighthouse keeper."

"What is this lighter house you keep speaking of?" Saffron started walking to the tower, picking her way over the rocky shoreline.

I struggled to keep up with her, but told her, "A lighthouse, not a lighter house, as in a place where there is light to mark land for anyone who sails. The old books spoke of such towers all along the shoreline of Torvald, as well as beacon and watchtowers here. They guarded the kingdom, helped warn of danger. I've read they even helped guide dragon riders through storms. Along with the

31

Dragon Horns, that was one of the ways the riders of Torvald communicated."

Saffron's head came up and she paused long enough for me to catch up with her. "The Dragon Horns?"

Spreading my hands wide, I told her. "Huge horns said to have been made in the earliest days, and encased in gold and bronze. Bigger than a grown man's height and loud enough to be heard for miles and miles. They were sounded to alert the Middle Kingdom of danger and they also sounded out for celebrations."

Saffron shook her head and started for the ruined tower again. "How can anything be so loud? But we haven't come to the Hermit for stories like that. We need his help—his books."

"Books!" I hurried to catch up with Saffron. "Why didn't you tell me he has books? This salt air isn't good for them, you know. Unless they're cared for, they can get moldy—it's too damp here."

"Why do you care so much for books?" Saffron said, the words grumbled.

I threw my hands wide again. "Saffron, books are more to me than just past knowledge. Everyone in Torvald has been forbidden to learn, but my father rebelled against that. He taught me the value of knowledge. And if this hermit lives in one of the old towers...well, what if some of his books are very old. He might know about the old lighthouses, and even the watchtowers and even where the Dragon Monasteries once stood. He could have maps and…and a dozen other things we need to know." I strode ahead of her, then had a second thought and glanced back. "But this hermit of yours—he's friendly, right?"

Saffron only shrugged an answer and headed for the tower.

As we got closer, I saw the tower was stones closely fitted against each other. It must have once stood three times its height. Stones that had once made up the upper part of the tower lay scattered around, looking as if they'd been blasted apart. That thought left me uneasy. Only a dragon could cause such destruction. Had the dragons torn this tower down? Or was it smaller to better hide it among the boulders of the shore?

One thing was for certain—it no longer acted as a lighthouse.

"There's no lanterns burning," I said when we reached a narrow door, blackened with age and salt. Someone had used panels and bits of sea-weathered oak to board up the windows and make the door.

I raised my fist to knock.

"Wait," Saffron said, reaching for my arm, but it was too late. I'd already rapped my knuckles against the wood.

I barely heard the knock over the rumbling surf that surged up against the beach, but it was still loud enough. However, no one answered. Maybe the hermit was asleep. I pushed at the door and it creaked open.

I glanced at Saffron. "It's not locked."

She pulled her bone-handled knife from its sheath. "It should be." She stepped into the dark room.

Swallowing hard, I followed.

A narrow entrance and short hall turned once and then opened into a larger room with a stone floor. Glancing around in the dim light that fell into the room from the open door, I could see nothing but what looked like a roughly hewn chair now broken apart, an iron grate set up in a crumbling fireplace and an old, sagging cot. Everything looked dusty and poorly kept. "Are you sure someone lives here?" I asked.

Saffron just waved for me to be quiet and stepped deeper into the tower room. A stone stairway led to an upper level where the floor and ceiling were made of wood. A fire burned here in another iron grate. This room held empty shelves and two huge chests that seemed to be more like seats, one set underneath each set of windows. Glancing down, I glimpsed a darker stain upon the wood. I caught at Saffron's arm. "Look…blood!"

"The Hermit might be hurt." Saffron pushed past me, heading up yet one more flight of stone steps. I drew out my knife and started up the stairs after her.

The stairs curved around the wall of the tower, narrow and steep. A solitary window let in a shaft of moonlight.

The uppermost floor revealed something like a storehouse with two lamps burning, an overturned table, and an odd array of glass tubes, most of which had been shattered on the floor. Bits of hand worked metal lay among the shards of glass.

For a moment, I thought this hermit of Saffron's must have left—and he had taken most of his books with him. I could see empty wooden shelves but no books. The room smelled of cherry-scented tobacco and a clay pipe lay on the floor, broken in half.

And then something groaned.

Saffron darted around the table and bent over what seemed to be a pile of rags that had been left on the floor. She tucked her knife away and lifted something, and I saw then that the rags were actually an old man's body.

He gave another groan and then coughed, spitting up blood. Saffron cradled the old man's head in her lap. I could not tell his age. His long beard gleamed white, but his short hair was streaked with dark hair still. He looked pale and battered, his face cut as if he'd been in a fight. A ragged, gray tunic stained with blood covered his chest, and heavy leather breeches and boots revealed skinny legs. Next to him lay a small crossbow, but there was no sign of any bolts, meaning he'd spent them all. But against what?

Saffron glanced up at me, blood on her hand and her face pale.

Fear flooded me, left my breath quickening and my hands shaking.

Someone had attacked this man—had mortally wounded him to judge by the blood now staining the floor.

Glancing around, I could see no windows in this room, and I wondered now if the blood we had seen below was that of this hermit or of his attackers.

Kneeling next to Saffron, I glanced at the man's wounds. I knew the marks of a sword, and this man bore them.

"This is your hermit?" I asked Saffron.

She didn't answer, but waved at me. "Find some water. Something to give him to drink."

I nodded, stood and glanced around.

Whoever had done this had not just gone after this hermit but had been savage with the man's few things. I could find splinters of glass and wood, scraps of paper and splatters of blood.

At last I found a small, metal flask and a scrap of cloth and took them back to Saffron.

She took them and told me, "We need to bind these wounds and get him to Zenema."

The Hermit coughed and put a bloodstained hand over Saffron's. "No need. I won't be long for this world."

I thought that once his eyes might have glittered fiercely under his thick eyebrows, but now they seemed dull and fading.

"No, we'll get you to Zenema," Saffron told him, her tone urgent and fierce.

"Zenema cannot heal me. Not this. Not now," the old man said, his voice weak and fading.

"Saffron." I knelt again by her side. "He's right. He does not have much time with us."

She shook her head, but she asked the old man, "What happened? Who did this to you?"

Instead of answering Saffron, the old man glanced at me and for a moment his eyes brightened. "At least I had the chance to serve the True King. I die without regret."

My skin chilled. I glanced at Saffron, but she was still bent over the old man, pressing the rags I had bought to his side and trying to offer him a sip from the metal flask I had also brought her. The old man pushed away the flask, and I asked him, "Why do you say that?" He could not know that I was in fact descended from the true kings of Torvald.

The old man gave a wheezing chuckle. "Knowing things—that was my life, my king." Turning to Saffron, he gripped her wrist. "Three men came to the island, flying no flag. I saw them at the village, heard them ask after a girl with red-gold hair and a lad with more knowledge than was good for him. The villagers told them about the dragon-girl. I came to tell Zenema that Enric has come for his blood kin. He found you, Saffron. As I said he would."

Saffron gasped. When I glanced at her, I saw her face had paled so every freckle now stood out. "You knew about me?" she said, her voice almost a whisper.

"That you are a Maddox? Yes, child. But it matters little what I knew now… All that…matters is to get you to safety. I bought you time. I shot one and he fell into the sea, but the other two tracked me here. One I wounded, but the last escaped with him back to their boat."

"You think they work for the king?" I asked.

The Hermit spat on the floor, and blood tinged his spittle. "Enric. That is what I think of him." He glanced at Saffron. "She's the only good thing to come out of the Maddox line… her mother and father—"

"You knew my mother?" Saffron stiffened. "Why did you never tell me?"

The Hermit sighed. "Such a kind soul..." He clutched his side and gasped. "No time now. I made a promise to hide you—and I kept it for as long as I could. Now, others must help you. Look to the north, to the Three-River clans..." A sudden spasm shook him. His face twisted with pain. His eyes fluttered closed and for a moment I thought he was gone. But he opened his eyes again and gripped my wrist, a surprising strength still in him. "Find what I've hidden for you, my king. Take back what is yours by right. Get to the clans. Stop Enric. Trust each other."

He let out a rattling breath and went still.

Saffron lowered his body to the floor. I scrambled to my feet. I had never seen death so close. Looking over to Saffron, I asked, "Who do you think came here?" I knew the answer, but I wanted to think we were still safe on Den Mountain. I didn't want to leave. "The dragons will look after us, won't they?" I asked her.

Saffron looked at me, her eyes bleak and her face still pale. "The Hermit of the Western Isles is dead. And I am certain King Enric's spies killed him. What can protect us from assassins who come in the night?"

*   *   *

CHAPTER 3

OLD CLOTHES & NEW FRIENDS

Bower and I buried the Hermit near his tower, piling rocks over his body. He seemed to weigh next to nothing, and Bower easily carried him down the stairs and to a rocky slope overlooking the tower and the sea. He had died to save me, it seemed. And to serve Bower as the new king. But staring at the pile of rocks over the Hermit's body, moonlight spilling onto the gray stone, I couldn't believe the Hermit had actually known who I was and never said a thing to me. Not once when he'd been teaching me to read had he even hinted that he had known my father and mother.

Amelia.

It was a good name. A forthright sort of name I decided. But it was all I knew of her. I had a scrap of cloth with her name on it— all I'd been left of her. I knew even less of my father. They had left me here on the shore of the island, and Zenema had found me and raised me with her clutch of dragons. I had grown up with Jaydra at my side. But now my heritage seemed to be coming after me.

Thinking of my parents now, I found no trace of hatred or pain that had once haunted me. I'd once thought they had abandoned me. But the Hermit said he had kept a promise to hide me. Had he promised my mother such a thing?

And had Zenema known who I was all these years? Was that to protect me? Or was it to protect the world from me?

I didn't know the answer, and now we'd been robbed of any help the Hermit might have given us. His warning also left me worried. Did Enric, my blood kin, hunt us because of Bower? Or was I the one Enric wanted to find?

Bower touched a hand to my shoulder. The eastern sky was beginning to brighten with dawn's first light. "We should look for what he said he hid." I glanced at Bower and followed him back to the tower, feeling suddenly tired and wishing I had thought to come earlier to see the Hermit—Bower and I might have saved him. Or maybe we would have been caught by Enric's men.

With a shudder, I stepped inside and out of the cold, dawn wind.

"I'm going to search upstairs." Bower said, moving quickly. He must be as chilled as I. We'd spent the night burying the Hermit and now…now I had no idea what the Hermit might have hidden for us to find. Had that just been the fancy of a dying man? Or had he really left something to help us?

The lower room seemed only a place to live, but I lit a small fire in the grate. The furnishings already looked broken into bits of wood, so why not use them as kindling? The Hermit had been something of a healer, and herbs hung from the wooden ceiling to dry. Cobwebs also clung to the corners and I glanced around.

What was there to find other than dust and mice?

Climbing the stairs to the next room, I moved the heavy curtains beside the narrow windows. I pulled them back, letting in the pre-dawn haze.

Below me the choppy waters of the sea washed over the rocks, leaving strands of kelp and white foam. Turning to the room again, I scanned it. What had the Hermit hidden? Some clue perhaps as to why my family had left me here?

Heading to the empty shelves, I searched them, but found only a dried scrap of thyme. I turned and headed to one of the chests. It opened easily, and I stared at more dust and chunks of wood that might feed a fire. I let the lid thud closed and headed to the second chest.

On this one, the hinges seemed to be rusted shut. It took my pounding on it with a fist and struggling with the latch, but at last the top creaked open with a protest. Bright colors greeted me.

Linens and clothes lay inside, all wrapped in pretty bits of silk cloth. I lifted out soft gowns and tunics in pale creams, pastel blues and greens. From the cut of them they seemed to be for a woman, and they reminded me a little of the clothing I had seen being worn in the towns of the mainland. But these were finely made, and of a different style than anything else I'd ever seen.

Digging deeper, I came across embroidery—a vine entwined around letters. And I knew then these had to be some of my mother's things for the embroidery was an exact match to that on the scrap of cloth that had been left with me.

Had my mother meant to return for these things—and for me?

Or had she left them for me?

I had always wondered why Zenema had taken me for lessons with the Hermit. Zenema had never wanted me to spend time in the nearby village, and she had hidden me from any passing sailors who stopped to provision from the island. Now I began to see she and the Hermit must have been hiding me from anyone who might take word of me to Enric.

"All this time…" I muttered the words and pressed a hand to the fine silks.

Had the Hermit meant to pass these things to me?"

Glancing down at the skins I wore—smooth and so comfortable they almost seemed like my own second skin, I doubted I could wear anything from my mother. But I dug deeper into the chest. And there I found a forest green leather jerkin and soft leather breeches that matched.

And these looked to me to be like the clothing I had seen on the cliff drawings—they were the clothes of a dragon rider.

Zenema had showed me the cliff drawings. They decorated the sea cliffs near where she had found me. On them, people rode dragons—always two to a dragon, and the riders had on leather jerkins in a dark green, breeches and boots and helmets. I found no helmet in the chest, but I could not resist the rest of it.

Putting back the fine silks, I repacked the chest. But I kept the leather jerkin and breeches. I pulled them on over my skins, letting my skin tunic and breeches act like undergarments. The green jerkin and breeches hung a little loose, but I liked the feel of them.

Oddly, they made me feel different somehow, more like myself—but like a self I had not even known existed.

Smoothing the leather, I knew I had not been forgotten.

From upstairs, Bower's voice echoed down to me. "Saffron, I think I found something!"

I ran up the stone steps and found Bower had righted one of the tables. He stood bent over it, his back to the spot where the Hermit had died. I avoided that spot, too. Sunlight streamed into the room through one of the narrow windows, and I noticed a hole in the wall where there had not been one before.

"What?" I asked, coming up to Bower's side. He glanced twice at my new, dark green jerkin but said nothing about it. Instead, he waved at the hole where he must have removed a stone to reveal the space. "Your hermit had a hiding place. Several actually. The other three were empty, but I kept thinking about how I'd had hiding spots in my library back in Torvald." Bower stopped and made a face as if remembering something sad. I didn't really understand why books mattered so much to him, but they did. He shook his head, his dark brown hair lank and falling into his eyes now that it had gotten so long. He pushed it back and pointed to paper spread out on the table.

It looked as if whatever Bower had found was both old and also missing chunks. I could see heavy black lines drawn on the paper, marking mountains and hills, marshes, lakes and even the forests.

Leaning over his shoulder, I glimpsed red lines here and there. These lines almost looked like dragon wings and a curl of flame. "We saw that mark in your city," I told Bower, pointing at it.

"Yes…it's the mark of the Salamanders. They're a group that defies the king's orders. They're—"

"Pirates? Thieves?" I asked.

Bower grimaced. "Yes and not exactly. They're like us— people who dislike the king's harsh rules and his unjust laws. They helped me escape the citadel the first time I left. And I think…I think my father was working with the Salamanders to fight back against King Enric."

Against the Maddox clan.

A shiver chased down my back. Why did my family have to be both powerful—and so hateful?

"Are they dragon-friends?" I asked. "Do they even believe in dragons? Is that why they use the symbol of dragon fire and wings?"

"They might be, but you have to remember that all the Maddox kings, from Hacon to Enric, have worked hard to make everyone think dragons are some kind of monsters from tales meant to frighten children. Most people don't really believe in them. But the Salamanders are at least trying to keep the old stories in memory—I think they're the reason my father collected the forbidden stories about dragons. That, however, is not as important as this." Bower waved a hand at the paper on the table. "This map proves your hermit—whoever he was—was connected to the Salamanders, or at least knew about them and knew where they could be found. It really is too bad we didn't have more time to talk with him about this."

Bower's words stung. It was partly my fault the Hermit was dead—if I had gone to him right away things may have been different. I turned away from Bower and his map. "Well, we didn't have time with him. And what good does this map do us?

It's just scribbles on paper. It's like those drawings on the cliff—it's all about the past."

"And that is just what is going to make the future!" Bower's eyes brightened. He walked over to the wall with the hole showing and pulled out a fat book. He carried it back to the table and opened it as carefully as if handling a fragile leaf. "This is the Compendium Atlas. I've only seen one other, and never one like this which seems to have been annotated by hand—by your hermit, I think."

"Will you stop calling him mine. He just lived near Den Mountain. And what's an atlas?"

Bower pulled in a breath, then said, "A compendium is a list of things, an atlas offers up maps of places people have explored. This does far more…just listen."

He turned the page and started to read.

"'It was my intent to tread the length of the Dragon's Spine Mountains all the way from their southerly end to whatever icy vastness held in the grim north…' And look, here's the map." He pointed to a drawing of mountains. "There's King's Pass marked and Valley of Cracked Willows, and the spot where three rivers converge—the Dangse, the Venge and the Oluk come together in one mighty torrent, cutting off this land of high meadows from the rest of the mountains." He grinned at me. "Do you see?"

47

Frowning, I shrugged. "I don't see anything but a book and papers you call maps."

Bower rolled his eyes and started to tap his fingers on the table. "Three rivers—the Three-Rivers clans. Your...the old man said that's where we should head. That we'll find help there." He pointed again to the spot on the page where three thin blue lines swirled through the mountains to come together.

I looked from Bower's face, which was almost glowing red, to the map and back again. "Do you know what you're saying. We're supposed to travel far to the north, across the land Enric holds, with him hunting for us, to see if there is a group of people who might want to help, and all on the say of an old man who might have been sane or might not?"

Bower put a hand on the book—his Compendium Atlas. "Well...yes. Or do you have a better idea? I mean, do you want to stay here and wait for Enric's spies to come back? Or for Enric to show up with his Iron Guard?" He waved at the map. "We have this—we know where we need to get to. And Enric won't know where we've gone."

I glanced over to the dark stain on the floor, and then to the window. The sun had come up and lightened the sea. The surf beat a soft, steady rhythm against the rock and the tower's foundation.

Bower was right—we could not stay. Enric's spies would take word to him of what they had found. *Unless we find them and stop them.*

But how could we do that? They were out in the ocean, and even a dragon would have a hard time finding them.

Jaydra's thoughts touched my mind as she woke. *You have dragon kin to help you. Always.*

She was right. But the den must be warned about what had happened. I glanced at Bower and nodded. "First, we must speak to Zenema." I smoothed my new leather jerkin. I was about to take a step as if off a cliff, and I knew my life would change. Perhaps never to be the same again. Pushing back my shoulders, I dropped my hands to my side and told Bower, "We need to formally ask for her aid and ask if any dragons will fly and fight with us."

*   *   *

CHAPTER 4

THE COUNCIL OF DRAGONS

Standing next to Saffron at the edge of the main cavern, I decided I'd never seen so many dragons. I didn't even know so many lived within the Western Isles.

The Council of Dragons, Zenema had called it.

Shafts of brilliant sunlight streamed in down the tunnels of Den Mountain. The main cavern looked more like a cathedral now, with the brilliant hues of the dragons. Everywhere I looked I saw dragons. The predominant colors seemed to be the sea blues, with a few greens, but I spotted three whites and five with mottled orange scales. Sadly, none of the dragons seemed to be the crimson reds I had seen pictured in the old books.

The younger dragons all chose perches on rock outcroppings within the chamber, and sat flicking their long, spiked tails, staring down with inquisitive eyes. The older dragons, however, seemed content to stretch out on their sides.

If I hadn't been living with dragons for a time, I would have been terrified to face so many, for a few of the dragons seemed to stare at me with a predatory hunger. Or maybe that was just amazement that a foolish human would be at the Council of Dragons.

Nudging Saffron with one elbow, I told her, "I hadn't expected so many." Trying to act as if I consorted with dragons every day, I leaned against the nearest wall. Saffron took up a position just in front of me. She was silhouetted against the bright sky at the end of a tunnel and stood so still that for a second I thought she might not have heard me.

But she answered in a low voice, "Neither did I. Zenema's called them from all over the Western Isles."

I thought I heard a tremor in her voice, but I didn't know if that was excitement or maybe a little fear. My mouth was dry and my heart pounding. I had no idea how I was supposed to behave.

When we'd told Zenema about the Hermit's death, she had emitted a long, mournful call that seemed to echo over the island. I'd wondered if maybe the Hermit had been a dragon-friend to Zenema in the same way that Saffron was to Jaydra. Zenema had listened to Saffron, and then said we must call the Council of Dragons.

The council met exactly one day later. Dragons had been arriving all through the night and day. The cavern smelled like smoke, dragon, and a little bit like fish, which left me hoping most of the dragons had eaten before coming to the council.

Suddenly, a roar and a skittering of claws on stone went up in the cavern. I jumped and almost wanted to duck down the nearest

51

tunnel, for it seemed certain to me the dragons were thinking of me as a dessert.

"It's Oloxia." Saffron nodded toward what looked to be an ancient white dragon, bigger even than Zenema, who had entered the cavern from another tunnel and was hissing and snapping at other dragons to get out of his way. And they did. "Stay far from him," Saffron said. "He's more reptile than dragon these days."

She didn't have to warn me. Oloxia swung opaque eyes in my direction and snuffled the air as if he could smell better than he could see. His scales seemed dull with age and his bulk was massive—it amazed me he could still fly. His tongue lashed out, lapping at his mouth. I sensed that if he had the chance, he would snap me up as a tasty treat—and maybe Saffron, too. One of the smaller, green dragons hissed at Oloxia. The ancient dragon swung around, lashed out with a spurt of flame and a fast swipe of a front leg, pinning the smaller green dragon's wing to the cavern floor.

The green dragon started to struggle and two other small dragons swept down next to him. I feared there would be blood, but a roar shook the cavern and a word echoed in my mind.

Stop!

Zenema swooped down and into the cavern, scattering the younger dragons from their perches, including Jaydra, who chirruped and settled again next to Saffron. Zenema landed in the middle of the cavern and lifted her head high above the other dragons.

The dragons all seemed to give way to her, except old Oloxia who huffed out a smoky breath, but released the younger green dragon who darted away with his friends.

I glanced around. I didn't know how many of these dragons were Zenema's kin—her children even, such as Jaydra. But it was plain Zenema ruled Den Mountain and held great sway with all the other dragons. And not just because of her size or age. Her stare swept the cavern and she held each dragon's gaze, intelligence and power in eyes that seemed to shift color and swirl with light.

"A den-mother is a great leader among dragons," Saffron whispered to me. "Even though there might be more than a few clutches of eggs from different mothers, there is still only one who rules, usually the oldest mother. Zenema is head of the whole family."

I nodded. I had wondered why Zenema seemed to quite literally rule the roost.

"The den-mother is like a queen. That one there?" Saffron nodded to a brilliantly blue-green dragon with silver-flecked eyes and a long neck. "That's Ysix. She's den-mother to another brood on another island, but she's also one of Zenema's daughters."

53

I edged closer to Saffron. "That makes Zenema an empress—a queen over other queens."

Saffron smiled. "You know, maybe you really are a dragon-friend. With words like that, you might even charm Zenema."

My face heated. I wasn't sure I could do any such thing. Next to these mighty creatures, I was feeling small and all too vulnerable.

Saffron didn't seem to notice, but told me, "Every now and again one of Zenema's daughters will have a clutch of eggs of her own. But, to become den-mother, she must go off first and find her own cavern, on her own island like Ysix did. And a lot of the dragons prefer staying under the protection of a more powerful dragon."

Zenema's thoughts rang inside my head again, so powerful that it was almost like the blare of trumpets. *Family and blood kin, this is the third council I have called and the first for many of you.*

Some of dragons let out chirrups and clicks—I didn't know if they were agreeing with Zenema or not, but Saffron didn't seem worried.

Zenema's thoughts softened a little in my mind.

A darkness once again rises across the land, and it reaches for us. We of the West thought our dens to be safe. We lived as wild dragons, always have, but without savagery. We grew strong—the oceans have been good to us!

A loud hissing rose up from some of the younger dragons. Saffron grinned, and I asked, "What was that? What did they say?"

"Just the younger dragons being silly, saying it's the fish that's been so very good." She shrugged.

I thought of how Jaydra always wanted to go hunt the oily ocean fish, but Zenema's thoughts echoed in my mind again.

But all things are joined at their center, as the old lore says. The darkness comes for us. It will come to try and put an end to us as it did so very long ago. For we are its enemy. We are the spark of life, the fire in the heart, the ray of light that shines even in the night.

I had never known a dragon could be so poetic. It almost seemed as if this might be something spiritual, but did dragons have a religion?

One of the other dragons hissed and screeched, and I looked to Saffron for a translation. She shook her head and turned to look up at Zenema, so I did as well.

I can promise you, in all my days and across three councils, as there is light, there is dark. As there are dragons, there is the shadow that seeks to extinguish them. We must decide not only our own fate, but that of others.

Hissing and chirps rose up from the dragons—mostly hisses from the older dragons and chirps from the younger ones. Even to someone such as myself who couldn't speak dragon, it was obvious that the dragons were arguing about how to deal with the threat that was going to come.

I imagined black war ships bearing Enric's colors of royal purple and gold, staffed with the unflinching, mechanical Iron Guard, and aided with the king's strange sorcery—could anything defeat such a fleet?

But these were dragons! I had read stories of dragons doing amazing things. However, the king's powers were daunting—Saffron and I had barely been able to escape the king and keep him from destroying his own city, all for the sake of wiping out any who opposed him.

Glancing around, I wondered how many of these dragons even knew how to fight?

Zenema's thoughts cut through the noise, which quieted as her thoughts seemed to reach not just me but every dragon as well.

Were it my choice alone, I would say we should give up on the humans who have brought our race so much suffering.

Another chorus of hisses and wing-beats answered her, and then Zenema rose up above the flurry of dragons.

Were this a generation ago, I would suggest we fly even further west and seek what new lands we might find. Or fly south until we leave the humans to their own petty cruelties. But we have found there are humans who still remember us, and who are still good and true dragon-friends. In them, there is hope the world might remember what humans and dragons were once. And even more importantly I see ahead and see that we cannot run. For in running, does not the prey learn that the predator always runs faster? And I will be no one's prey.

Old Oloxia let out a burst of what sounded to me like angry hissing. Zenema shook her head and spread her wings and the noise quieted.

I hear your arguments. Life has been better, living wild. But are we dragons to run when chased? Once we had no choice. We had to flee or face destruction. But our numbers are vast now. Many of you cannot recall how life was in the times before, but there was a time when humans and dragons lived and worked together. There was a time when humans brought us food and helped make our homes. There was a time when the dragons did not die of scale-rot, or flame cough or any other illness because humans would bring healers and together we lived better lives. If humans remember us, is it not time for us to remember ourselves? Let us remember our past—and look to our future. Step forward,

57

adopted den-daughter of mine, Saffron Maddox, and dragon-friend, Bower of Torvald!"

I gulped and straightened, my heart thudding into my chest. Glancing at Saffron, I saw she was looking pale, her freckles standing out. But she held my stare and gave a small nod. She stepped into the center of the cavern, into the midst of the dragons. I could not fail her now.

Compelled by the moment, I followed Saffron only to be surrounded by what seemed to me to be suspicious, skeptical and hungry-looking dragons.

Saffron lifted her hands over her head.

The air around us seemed almost unbearably hot. Sweat trickled down my back and beaded on my forehead. The sandy ground in the cavern gave under my boots and the rustlings of dragon wings seemed to fill the cavern for a moment.

Saffron looked around her much as Zenema had. She seemed to be trying to look at as many of the dragons as she could, turning to include not just Zenema and Ysix, but also the smaller dragons and even old Oloxia, who lay at the back of the cavern now.

There was something about the deeply textured, inquisitive eyes that always made me think dragons could read my darkest secrets.

Saffron lowered her hands and silence fell.

Instead of thinking her words, Saffron spoke to the dragons. "Many of you have known me for my most of my life. I am den-sister to Jaydra, and I have flown, hunted, ate and slept alongside you. For sharing your home with me, I can only say thank you. You have shown me how wise and gracious dragons can be and taught me better than any human family could." She bowed her head and put a hand to her chest.

Was it just me or had I heard a slight hitch in her voice when she had said that last part?

Looking up again, Saffron balled her fist at her side. "But now the time has come when I must ask more from you. I have traveled into the human world and discovered a danger that threatens the den."

A few dragons hissed, and some reared up, beating their wings. I wondered if that was dismay or an offer to do battle.

Saffron raised her voice so she might be better heard. "The Middle Kingdom of Torvald is ruled by an evil sorcerer, a man called Enric Maddox, who is blood kin to me. But he is not content with what power he has. He wants more. He will never be satisfied until the entire world bows to him—and all threats are gone. Meaning he seeks to destroy all dragons—and create only the memory of dragons as enemies."

More hisses answered these words, and this time I could feel the anger behind those sounds. These dragons weren't happy.

Saffron's shoulders tensed. She lifted her chin and called out, "Enric sent his spies here, to this very island. They now carry word back to Enric that dragons live here. Even worse, these spies killed the Hermit who lived next to us and in the shadow of Den Mountain for so many years. Enric will stop at nothing in his quest to control the world. But I cannot allow this to happen. Enric seeks my death, too, or control of me. And so I'm asking you to fly with me, for I cannot fight without your help."

She let out a gasp, as if this speech had taken too much out of her.

A moment of silence answered, and then the cavern erupted into whistles and hisses from the assembled dragons. Even though I couldn't understand what they were saying, from the way they were snapping at each other and swiveled their long, scaled necks to hiss, it was obviously an argument, with some wanting to help Saffron and others spitting out fire in clear rebukes.

A heavy thud from Zenema as she slapped her tail against the cavern floor had every dragon turning to look at her. The air now smelled of smoke, and I tried not to cough.

Zenema's stare swept the room. She looked from Saffron to gaze at me and my insides quivered under that hard, swirling gaze, as if Zenema was seeking something from within me.

At last Zenema turned away from me, and I resisted the urge to wipe the sweat from my face. Saffron stood even straighter as Zenema asked, *Why would humans seek to be friends with dragons again? Why should we not stay out here in our dens? What if this generation of humans are as frightened of us as the island villagers? What do you answer, Saffron, to the questions put forth by so many dragons?*

Saffron turned and pointed at me. "The world changes because of him."

Every dragon's gaze turned to me. My throat tightened and my heart seemed to almost jump from my chest. I stood still, heart hammering and wondering why Saffron had said that.

She came over to me and put her hand on my shoulder. "Bower is the rightful King of Torvald. Through him the great bloodlines of Flamma and Torvald have come together, and only he can bring peace to the Middle Kingdom…to all kingdoms. He is the bridge between the dragon and human worlds. You all can sense in him that he is a true dragon-friend. You know this or you would not have allowed him to live as he has within Den Mountain. If we see Bower restored to the throne, we not only save those who now live under a terrible rule and terrible lies, but

61

we also will see dragons restored to their rightful place in the sky—so that dragons may live wherever they wish and need not run from this Enric like sheep."

I'm still not even certain I want to be king.

The thought left my face hot and I shuffled my boots in the sand. Under the gaze of every dragon in the cavern, I felt more like a fraud. I was no warrior-king, riding at the head of dragons and battling a dark sorcerer for a throne. My skills were better used with me being the one who chronicled great deeds.

A sound like the hiss of steam escaping a kettle started and grew louder until my ears ached. Then Ysix rose up, spread her wings and gave a roar that silenced all the dragons.

I glanced at Saffron and saw her freckles standing out as her face paled.

Looking up into Ysix's swirling, silver eyes, I thought she had judged me unworthy and was going to eat me.

But Zenema's voice echoed in my mind. *Bower of Torvald, den-mother Ysix challenges you, asking if you have the strength to be the Dragon King. Do we wait until another comes along who is braver? Can you lead as a king must? What do you answer?*

Her words cut through me, punching into my gut like a fist. What could I say? Ysix was right. She had seen into my thoughts and knew I was more of a scholar. I had been raised with books, not with battles. Oh, yes, I'd had a sword in my hand, as did all nobles. But my parents had worked hard to hide my real heritage—and they had done such a good job that I hadn't even known I was supposed to rule the Middle Kingdom.

Glancing at Saffron, I wanted her to tell the dragons to follow her—not me. She was a leader. She could fight. She had magic, even. I had...I didn't know what I had.

Slowly, Saffron nodded and mouthed the words to me, *I believe in you.*

Well, it seemed I had Saffron. Saffron who believed, who trusted, and who was now staring at me with worry tightening her expression. She no longer looked like the half-wild girl I had met in the woods, but instead seemed a young woman teetering between hope I would do the right thing and despair that I might not.

How could I betray her trust?

Pulling in a breath, I faced Ysix. My throat seemed dry, but I knew I needed to prove there was more to me than a skinny youth who'd barely been tested. "I thought...I once lived only for the stories within the pages of old books. I read about dragons—and did not think them real. I wished...I wished for more. And I found that with Saffron. I have faced danger and battles, but I have not enjoyed them. But I would not—cannot—go back to my old life. You—all of you—have shown me a better world. A world with dragons. A world where dragons and humans join to be so much more together."

Ysix huffed out a breath. I held my own breath and tried not to choke or cough or wave away the smoke in front of my face.

Turning from Ysix, I spoke to all the dragons. "I am not one of the heroes of old. I do not come here seeking the heads of my enemies. It is true. I would prefer to talk to someone to reach a resolution. But I do come to you with a passion and a love for dragons and the past that has been with me ever since I first could look at the sky or stare at an old drawing of a dragon. I may not be the great king you were hoping for, but I will be one who will try every day to be better and to understand more how humans and dragons can live together. I wish for there to be peace between our species, and I am willing to fight for that. I will fight for those who need my help, and for the Dragon Riders to return to the skies!"

Glancing at Saffron, I hoped she thought I had done well. Her mouth curved in a small smile and she gave me what seemed an encouraging nod.

The flap of beating wings and hisses answered me as the dragons argued over what to do with me and my words.

Ysix raised her voice once again above the tumult and this time her voice echoed in my mind. *Bower of Torvald, words come easy to humans so let your actions say more. You are challenged to a test that will prove if you can do more than try.*

Glancing around, what would Ysix would have me do? Wrestle a Grim-bear? Battle one of Enric's undefeatable Iron Guard? What feat would make a dragon trust a human?

Saffron pushed an elbow into my side. I glanced at her. She shook her head and glared at me, trying to say something without saying it, but I had no idea what she wanted. Instead, I looked at Ysix and told her, "I accept your challenge."

What else could I say? If we did not have the help of the dragons, we were as good as dead. Without them, Enric's men or his spies or his assassins would find us and we'd be done. Or I would be. I knew Enric wanted Saffron for her power—but Enric had no use for someone who had a better claim to the throne of Torvald.

Ysix glanced once at Zenema. The other dragons fell silent, and then Ysix's thoughts echoed in my mind. *Bower must prove he has the blood of the true Dragon King in his. Bower must show he can mend the distrust between human and dragon. Go to the villagers of this island and make those humans into dragon-friends. Do this and Ysix herself and her brood will fly for you.*

*   *   *

CHAPTER 5

A DRAGON'S PEACE

I kept trying to explain to Bower just what he was facing. "One of the things you have to understand is that the villagers really don't like dragons."

He nodded and then shrugged as if he was only half-listening, but he said, "I know, I know. The people in Torvald are the same. Those who ever dare to mention dragons do so only to tell stories of how dragons are monsters from nightmares. But I know what to do. People just need to see what dragons are really like. They just need to meet them."

Rolling my eyes, I wanted to punch Bower. He was underestimating how difficult this challenge was going to be. The villagers had already met dragons and still didn't like them.

We had left Den Mountain at once. Glancing back, I could see the visiting dragons swirling around the warm updrafts that circled Den Mountain. It had taken most of the day to reach the nearest village, and we were almost there. Despite Bower's insistence that this was something he could do alone, I'd told him I was going with him.

It was, after all, partly my quest and it had been my request to have the help of the dragons. The way I figured it, everything depended upon Bower, and if the villagers turned nasty, he would need someone who could fight at his side. Zenema had agreed with me. Jaydra had also insisted she was coming with us. That had kicked up another argument with the dragons, but Zenema simply said Bower needed to have a dragon with him if his task was to convince the villagers that dragons could be their friends.

It's not that Jaydra does not like villagers, Jaydra mused, her thoughts reaching mine. *Jaydra just does not like arrows or their long spears.*

I glanced up to where Jaydra soared overhead. *Maybe they threw those at you because you ate one of their forest pigs last week.*

Jaydra gave a loud snort of displeasure that carried to me.

Travelling with a dragon usually had its benefits in that you got to fly on its back, but Bower had insisted we arrive on foot. He was right in that dragons were big—and also a dragon flying low over a village usually sent every villager running. So Jaydra had to stay high above the clouds or down on the ground and out of sight—at least for the moment.

Glancing at me, Bower said, "You are going to let me try to do this my own way, aren't you?"

"I know you have to prove yourself, but I don't think you realize just how many generations of bad blood there are between

67

the islanders and dragons. The villagers try to steal dragon eggs, and the dragons in turn steal livestock from the villagers. Mostly, the villagers keep to themselves these days, but there are stories the dragons tell of wars even between dragons and villagers!"

"And the villagers probably have their own sagas as well about what happened when dragons first showed up, or when villagers came to these islands." He huffed out a breath and strode ahead of me. I was stunned by this reaction, and felt vaguely ashamed, like I was being a traitor to my own kind—to dragons.

Hurrying to catch up to him, I told him, "Bower, the villagers even set fire to the forest once. Who does that?"

Bower glanced at me, his face pinched with worry. "I understand. I really do. I grew up in Torvald, where even talking like we are now would have you imprisoned—or killed. I know how horrible some people can be, but that doesn't mean you give up on everyone."

I suddenly blushed, remembering how Bower had been tortured at the hands of the king. And I had been the one who had dragged Bower back to his city when really he was trying to escape from it and the king—from someone who had proved he really was terrible.

"I'm sorry." I kicked at a rock in the path. "I just wish you had suggested Ysix pick a different challenge."

He hunched a shoulder. "Ysix was right! I do have to prove myself. If I can't negotiate a peace between dragons and humans here, how am I going to do this anywhere else? This is important. And it's not just...well, I've given up a lot. My home. My friends. Even my books. I have to know that I really can do what everyone seems to think I should be able to do."

Pushing a long-leafed palm from our path, I told him, "But, Bower, maybe you just need more training first?"

He gave a short laugh. "In a way, I have been training for this for a long time. I was a scholar before I had to leave Torvald. I read every book I could, a lot of them old ones, and most of them were ones the king didn't want anyone reading. I read the *Strategicus*, *The Manuals of Mordecai*, which noted ways of dealing with dragons and how to fight beside dragons and a whole lot more. If I can apply even a little of that learning, I might be able to do this."

Bower stopped and glanced at me. For a moment, he looked taller and more confident than I had ever seen him. Sunlight streaked his shaggy brown hair and his dark eyes seemed suddenly far more knowing.

Maybe he has the blood of the true kings in him after all.

From above, Jaydra's thoughts came to me. *Just so long as Bower can get villagers to stop firing arrows at Jaydra.*

I led the way down to a clearing just in front of a river. On the opposite side of the wide, slow flowing river, huts stood on stilts. Wind chimes of shells from the sea and carved wood beads rattled cheerfully. The villagers seemed busy with their day, going in and out of the big, wooden huts with their peaked roofs, mending fishing nets, or just sitting and talking to each other.

Someone noticed us, for a horn sounded a short blast. Everyone in the village seemed to stop what they were doing, and a boy pointed at us.

Bower let out a breath and said, "Well…here's to at least trying." Stepping forward, he walked toward a planked, wooden bridge that crossed the river at a narrow spot.

I put my hand on my knife hilt at my belt and followed him.

The bridge, while simple, had posts at either end that had been carved into fantastical versions of dragons. I wasn't sure whether to be impressed or insulted by the way they had depicted my family as being all teeth and wings and claws.

As soon as we stepped off the shaky bridge, a thin man with a beard, a tunic of cloth, leggings and boots stepped in front of us. He lowered a long spear at Bower and called out, "Halt."

Bower held up his empty hands. I was wishing now that I had a bow and that Bower had his sword. We stopped. The villagers all stared at us with wary eyes, and behind us the river babbled

70

along. I didn't like that we had our backs to the river, but if we needed to run, we could get across the river fast enough that Jaydra could swoop down and protect us.

Bower wasn't thinking about any of that. He smiled and said, "We come with a message of peace."

The man with the spear stared past Bower and at me, his eyes widening. "The dragon-girl? You brought the dragon-girl with you?" He glanced at Bower again, a frown pulling his sandy eyebrows tight. The spear shifted to aim more at me.

"Saffron. Her name is Saffron, and my name is Bower." Bower stepped between me and the spear—not a wise move. I glanced around. A crowd was beginning to assemble. Some of the villagers carried bows notched with arrows, the children had rocks in their slings, and several of the men hefted more long spears. They did not look welcoming. No one was smiling.

"Bower?" The man stumbled over Bower's name. It was not one common to the Western Isles. He nodded at me. "Our shaman will have to decide what to do with her now you've rescued her from the dragons."

"Rescued?" Bower's eyebrows shot up. "You think the dragons were holding her captive? No, that's not it at all."

From the crowd, an old woman stepped forward and called, "What is this? What is happening?" She pushed through the other villagers, hobbling forward with the aid of a tall staff. Shells and wooden beads decorated her long tunic, which was white and fringed. More shells were woven into her graying hair, and bones rattled as she walked. Long, gray hair framed a brown, wrinkled face and gray eyes stared at us with a measuring look.

She had to be the shaman.

The man with the spear stepped back and said, "Grandmother, it is the dragon-girl and a dragon-boy come to us. He speaks of peace."

The old woman stepped closer, the dried skulls of birds and even a few teeth, clattering as she moved. She squinted at each of us in turn, and narrowed her eyes. Her nose wrinkled. "Are you with the others?"

"What others?" Bower asked.

I nudged Bower with my elbow and shook my head. I wasn't sure if the others were the king's men who had killed the Hermit or maybe someone even more dangerous.

Bower glanced at me, frowned as if he didn't understand what I was trying to tell him, and then faced the old woman again. "I am an emissary from the dragons of Den Mountain and I come with their promise of peace."

The shaman gave a sharp laugh. "Peace from a dragon? What trickery is this? Seize them!" The shaman stepped back and waved for the four men with spears to come forward.

I pulled out my knife, and Jaydra roared and fell from the sky, landing in the river with a huge splash. The villagers all fell back and some screamed. Jaydra raised her neck and head high over the bridge and over us. With one smash of her tail, she could destroy the bridge and then she could lay waste to this small village.

A cry went up at once, with the villagers shouting or screaming. The four guards with spears moved away from us to stand before their shaman, raising their weapons in an obviously defensive move. Children fled, women gathered them up and headed into the jungle as if to hide.

"Wait!" Bower shouted, raising his hands. "Jaydra means you no harm, she is only here to protect myself and Saffron," He moved to stand almost directly underneath Jaydra's jaws.

Jaydra set fire to their puny village. Jaydra asked me with her thoughts.

No. Let Bower talk. I thought to her, even though my fingers were tingling as my magic started to rise. I bit down on my lower lip and tried to hold it back. I couldn't let it go now—I had no idea what it might do.

My magic had always been more wild than controlled. At times, I could use it to hide myself and Jaydra as well. Other times, it burst out with such power that it frightened me. I'd once almost killed Jaydra by accident, and now I didn't want to harm these villagers—not if I didn't have to.

I watched as Bower and Jaydra stood still, letting the shaman and her guards back away from them.

Turning, Bower pointed to Den Mountain, where dragons whirled around the peak. I had no doubt the dragons had their ears and eyes trained on what was happening here and were readying to attack the village to save Jaydra and me. "Look—look at the dragons of the Western Isles who now watch you to see if you mean peace or not. To see if you can be trusted."

The shaman glanced at the mountain and then said, "I see dragons—ready to attack!"

"But they haven't," Bower said. He waved at Jaydra. "She could destroy your village and drive off your livestock, but she has not. We came here to offer peace. Think how much more fish you could bring in if you had the help of dragons. And look at how many dragons there are in the Western Isles. They could have driven you from this island years ago, but they have allowed you to share this land with them. But they could do so much more for you. Or…if you fight, they could drive you and your families from these shores forever."

"Are you threatening us, dragon-friend?" The shaman made the word into an insult and then spat on the ground in front of Bower's feet. Holding up a bird skull, she rattled it at Bower.

Mouth pulling down, he stepped forward. He looked far more like an insulted dragon right now, with his chest puffed out and his face reddening. "I am a dragon-friend, and a proud one at that. I have come to talk with you, not threaten you. I come to make peace—one in which if you will promise to live in harmony with all dragons, they in turn promise not to attack you or eat any more of your livestock."

Jaydra glanced down at Bower and blinked in surprise. I could feel her shock in my mind and begged her to just let Bower keep talking. But I was certain no human could ever hold a dragon to a promise not to eat pigs or goats or sheep.

"Lies!" the shaman cried and rattled her skull at Bower again. But some of the spears dropped a little bit lower. Glancing around, I could see some of the villagers were swapping glances and thinking about Bower's words. The old woman seemed to notice this as well for she turned on the men. "Remember what the messengers said. The dragon-girl has been entranced by dragon magic."

"Well, I'm not entranced," Bower said, his tone amiable. The spears drooped even lower until their tips touched the ground. "There are enough dragons up there to destroy not just this

75

village, but every single village on every island for miles around. Dragons haven't been your enemy. Ever. If anything, they've made this a safer place to live. Do pirates come and raid your village? No—because dragons are near. Now all the dragons ask is that you take a step closer to them, that you become friends. Why is that so hard to believe?"

The shaman's mouth worked, but no sound came out. She seemed to be struggling for an answer and not finding one.

The first man we'd met stroked his beard and said, "That makes some sense."

Bower nodded. "It does, doesn't it? You all live on the same island, but instead of raiding each other—or trying to get the others to go away—why not work together? There is plenty of food, both on the island and in the sea. So the dragons like the taste of your pigs. Raise extras every year and trade with the dragons. They could fish the deepest part of the oceans for you, for food you would never have otherwise. They can tell when storms are coming and warn you. They can protect you from all enemies, not just pirates but other dangers, too. There is no need to keep acting as if you live on this island on your own—or to act as if dragons are here to kill you."

Some of the men nodded. And something else was happening.

Women and children had edged out of the jungle as if drawn by Bower's voice or his words. He sounded so calm and reasonable that the men of the village were nodding to each other. Only the old shaman glared at him.

As he spoke, Bower was waving his hands and walking back and forth and looking directly at the villagers as if they were his friends. Even to me, his words were having an impact. I was starting to think it really didn't make any sense that villagers and dragons couldn't find a way to share such a small island.

"But they always fight—with each other and then with us," one of the guards said. "And messengers came to tell us dragons were getting ready to fight again. But help is coming."

The old shaman kicked the guard hard in the leg, causing him to grunt. He shot her an irritated look and stepped away.

Bower held up his hands again. "Do they fight? Or do you just hear them making noises? Dragons are loud." Jaydra gave a low roar as if to confirm this. Bower walked over and put a hand on her side. That seemed to impress the villagers more than anything. Glancing around, Bower said, "Let the dragons prove they can fight for you. That is surely better than having to climb Den Mountain to battle flying, fire-breathing dragons." He grinned, making the idea seem ridiculous. He even got a few uneasy smiles. Moving away from Jaydra, Bower asked, "But who are these messengers you speak of?" The shaman stumbled backward, holding her staff in front of her as if to fight off anyone who might stop her. "It's evil magic he is using. Say nothing. Shun these two. They'll kill us all!" She ducked into one of the smaller huts that wasn't on stilts.

The villagers in front of us swapped uneasy glances, and a cold trickle slipped down my spine. I tightened my fingers around my knife. Had the shaman just undone all Bower's good words?

The man who had first stopped us glanced at me and told Bower, "The messengers came to look for her."

Bower's head jerked up and he said, "Did they also go to see the Hermit?"

The man stroked his beard again. "Yes, when we told them a hermit lived on the island, they seemed to want to see him." The guard shrugged. "I told them he was just a crazy hermit and lived too near the dragons, but they said they had boats. We didn't see them after that. But they said the king was sending his ships to protect us."

Bower grimaced and muttered, "Enric."

My heart seemed to stutter. Enric was sending ships? How many?

Jaydra suddenly lifted her nose into the air and snuffed deeply. *Wood. Iron. Black-powder. Hatred.* She breathed in the winds of the world and then looked to the east.

Where? How far? I thought to Jaydra and then edged closer to Bower. I tugged on the sleeve of his skin tunic.

"What is it?" he hissed. "These are delicate negotiations and—
"

"Something's coming. Jaydra smells it." I glanced over at Jaydra, who was now spreading her wings and looking ready to take flight. "Jaydra smells wood and metal." I left out the fact that dragons could also smell emotions. That didn't seem as important as finding out if these were the king's ships coming to the island.

Zenema's voice slipped into my mind. They are, Saffron. Ships come from the east. Tall, belching smoke and with soldiers. They will be here before long.

The air shook with a distant boom. The villagers ducked as if thunder had sounded.

"What is that noise?" one of the villagers asked.

"Cannons," Bower said. "It's not a good sound. It's a huge gun, shooting fire that is more destructive than any dragon's breath."

The villagers started to mill around, and one man ordered the others to stay calm. Children were crying now, and women huddled close to the huts.

A cackling laugh broke out. The shaman stepped from her hut, carrying a cloth bundle as if she intended to flee the village. "You think you are the only one with tricks, dragon-girl? I once studied with the Hermit, before he thought me not pure enough!

Well, I have hidden the king's boats from you until now, just as you hide your dragons from us. The king will reward me when he finds out I, the witch of the Western Isles, lured his dragon-girl into a trap for him!"

She vanished into the forest.

Bower looked from villager to me and asked. "How far aware are the ships?"

Close. Three ships, Jaydra told me, and I told the same thing to Bower, for I wasn't certain he would hear Jaydra's thoughts.

Another boom shook the trees and something crashed into the forest, knocking four tall trees into splinters. I didn't know if these were warning shots, or some sort of signal, or if the ships testing the range of what Bower had called their cannons.

Bower strode into the village. "You have to get your people to safety. I don't think those ships care what they smash, meaning your village could be destroyed. Go to the Den Mountain and hide in the caves—the mountain is too strong for the cannon, and the dragons will not harm you. They have given their promise to be your friends. But you must go."

The villagers started to shake their head, and Bower raised his voice, "When the king's soldiers come, they will not leave until every man, woman and child is dead. You know the truth—that dragons exist. This means they cannot…they will not leave you alive. Please, you must go. Hurry."

Heads were shaking, but I could see worry and hesitation in the eyes of the villagers. I stepped forward. "Bower is right. Those messengers? They killed the Hermit. His grave is next to his tower. Go and see his grave of piled rocks if you do not believe us."

Bower nodded and called out, "Any of you who can lay a trap, do so. Make your village unsafe for any who invade it. And go to the dragons. They will defend you."

"You ask much of us," a woman said, holding her child close to her breast.

Bower shook his head. "No, I only ask that you put your trust in the dragons you know and not the strangers who are coming and who have weapons that can do that." He waved at the fallen trees, now starting to smoke and burn.

"Bower," I shouted. "We have to go as well."

"Send a message to Zenema!" he said. "Ask her to take in the refugees from the village. Den Mountain can withstand an attack, and we need to do what we can to repel these ships." He reached for my hand and held it tightly. "I am sorry, Saffron. I failed to protect you. Enric found you."

Bower did not fail. A shadow rippled over the ground. Ysix flew low overhead, her scales gleaming in the sunlight.

Bower has proven a worthy leader of humans, but Ysix still does not know if Bower is fit to lead Ysix's brood just yet! Go with my blessing. Ysix and her den will see how well these little ships burn under dragon fire. The false king will never even hear where they sank. But know this, Bower of Torvald, when you have need for dragons, call. We will come.

"Thank you, Ysix," Bower said, the words almost hushed. He turned back to the villagers and shouted, "Take only the essentials. The dragons can fish enough to feed you, but go now. Quickly!"

For a moment, they hesitated, and then the man who had first met us waved at the trees and shouted, "You heard him. Let's go before our huts our smashed just as those trees were and our bodies, too."

I stepped closer to Bower and nudged him with my hand. "It looks as if you have finally started to find out who you really might be. And that might be a king."

*   *   *

CHAPTER 6

NORTHWARD

Chaos erupted in the village, leaving Saffron and me standing there and trying to help. I had always thought a battle would be terrible and scary, but this wasn't even a fight yet and it was already confusion, with villagers falling and running and sometimes shoving at each other. Thankfully, a few of them seemed to keep their wits and they were able to get the others organized. Saffron and I couldn't do much more than lead the way to Den Mountain, the villagers following in clumps. Saffron asked Jaydra to fly and scout out the ships and keep an eye on them.

Jaydra rose into the air at once, and disappeared up into the clouds that almost always dotted the sky over the islands toward the end of the day. And that might be something that helped us— it was nearing sunset and I wasn't really certain the ships would try an attack at night. Not if they couldn't see any fires—and there would be no moon tonight. That might give us a few hours to prepare.

I wasn't really sure the villagers and the dragons would get along. Would the villagers treat the dragons with respect? Would the dragons understand the panic the villagers were in? I was worried for them, I had to trust in Zenema and the other dragons.

We reached Den Mountain and started to climb the rocky sides. The villagers had trouble and I almost wanted to urge them to let the dragons take them up to the caverns and tunnels, but it was difficult just dealing with dragons overhead. I could hear their wings flapping, their calls and hisses. It seemed as if there were dragons everywhere, flying around the peak in ever contracting circles. I could feel their agitation, and my hair and clothes were buffeted by the breezes their wings created. I had never seen an entire flight of dragons, and they reminded me of the way birds flock in gigantic groups. The only creature still calm seemed to be Zenema, who sat at the edge of one of the stone perches, staring out to the glittering blue sea to the east.

King's ships bring their filth with them. Zenema's thoughts held such scorn that I almost tripped. I would not want any dragon, but especially one as powerful as her to ever be angry at me.

Looking out from high on Den Mountain, I could see three fat-bellied ships, their dark wood blackened with tar. They seemed wide and slow, and their sides bristling with cannons. The vessels seemed to have anchored in the largest bay in the island, not far from the village where we had been. The ships had no masts, but each vessel had a strange metal chimney from which belched forth oily, black smoke. A black sweep spoiled the water behind each vessel, spoiling the pristine blue waves. More of Enric's magic I guessed.

84

Ysix and her brood swirled over the ships, diving in low and fast every now and then, but I noticed the flames they shot at the ships did no damage—there were no sails to catch fire and the decks seem protected by metal. However, Ysix and the other dragons at least kept the sailors and soldiers from coming onto the decks.

The sun was setting and I wondered if the sailors would try to land at night and would they try an attack directly at Den Mountain? Or would they raid the village first? I wasn't sure, but the first order was to get the villagers settled.

Thankfully, Saffron told me that Zenema had commanded one tunnel to be kept for the villagers alone. Saffron and I were able to settle the villagers there, and once they figured out the dragons weren't trying to attack them—or eat them—they got down to sorting out sleeping arrangements, food and water.

Leaving Saffron to help sort out supplies for the villagers, I headed back outside to stare at the dark waters and the darkening sky. Every now and then a boom shook the air as one of the ships set off a cannon. I could see fires in the forest below, and I wondered if the ships would simply stay in the bay and try to pound the island into dust. Ysix and the other dragons returned to Den Mountain, and then Zenema's voice echoed in my mind, commanding me to attend her.

I climbed up to the higher rocks where she perched, my heart thudding and even more nervous than when I had faced the villagers.

Speak to me, Bower of Torvald, Zenema asked, her thoughts rumbling. *The last time I flew against any human was well over a hundred years ago at the fall of Torvald itself.*

"You were there?" I stammered, amazed. "Is that why you sent Saffron to the mainland to learn the truth of her heritage? Do you know of the Flamma-Torvalds? I am—"

I bit off the last words. I wasn't sure if I wanted to know if I were anything like one of my ancestors.

Zenema growled at me. Her wings fluttered and her words came into my mind again. *When the time is ripe, I will tell you of these things. But if Bower wishes to do his ancestors proud, advise me now.*

"Well, uh…why are you asking me for advice? I mean, I've read *Strategicus,* but don't dragons know how to fight?"

Against villagers. And in the old ways. But Bower grew up in Torvald. Bower knows the creations of Enric. We do not.

I thought I caught a hint of sadness in her words, and it seemed wrong that so powerful a dragon should feel sorrow at not knowing how the world had changed. I stood a little straighter. "I'll do my best to remember what the old books and manuals told me—and mix it with what I know of Enric and the mainland. There have been a lot of battles recorded. I read General Berison's chronicle of his exploits and his military manuals. But that was a long time ago. And…well, a lot of our history has been twisted and blotted out."

Speak of what you know, Bower.

"Well, one of Berison's tenets was study your field." I looked to the darkening vista before us. The water had darkened, with the setting sun leaving a streak of gold across the waves. The island seemed darker than usual, with no village fires burning. The island itself was shaped a little like a squashed star, with points of land sticking out into the water, shallow bays, and Den Mountain rising up at the very center. Rivers wound through the island, with the largest river making a wide loop and then emptying out into the largest bay. Forests covered most of the island, with clearings here and there, and the villagers had their settlement near the river, not far from the bay edged with golden beaches.

Crossing my arms, I told Zenema, "Enric's ships look to have anchored in the bay—they must know the river is the fastest way to the village. But it's Den Mountain they have to conquer if they want to wipe out the dragons."

Jaydra and two other of the younger—or at least the smaller— dragons flew back to Den Mountain, gliding low over the forest.

Plumes of black smoke lifted from two of the anchored vessels, followed by the heavy, echoing booms of cannon.

I waved a hand at the ships. "Those cannons have shot that's powerful enough to punch a hole through a dragon's wing or break a skull. That's their advantage. Ours is that the cannon's range can't hit Den Mountain. Look you can see where the shot crashes into the forest. It's demolishing ancient trees and cracking boulders. But to get to Den Mountain, the ships will have to land troops on the island."

I do not want to send the young ones against those black guns, Zenema thought at me.

I shook my head. "That is wise. But they may try to keep you pinned within the mountain. If that happens, that could lead to trouble.

Villagers. They must eat and drink and will become restless. Dragons would just burrow deep and sleep.

Zenema lashed her tail and I edged away so the spikes on the end wouldn't hit me. How nice it must be to be a dragon who could sleep until troubles went away. Or who had the power to fight, or even to fly away.

I rubbed at my chin. My beard had not yet come in—I wasn't old enough to grow one. But sometimes my jaw and cheeks seemed to itch as if hair would sprout any day. "On one hand, here on the mountain is the safest place for everyone, but on the other, we can easily be trapped here by the ships. But I read something once about how if you have allies then you should always choose to hunker down during a siege. You can survive longer than an encamped enemy as you wait for reinforcements. But we've got all our allies here. So…if we don't have allies coming to help us, we must find a way to break the siege."

Zenema huffed out a warm, smoky breath as if she did not care for my reasoning aloud.

I cursed myself. If I was a True King, why did I not know the answer to this problem?

A wave of anguish knotted my insides as I wondered if perhaps Ysix and the rest had been right about me. I was not ready to be any sort of leader. All I knew about were the dusty and dead lessons from books. What sort of king relied on that alone without any experience to guide him?

I heard a scatter of rock behind me and turned to see Saffron climbing up to the perch. With me, Zenema and Saffron, it seemed crowded. I reached out to give Saffron a hand, but she simply glared at me and climbed up to stand in front of Zenema.

Saffron and Zenema swapped stares as if Saffron was asking if it was acceptable to intrude. Saffron was dressed in her heavier travelling breeches and what seemed a new, green leather jerkin. A heavy backpack hung from one shoulder along with a rope.

Looking away from Zenema, Saffron waved a hand at me and said, "You should get changed if we're flying north. It will be cold." She glanced behind her, looking to the black, oily boats now almost lost in the gathering night. For a moment, her expression seemed bleak.

Something in me snapped.

I would have to go—I must. But I could not leave the dragons and these villagers in trouble. I might not be a great general or the perfect king, but I could not let Saffron and the others down.

Looking up at Zenema's white bulk, I told her, "You need to stop those cannons. Without cannon, those ships have no power, no control over the island."

One hit will kill any dragon.

"They have a weakness. I saw it a few years ago when Enric had had a great celebration to unveil the creation he had used against some of the southern tribes. The cannons use black powder to fire a heavy iron ball that can smash whatever is in their path. But the alchemical primers I read that talked of this magic spoke of how the powders are unstable. One man must mix the powder just right, another two have to load the cannon, another one arms the mechanism and lights the fuse. They have to aim the cannon and all of that takes time to fire them. That is their weakness—the long delay."

Zenema huffed out another smoky breath and I thought I saw the hint of a scowl pulling down her wide dragon mouth.

Remembering one of the main lessons of battle that I'd ever read, I told her, "Pit your strongest points against their weakest—that is the way to win."

Zenema's thoughts swirled in my mind. *We can fly. We breathe fire. We are strong.*

"And you are together—you outnumber the enemy!" Glancing down at the black water where I could only make out the ships as small fires they had lit, I told Zenema, "Look at the way they huddle so close. They are far from home, far from the mainland, far from their allies. And they think dragons can only fly."

But I knew better—I had seen dragons fish. I knew how Jaydra loved swimming in the river.

Just like one of the many puzzles that I had once solved in my study in Torvald so very long ago, I suddenly saw the way that the battle had to go if we were to win. I started to explain everything to Zenema and Saffron.

*   *   *

At dawn, the dragons were ready. So was I—I hoped. Zenema had spoken to Ysix and the other dragons and since they thought it was her plan, they were willing to follow her. While the sky was still dark, the dragons left Den Mountain, flying high up into the morning clouds.

I stood on the peak where Zenema had sat last night, Saffron at my side. "This had better work," Saffron muttered.

I said nothing—I could say nothing. I was too nervous to talk. Too nervous to do anything but stand with my hands clenched and hoped this would succeed.

At Zenema's commanding roar, the cloud of dragons whirling in the gray, early light above us parted. Four of the biggest, most mature dragons broke away from the others. One of them was huge, lumbering Oloxia. The four swooped around Den Mountain and skimmed low over the trees, racing to the other side of the island. There they plunged into the water, sinking out of sight.

I watched the waves, wondering how long it would take them to swim around to the bay, wondering if the plan would work.

It is a good plan, Bower of Torvald, Zenema thought to me. *Almost good enough to be worthy of a king.*

Above us, the other dragons began to roar and shoot fire into the sky. Even from this distance, I could hear the clang of warning bells from the ships. "Look up…keep looking up," I muttered.

Dawn streaked the sky and now I could see the ships—three ships anchored in the bay.

The soldiers on the ships readied their cannons and fired, but the dragons in the sky dove and darted away, unharmed.

That's when it happened.

Great spouts of water rose up under the boats. The ships all rocked—and dragons roared up from the water, grabbing the ships' hulls with sharp claws. The soldiers on the ships had no time to reload their cannons. The ships rocked wildly, and one dragon—Oloxia—dug a huge hole in the ship's hull. The ship next to it flipped upside down and now dragons descended from the sky onto it. The third ship tried to fire up its engines and turn to run, but two dragons surged up from the water, crashing down onto the ship with all their weight, sinking it in an instant. The water foamed and dragons tore from the sea, heading back into the sky to swirl over the broken ships. It was too far for me to see if any of the soldiers had survived, but I could see dragons plucking small shapes from the water, and I turned away.

Above me, the dragons wheeled once around Den Mountain and then broke apart, some flying low over the sea and others swirling over the sinking ships. Every now and again a scream or a wail drifted to me on the wind, and I cringed.

But I had to remember the horrible things Enric had planned— how he had tried to destroy his own capital city, how he had sought my death, how he had tried to steal Saffron's magic, and how even now he hunted us.

My resolve hardened—Enric had to be stopped.

Even if a few soldiers escaped, they would be stranded on the island—and either villagers or the dragons would take care of them.

"It will buy us time," I told Saffron. "Time to find another island. Time to evacuate the villagers."

Saffron glanced at me. "But we still lose Den Mountain. The villagers still lose their village. How is that just?"

I shook my head. It wasn't. But we were now at war with the king.

We didn't wait for the celebration. I went and told the villagers what had happened, how the king's ships were no more, how they must find a new home, another island. A few grumbled, but some of the younger villagers were starting to get bold about getting closer to the younger dragons—maybe this alliance would last. I hoped so.

I packed up the few things I had—the few books I had salvaged I would leave with Zenema. She would have to care for them.

When I took them to her and gave them into her care, Zenema looked at me for a long moment, her eyes swirling and bright, before she nodded. *Once we have a new den, the dragons I can spare will follow you. Go now with my blessing and wishes for a swift flight and steady wind.*

I left her and headed back to where Saffron was waiting, her own gear still packed. She gave me another long look, and I asked her, "What?"

"Nothing." She shook her head and pointed to two leather pouches. "Food and water. We have to get them on Jaydra. Then all we have to do is get you to learn how to fly, fight, shoot and generally not look so sheepish all of the time."

I mumbled something back to her that was more of a complaint about her.

We tied the pouches to Jaydra. And Saffron barked, "Quit moving, Jaydra!"

I glanced at Saffron and saw her cinching a strap around Jaydra.

Jaydra fidgeted, craning her head to look back at what Saffron was doing to her.

Somehow, Saffron had managed to create two makeshift saddles out of old blankets and bits of leather and ropes. The straps to hold them on Jaydra seemed huge, and Jaydra squirmed as Saffron pulled them tight. The saddles sat between Jaydra's spines, and from them hung our pouches of food and the maps we had found in the Hermit's tower.

We were about to become dragon riders it seemed.

Saffron climbed into her saddle, tested it and lashed an old belt around her. She gave me a hand and I climbed into my saddle. She had fashioned a belt for me as well.

"We have a long way to go and we're going to be sleeping on the go," she said.

"And you don't want me falling out. You know, they once had a dragon rider academy, and saddle makers as well as harnesses for dragons. Every dragon had a custom harness that wouldn't chafe or itch."

Just then Jaydra shook and I had to cling to a dragon spine not to get tossed off.

Saffron glanced back at me. "Now you have Jaydra wanting just that. She doesn't think much of my skill with rope." Jaydra tensed and gave a high-pitched call. I felt a thrum of connection between her and Saffron. Saffron leaned down to hug Jaydra's neck and then she straightened.

"Ready?" Saffron asked.

"No," I said.

"Me neither."

Jaydra threw herself into the air. Wind stung my eyes and face and pulled on my hair, and I vowed I was going to create a helmet to wear. Even though Saffron was always telling me not to look down, I did. And then I could not tear my eyes away from the wreckage of the king's ships.

A black slick coated the bay, and the golden sands now seemed stained and strewn with bits of flat metal and chunks of wood. Thankfully, I could see no bodies in the water—but I knew that meant either the fish had eaten them or something else had. I didn't want to think about that, so I looked up again.

The island receded at an alarming rate, becoming the sort of image that I might see on one of the best maps. Jaydra beat her wings in a steady rhythm, taking us into the clouds and then above them. The sun beat down on my head and back. I held onto my harness and Jaydra's spines, my heart thudding, and my motions mixed.

We were on our way to perhaps find an army—or allies who would help us. But I wanted to look back at the island. I wanted to know the villagers would be safe with the dragons and the dragons safe with the villagers as new friends. I wanted them to find a new sanctuary, and yet I knew I could not stay to help them with that task.

Seeing the same tension in Saffron's shoulders as she sat hunched and tight, helped a little. She was leaving far more than I was.

97

The mainland loomed ahead of us, a darkened haze on the horizon, as we flew toward our future or our doom.

CHAPTER 7

SAFFRON'S LESSON

The air was changing, growing colder. I could feel it in my
bones, in just the same way as I could smell it and taste the
change. And I could hear Bower's teeth clattering. Were it not for
the dragon-in-my-mind—the place that was part me and part
Jaydra—I wonder if I still would have been able to detect all of
this. The air to me seemed to lack the soft smell of ocean. It held
a hint of pine and something bitter.

Northern snows, Jaydra informed me, and her thoughts seemed
unhappy. It was one of the few things she had shared with me
over the long hours we'd been flying. I sent her my agreement,
not knowing whether there was anything I could even say to
make her happy about snow and cold winds. Like me, she had
grown up with the warm trade winds of the Western Isles. And,
like me, she had just left her family again to come with me. But
this time we weren't leaving Zenema and the other dragons safe
in Den Mountain. Would Jaydra forgive me for taking her away
from her family right when they were in need?

Jaydra's thoughts butted into my mind. *Saffron is Jaydra's
family. We are one. We are not the same, but we come from the
same spark.* She did not sound like the playful Jaydra I had
always known. She sounded older and wiser. I wondered if

dragons matured not in years but from events such as this one, suddenly turning a corner and becoming cleverer by leaps and bounds.

Just like Bower has.

When we had first met Bower, he seemed a gawky youth, unable to survive in the wilderness. It was not that long ago that we'd first met, but events had changed him. His plan to deal with the king's ships had been a good one, hitting them from below when they were looking up at the skies and expecting dragons to fall on them.

For a moment, when he had been telling Zenema his plan, I had seen the worry rise up in his eyes—that old uncertainty that I'd seen before in him. But then something changed. He had pushed back his shoulders and had seemed to accept the role being pushed onto him.

Now, however, I heard him cough. I turned to see his face now white and his hands just as pale as he clung to one of Jaydra's spines.

"Losing sensation?" I shouted. The wind took my words to him. He pressed his lips tight and just nodded, as if he was too cold to even manage words. "Cold from the north," I pointed to where we were heading, and then rubbed my hands over my arms and legs. "Keep moving. Get blood in them!"

Bower nodded and tried to wiggle his legs, but ended up shifting his weight. Underneath us, Jaydra shifted as well, trying to adjust to Bower's movements.

Where does he want me to go? She hissed, sounding more than a little annoyed with Bower.

Just keep heading toward the mountains and the snow. Ignore us for a while.

I sent her my feeling of sympathy for everything she was going through, hoping she would be patient with us. We were all tired, and worried for those left behind. But right now I had to make sure Bower knew how to deal with a long flight. I also had to teach him not to send more wrong signals to Jaydra.

Unclipping my belt, I stretched and then swung my legs up and around, so I now sat facing backwards, facing Bower. The cold breeze plucked at my hair and clothes. Bower's eyes widened, but I held up a hand to let him know I knew what I was doing. I had been riding Jaydra's back far longer than Bower had, and I was used to the way Jaydra flew. I could anticipate her movements, and since her senses were connected to me just now, she also knew that I needed her to fly steady and straight.

And Bower had to learn this lesson as well as others.

Pulling my legs up, I crouched on the blankets I had set between Jaydra's spine ridges. I waited for the tingling in my legs to stop and then I shouted, "I'm coming over to you!"

Bower frowned. "Are you certain that is wise?"

Ignoring his question, I eased over Jaydra's spine, spreading my feet as wide as I could and keeping one hand on the spiky ridges on her back. Once I was in front of Bower, I waved for him to unfasten his own belt. "I found out the first time I flew to the mainland that you have to get up and move or land and stretch your legs every few hours. Your muscles will seize up otherwise."

"Can't we land?" Bower shouted, hunched over and hugging his arms around his body.

"If we had island-hopped, as we did when we escaped Torvald, we might have found land every few hours or an atoll. But it's not wise for us to cross the skies over the Middle Kingdom, so Jaydra is taking us north over the sea and then we'll head to the mountains in the north to try and find this Three-Rivers clan. It will be a day or two that we'll not find islands out here."

"Can Jaydra fly that far?"

"Good question—it is one you need to know. You also need to deal with things that go wrong. It's a key lesson in flying, one that every dragon learns early. Sometimes you don't know if you can escape that storm or if you are fast enough to avoid the obstacles. You have to find out your limits by pushing up to them. You have to know what you can survive."

Bower undid his belt and I could see him working hard not to look down. This was one of the hardest lessons I had to teach him—he had to learn to trust that Jaydra would never allow him to fall.

I waved for him to stand. "Don't worry. A dragon can sleep on the wing, by putting half her mind to rest and just gliding. Dragons can lock their wings. Jaydra will probably snooze once we've stretched. Now, up you get."

Bower took a deep breath, grabbed my arm and one of Jaydra's spines and struggled up into a crouch.

"You have to do this every few hours. You have to stand and walk around while in flight." I stood straighter to show him it could be done. It was colder standing, for I no longer had Jaydra's spines blocking some of the wind. I staggered a step to find a better balance.

Bower watched me but did not rise from his hunched over crouch. "This seems a very bad idea."

I shook my head. "We'll be through the worst of it soon. Right now we're getting a mix of winds—cold ones from the north and they're hitting the warmer currents from over the sea. It gets a little choppy where the two meet."

Which is why we don't usually fly north over the sea, Jaydra added, her thoughts sharp and still unhappy.

Yes, but this is a good lesson for Bower to learn! I held out my hand to Bower. "Come. Stand up."

"I don't think that I can," Bower said, still clinging to Jaydra's spine.

I grabbed his wrist. "How is any dragon going to follow you if you cannot trust just one dragon, and a dragon who is your friend? Now, if you don't stand, your legs will cramp and when it comes time to land, you'll end up falling off Jaydra's back and that's high enough up that you could end up breaking a bone. So get up!"

I felt bad forcing him to do this, but my words worked on him. He nodded, turned his hand to grip mine and slowly rose to his feet.

He lurched to one side as if his legs were cramping, and he almost stumbled back down to one knee.

"Find your balance. Use your arms and keep your knees bent a little." I kept hold of his hand. "It's actually hard to fall off a dragon. Look how broad Jaydra's back is, and look at all the spines and scales you could catch onto. Just take a breath and relax. Feel how Jaydra moves underneath your feet. You need to learn to trust your dragon will hold you up."

Bower's face was still pale. And his one leg kept buckling. He leaned to one side, as if to compensate for that weaker leg and in doing so, lost his balance.

"Bower, stand straight," I shouted, latching onto his wrist so that now I held his hand with both of mine.

He jerked upright, but his weak leg bucked and he slipped to the side and slid off Jaydra's back, pulling me with him.

Freezing wind howled in my ears. A thousand tiny flecks of ice bit my cheeks. I let go of Bower and tried to grab for Jaydra's scales, but my fingers slipped, for she was as icy as the rest of the world. Spinning now, I fell through swirling, misty clouds.

From somewhere just below me I heard Bower's scream. Glancing down, I saw a darker shape. I rolled and spun myself and shouted out Bower's name, but the wind whipped away my words.

Jaydra's thoughts burst into my mind. *Can't see Saffron, but Jaydra can smell.*

Through our connection, I felt how she was being buffeted by the mix of winds—the warm currents trying to carry her higher and the cold ones pushing her down. I didn't know if she could reach me before I hit cold, hard water.

The clouds cleared suddenly, and now I could see dark water below us, the waves capped with white. Bower tumbled over and over again. We'd hit the water like two thrown stones. If the impact didn't kill us, those icy waves would.

With a sudden pulse, my magic swirled from within me. Power tingled in my fingers, spread up my arms and burst into my chest like a blazing fire. The power that coursed through my veins was always waiting to bubble up. I didn't really know what it was or where it came from—only that it had something to do with dragons and I had at least learned how to summon it. My hands moved in complicated patterns of their own accord, and power poured from my fingertips.

I threw out my hands at Bower. A golden-green light erupted and wrapped around Bower, catching him. With a jerk, his fall slowed. The light pulled him to me, as if it was a rope that I could pull on.

I spread my hands wider, turning the light into wings. We soared over the white-capped waves on my magic. The wind seemed to disappear as if we were part of it now, not separate and fighting it. We weren't falling. Willing it, I changed our direction, and sped us forward. But I was already exhausted and knew I could not keep us in flight for much longer. The magic wobbled and the green-golden wings of light shrank. We dropped closer to the ocean.

I can't control it—we're going to fall.

Above me, Jaydra roared. She swooped down, catching us back onto her back. Smoke wisped from Jaydra's mouth. I clutched at Jaydra's spine ridges, and my magic evaporated, leaving my legs shaking and my breath rattling in my lungs.

Bower righted himself on his saddle and asked, "What did you do? That was unbelievable." He grinned.

I crawled to my saddle and fastened my belt again, my hands shaking. Jaydra held her wings wide and steady, and swooped down to a lower height where the air seemed a little warmer.

Bower shouted to me, "What were you trying to teach me again?"

I glanced back at him. "Not to be scared of flying."

Bower laughed. "I don't think much of anything will frighten me after that. That—that was magical flight. It makes sitting on a dragon seem easy."

Turning to face front, I hunched over and clung to Jaydra's spine. I had wanted him to just try to stand up on Jaydra and walk on her back.

Instead, I had learned something about myself.

Could I repeat that same magic again? Could I summon it when I had need again?

Jaydra's thoughts slipped into my mind. *All that matters is that Saffron saved Bower, and Jaydra saved Saffron. That counts a successful hunt!*

Dragons have a much simpler way of looking at things, I told her.

Glancing down at my hands, I tried to will the magic to return. My fingers tingled and a glow spread over my skin, but it seemed as if I had used up whatever store of power I had. It would have to build up again. My hands had moved more of their own accord, as if they knew what to do while my mind did not. Why was it that I seemed to have to be in dire peril before I could even use magic?

I had to find a way to strengthen my powers, to be able to control my magic when I wanted to use it, and not just hope that it would come to me out of desperate need.

*   *   *

PART 2

LEARNING TO FIGHT

CHAPTER 8

WARNING SIGNS

On the third day of flying we spotted land. Despite the cold and my aching muscles, despite Saffron seeming to want to show me how dangerous flying was by almost getting us both killed, I was learning to love this.

I was riding on the back of a dragon.

It was like one of the old tales I had read, only it wasn't some peasant boy who got to ride dragons. It was me!

The dark oceans below gave way to a narrow beach and jagged cliffs. Far below I could see hundreds of sea birds trying to nest above the spray of the waves, suddenly disturbed by our flight. I would have thought by now I might have gotten used to looking down at the land from on high but it still felt fresh and exciting to me. I could see for miles, for what felt like a day. Below us was a patchwork of the light green of occasional, overgrown meadows and the deeper green of the wildwood forests. Beyond them came the river valleys and the mountains, their heads layered with snows. On the horizon I could see the distant shapes and humps of the distant northern mountains that I didn't know the names of. I looked to my right, to the east where, somewhere beyond the horizon, Dragon Mountain and the citadel of Torvald stood.

It felt like if I could peer far enough into the distance, I might even see my future staring back at me. It was a feeling of total freedom like I'd never experienced before. But we had to find a place to land, as Jaydra was getting tired. She barely beat her wings now, just letting the warm thermals carry her ever deeper and lower over Middle Kingdom.

Pointing to a ribbon of gray that cut across the green land to the south, I called out, "Look there."

"What is it? A place to land?" Saffron said, glancing back at me.

"No, that must be the Great Western Road. It is the same one I was travelling when I met you, and you saved me from that grim-bear. It runs right from Torvald all the way to the coast, or so they say." It felt like that had all happened years ago, when in fact it was not that far back. I strained to see some sign or indication of my home city—the hearth fires or the great wall that surrounded Torvald. But I could only make out the peak of Mount Hammal, which now seemed far to the south of us.

Saffron's shout pulled my attention back to her and she waved to the north and frowned. "Do you have a clear idea of where we're heading? Where the three rivers met on the map? It all looks different now."

She was right.

The Hermit's map had shown flat lines and marks on a paper. Now we could see snow-capped mountains and valleys that offered up winding rivers, forests of green and bright reds as the trees changed colors. But it was starting to make sense to me as I looked at the rivers that crossed the land and matched them to what I had seen on the map. I doubt I would have noticed the pattern if we hadn't been flying, for the Hermit's map relied upon an aerial perspective to make sense of the different colors and lines that represented hills or mountains, fields or forests. Looking down to a ridgeline, I glimpsed the silvered foam of a waterfall that fell into the river, and a lake nearby.

I had the Hermit's map in my pack behind me, but I thought I remembered the snaking blue lines of the river and the arrowhead-shaped lake

"If the map is accurate, we still have a good way to travel up to reach where the three rivers meet, but we are closer," I shouted.

"Good," Saffron called to me. "Jaydra needs to feed. And we should hike for a bit so she can ease her wings for a time." Leaning forward, Saffron whispered something to Jaydra. The dragon angled her wings toward the lake and began a spiral down to a landing spot.

Being this much closer to finding the Three-Rivers Clan left me wondering if I really could raise and lead an army. But I had helped broker a peace—I hoped—between the villagers and the dragons, and Zenema had asked for my advice in defending Den Mountain. But this seemed a far more daunting task.

I'd known the dragons of the Western Isles—and the villagers had seemed a small group, far easier to approach than a clan that I knew nothing about. My stomach knotted, even though I kept trying to tell myself I could do this.

Jaydra swooped over the tops of the trees, the wall of the mountains ahead of us, and I tried to push my worries aside. Jaydra skimmed the surface of a clear mountain lake, and the spray of water kicked up by her wings brushed my face.

Jaydra's claws dug into the water, splashing up waves. She settled like a swan landing, let out a breath that seemed to be one of pleasure, and paddled toward a rocky beach.

I scanned the tall pines that lined the beach. We should be safe. We were far north of Torvald, probably a week's ride by horse and much longer by foot. But that didn't stop a trickle of fear sliding down my back. Enric had a long reach, and being back in Middle Kingdom meant we needed to be on guard against Enric's army and his Iron Guard.

Jaydra reached the shallows, and Saffron slid down Jaydra's shoulder, landing with a splash in the lake.

"Come on, hurry up," Saffron called. She waded up onto the beach, her boots crunching on the rocky shore as she looked around. She pointed to dead branches bleached white by time that lay under the trees. "We'll build a small fire and shelter it with rocks. We can stay the night. Maybe even snare a rabbit to eat."

I grabbed our gear from Jaydra, slid off and splashed into the shallows. The water was freezing, but clear enough I could see the bottom and the darting silver of fish as they flitted away.

"How about fish instead?" I asked.

Jaydra chirruped happily.

"That's a sure way to a dragon's heart," Saffron said. She headed to Jaydra and undid the straps to our saddles. We could use the blankets for bedding. Freed of the straps, Jaydra swam out to the deeper waters and began hunting for food, diving and resurfacing. I waded to the shore and glanced around, settling our gear onto the rocky shore.

The ground near the trees seemed softer, so I looked for a place where we might sleep. Something not too closed in—I had learned a few things from Saffron. She headed to the trees and started gathering wood, talking as she did so. "We can follow the river to the place the Hermit spoke of tomorrow and fish in the rivers whenever we need to."

I nodded, still uneasy for some reason. Was it the lack of birdsong? Or animal chatter? It seemed oddly quiet, but Jaydra might well have frightened off any other creatures. Nothing seemed to be here—no huts, no smoke rising up from some woodcutter's home. It was far cleaner than the city, the air crisp and clear. Everything seemed calm and peaceful

And then I saw a skull on a stake.

It looked to be a human skull and I froze. Saffron must have seen me standing still, one bag of food still in my hands. She glanced at me, straightened, and then followed my stare.

The macabre sight stood at the mouth of a narrow path that wound from the lake and headed along the woods, toward the nearby river. I thought the message seemed clear—do not come this way.

"Uh…Saffron, maybe we want to find another place to camp?" I told her. Glancing around, I could still see no sign of any settlement. But someone had posted that skull here. Or was this just a grave site?

Still with an armful of wood, Saffron came over to my side. "Is this a usual thing for people of Middle Kingdom?" she asked. She walked up to the skull. "I didn't spend enough time on the mainland to find out."

I shook my head. "This is not normal, but the king's laws and his army might not stretch this far north. And that should make me feel safer, but given that skull, I'm starting to have second thoughts. This could be a cursed spot. Or a gravesite. Or...or we might want to take to the skies again tomorrow."

Saffron nodded and settled to building a fire.

Even more uneasy, I spread out our blankets, but I kept glancing into the woods.

Saffron soon had a cheerful fire going, and I sat near it, my hands spread to it, welcoming its warmth. We had dried bread and Jaydra brought a mouthful of fish to us, which Saffron cooked on long sticks she scavenged. Jaydra settled not far from the fire, the light glittering on her scales. It comforted me a little that Jaydra fell to sleep at once. At least she did not think any danger was near.

I slept poorly that night, startling every time Jaydra shifted, dreaming of flying—and falling. Every time I woke, I fed a little wood onto the fire to keep it burning. We slept next to Jaydra and she warmed our backs, but the night grew chill, and I found more comfort in the bright orange flames that held back some of the night's shadows.

The first rays of light woke me again. Stiff and puffy-eyed, I stretched, rose and put the last of the wood Saffron had gathered into the fire. Dew had fallen and left the wood damp and it smoked. Saffron soon woke and that woke Jaydra as well. We filled our water skins from the lake and ate a little of the bread and fish. I kept glancing at the skull as if the jaw might move and it might tell us why it had been placed there.

"Staring won't answer your questions," Saffron said.

I glanced at her. She'd brushed and braided her hair and looked far more rested than I felt. But Saffron had always been fine with sleeping on the ground. I still missed my bed back in Torvald.

Standing, Saffron started to gather up our gear. I moved to help her, pulling out the maps just in case we needed them close to hand. We soon had our saddles on Jaydra's back and our food and equipment secured. "Just in case," Saffron said. I nodded back to her. It seemed wise to be able to jump on Jaydra's back to escape any threats.

With one hand on her knife hilt, Saffron started up the narrow path, walking past the skull as if it did not exist. I hesitated only a moment and then followed, making sure to give the skull a wide berth.

"How far should we follow this path?" I asked.

Saffron shrugged.

The thin track appeared to have beaten-down grass as if it was used infrequently—it would have been dirt only if used often. But the bent grass meant someone had been here recently. Ferns and other undergrowth choked the sides. I glanced back at the lake and saw Jaydra emerge from the water, gulping down fish before she pushed into the forest after us. For so large a dragon, she was very able to move quietly, the brush of her scales against the trees sounding more like the wind that whispered through the pines.

Having our gear on Jaydra—our cloaks, ropes, food and water—made the hike a little easier. But the path widened and became steeper, leaving me panting and my legs aching. I'd already gotten used to riding a dragon and not walking. "Are you certain we are going the right way?" I asked.

"You tell me." Saffron waved a hand at the trees and the mountains that appeared just behind the top of the pines. "On the island, all rivers lead to the sea and they always fall from the mountains down to the coast. It makes sense they will do the same here, so if we head upstream, we'll reach that spot where the three rivers join at the base of the mountains."

I paused and glanced at the Hermit's map, wishing I'd had a better education in map reading. My father had done his best, but my education had been more fitting to a noble, meaning I could read, write and do sums, but trying to figure out the map from here on the ground seemed far more difficult than it had from the air. The map seemed to indicate that we should search for a high meadow that would be surrounded by where the three rivers met.

That was the spot marked with the Salamander's sign of a stylized flame and two wings.

But what if the Hermit's map was in fact old and far out of date? My hands chilled at the thought. Might the Salamanders who had lived here moved on? What if the rivers had changed course? I tried to cheer myself by remembering the Hermit had told us to come here—that must mean there was still help to be had.

Putting the map away, I followed Saffron.

We hiked all morning and into the latter part of the day. The air warmed, for the sun was up and bright. There was still an odd lack of birds in the air or other animals. The only sound was our soft boot falls, the wind in the trees, and Jaydra's soft swish as she made her way through the trees. I started to become bored, and to amuse myself thought back to what I'd read in the *Compendium Atlas* about this area.

'A place the local people call the Three Rivers, where the Dangse, the Venge and the Oluk come together in one mighty torrent, with alpine meadows lush and with good grass, and wooded ravines that lead up into the mountains...'

The southernmost river on the map had to be the Dangse, and I wondered if that was the river we were following. I paused and thought I could hear the river to our left, the water making a soft babbling as it fell over rocks. Looking around, I realized I'd lost sight of Saffron, so I hurried to catch up with her.

Saffron had stopped at a slight rise in the path, and I hoped from there we might have a view of where we were.

Pulling out the map, I hurried to Saffron's side, trying to trace where we might be if it really was the Dangse we followed. "I think I might know where we are," I told Saffron. "It looks as if the Dangse opens into the lake we left, so that means we're here." Holding the map in front of Saffron I tried to point to where we must be.

Voice low and urgent, Saffron just said my name in a tone that made me look up.

I stared straight at a notched arrow and a bow held by a woman clad in patchwork leathers. Brown and ochre paints smeared her face, making her blend with the woods around us.

"Oh," I said and blinked twice.

The woman gave me a grim smile. "Oh indeed."

Two more women stepped from the trees, blocking our path. Each held a bow, and all three had black hair pulled back into long braids.

Saffron told them, "You should be warned—I have a dragon with me."

The three women looked very alike, but the tallest one stepped forward. "So do we."

I elbowed my way past Saffron, the map rustling in my hands. "You have dragons? But that's impossible! There are no dragons in Middle Kingdom. Everyone knows that."

The woman's mouth curved. She gestured and the woman with the knocked arrow lowered her bow. However, she did not remove her arrow from the bowstring. The tallest woman turned back to us. "You two have a lot to learn."

"Do we now?" Saffron put her hand back on her knife hilt, and from behind us, Jaydra rumbled. I didn't want Saffron's quick temper—or Jaydra's—getting us shot full of arrows. Holding up one hand and struggling to hang onto my map with the other, I said, "We have no wish to fight or spill blood."

Saffron narrowed her eyes, her mouth pulled down, but Jaydra quieted. I wondered what Saffron had said or thought to Jaydra.

Before I could ask, the wind caught at the map, pulling it from my hand. It fluttered to the ground and the woman with the bow and the arrow still strung tight stamped a booted foot down on it. She glanced at it and glanced back, her eyes going wide, then said, "Nerys? Look." She waved with one hand at the map.

Nerys—the tall woman—glanced at the map, and then looked from me to Saffron and back again. "How do you know this symbol?" She pointed to the fire and wings drawn onto the map.

"The fire within," I said breathlessly. "Are you with the Salamanders? The rebels who fight the king? That's who we seek."

CHAPTER 9

A TRUE DRAGON FRIEND

"Come," Nerys said. She turned and slipped off the main path and onto another one that twisted off to the left. The two other women followed her. Bower glanced at me, shrugged and followed after them.

I didn't like it. Not one bit. Neither did Jaydra, but I thought to her that now was not yet time to fight. Bower seemed to think these might be the people we were seeking—the Three-Rivers clan. I wasn't convinced. These three women reminded me too much of the villagers back on the island—too ready to draw a weapon first and talk after the fight. How could they claim to have a dragon or know about dragons if they didn't seem to think anything of facing a dragon in battle??

Give Jaydra a sign and Jaydra will tear out each of their hearts, crunch their bones and set fire to their forests. Jaydra sent images to me of doing just that.

Wait, my sister. This is Bower's kingdom more so than ours. And he was good at talking to the villagers. We have to learn if these people are the ones we must find.

And if they are true dragon-friends. Jaydra snorted out a fiery breath that all must have been able to smell.

I could tell she didn't believe these women were dragon-friends. But Bower seemed to want to at least talk to them. And I had to admit he'd managed to get them to ease their guard and unstring their notched arrows. He had a way of getting people to like him somehow. Was that the mark of a good king? Didn't a leader have to know how to fight?

Ahead of me, Bower hurried to catch up with the Nerys and the other women and asked her, "So, you have dragons you say? How many? What colors? I have a theory that the dragons from Torvald and the Dragon Academy that once existed there fled west, but it would be amazing to think some might have gone north."

"Dragon Academy?" Nerys glanced at him over her shoulder, her black eyebrows low and tight. "The old monastery you mean?"

"You know of it?" Bower jogged a little faster to catch up with her long stride. "How do you know of it? Did your people come here from Torvald originally?"

"The stone city?" Nerys shook her head. "No, I was born in meadows of the north as was my mother and my mother's mother. I'm Nerys, daughter of Nurita, who was daughter of Niall. My mothers have lived in the mountain meadows for as far back as memory goes, or at least we lived there until the metal men came to burn our villages. We fled deeper into the mountains and we fight back when we can, but we have never defeated the metal men."

"The Iron Guard," Bower said. "That is what we call them. They are the king's creation—some sort of magic makes them move and act."

Nerys nodded. "Others have joined us. Refugees fleeing the cities and a few old warriors. Some of them drew that sign you have on your map—the one of the flame and wings. They said we would one day need dragons and helped us capture some."

"Capture dragons?" I muttered. Reaching out, I snagged Bower's tunic hem and made him slow down and drop back with me. "What is she talking about? I thought you said the Salamanders are dragon-friends, but she doesn't sound a friend at all."

He lowered his voice and said, "She says others had the symbol of the Salamanders, so I think these women may be descendants of the old northern tribes." He hurried forward, and I glanced back to see Jaydra was now swimming in the river.

Our path kept us near the rocky banks. The path turned and headed uphill. The trees started thinning as we progressed to rockier territory. Soon, everyone except Jaydra had to scramble over boulders as we struggled along the path.

Jaydra leave river—wild currents not good for fishing or swimming.

Then fly above us, sister, that way you can swoop down if you have to, I counseled her. Jaydra took to the air, leaving us on the ground, the river water turning white, rough and roaring.

"That must be the Venge," Bower said, pointing to the river.

Nerys stopped near the top of a rocky rise. Her two friends went ahead of her. Bower scrambled up onto the boulder and I followed him.

Looking down, I could see an impressive gorge now where three rivers met—one streaming down from a waterfall, one wide and slow, and the one we followed cut out from this joining. The path wound down to the river and led to a rickety, wooden bridge that crossed the rough waters below. Once across the river, we'd be in a wide and long meadow that stood between the three rivers.

"Are you sure that bridge will hold?" I asked Nerys.

She shrugged, and then Jaydra circled overhead, casting a shadow over us. Nerys glanced up, raised her bow and knocked an arrow.

Stepping forward, I knocked her bow down. "You should know an arrow will do little against a dragon's scales."

Nerys narrowed her eyes but she did not lift her bow again. "Depends on where your arrow strikes. Our dragons are dark, their scales black or a very deep blue. So that is your dragon?"

"Mine? Dragons don't—"

"You ride wild dragons?" Bower said, interrupting. He turned to me. "The black dragon of the North Mountains is supposed to be the fiercest of all. It's said to be a little smaller than Jaydra, with spikes on their tail, and barely civilized."

I glanced at him and then turned back to face Nerys. "Jaydra is with me. But she is not mine."

"Well, see to it she keeps her distance." Nerys unknocked her arrow and returned it to her quiver. She followed the other two women down to the wooden bridge, glancing back to shout at Bower, "And as for riding a dragon, who would be fool enough to try such a thing?"

Bower glanced at me, his expression worried, but he followed Nerys down to the bridge. I noted how Nerys held to the ropes that acted as handholds on either side of the bridge. The ropes creaked and the bridge swayed as she crossed. The other two women crossed as well, one at a time.

"How could the Iron Guard get across this?" Bower muttered.

I glanced at the deep waters below us—the river was not so fast here, but the smooth surface might hide fast currents. "Maybe they just walk through the water. I'll go first—you follow me."

The wood of the bridge was slick with water splashed up by the river. I took my time crossing. The bridge and the wood creaked like a dying animal. Several of the boards looked rotted to me and I stepped over them. This bridge was as much a death trap for the unwary as anything.

When I reached the other side, Nerys gave me a grudging nod, as if she approved of me. I turned to find Bower already on the bridge and crossing.

"Watch the boards," I called out.

He nodded, and clung to the rope handholds, his knuckles almost white. For a moment, I thought he would cross safely, but as he neared the last quarter of the way, a board cracked and split. Bower's foot slipped through the wood and he clung to the rope, staring down at the fall to the water below.

I started to cross back to where he was, but Nerys grabbed my shoulder and held me back, calling out, "Too much weight on the bridge and it will collapse. It is made for one person at a time."

On the bridge, Bower had frozen, his booted foot dangling through the gap in the boards. Magic tingled in my fingertips and welled up in my chest. But I feared releasing it. Perhaps I could use it to fly him across the river, but what if the power burst out too strong and took out the bridge completely? I could end up sending Bower plummeting into the river below? But another could help.

Jaydra?

Bower in trouble—Jaydra sees.

With a shriek, Jaydra swooped down, claws extended. She snatched Bower up by his shoulders, as if he was a tasty, large fish. Beating her immense wings, she soared up and then deposited Bower not far from me.

Thank you, sister.

"Th-thank you, Jaydra!" Bower said, gasping for breath, his face red and his voice shaking a little.

"By the mountains!" With an arrow again knocked, Nerys looked from Jaydra to Bower. She'd hunched down as if fearing Jaydra would grasp her next, but now she straightened and said, "Your dragon—didn't fly off to eat him—why not?"

I faced Nerys. "No dragon would ever take advantage of a friend in need. And no dragon would ever eat a friend." Hands on my hips, I stared at her. "You might as well suggest that we try to cook Jaydra for our supper tonight!"

She could try, Jaydra thought to me as she soared back up into the sky. Heading over to Bower, I asked him, "You well?" He nodded, and I lowered my voice and said, "I am starting to get an uncomfortable feeling about the people of the three rivers if that's who they are."

Bower straightened and shook his head. "Maybe…maybe this isn't the right clan."

I gave a rude snort. So far I didn't think much of these people.

Nerys turned and with the other two women strode down into the meadowlands. A narrow path wound through grass as tall as our hips, and then the path opened and I glimpsed smoke from a settlement. Clusters of small huts dotted the meadow, with perhaps two dozen or so huts in total. I heard the bleating of goats and the lowing of cattle, and all too soon I could smell the smoke and the scent of people and animals.

But no dragons in the sky.

Birds soared overhead, but why didn't dragons swoop from the caves in the mountainsides that I could see. Were there even any dragons here?

Jaydra can smell dragon, my den-sister informed me. *But as if very far away. They are not like island dragons.* Jaydra's hisses carried to me from overhead, a sign she was distressed at what she was uncovering.

Ahead of us, Nerys waved an arm and called out, "Welcome to the Three-River Clan,"

So much for these people being the wrong ones—they were indeed the clan the Hermit had said we should find. I was starting to think perhaps the Hermit had not been in his right mind when he'd said such a thing. He'd been dying at the time, and perhaps had mistakenly sent us to the wrong place.

Bower, however, started to smile and the tension eased from his shoulders. I could only guess that to him just the sight of people living far from the rule of Enric and his Iron Guard was enough to be an inspiration.

Glancing around, I kept wondering where their dragons lived? If they were dragon-friends, why keep their dragons so far from their homes?

Sending my worried thoughts to Jaydra, I told her, *Stay near, but not too near. And stay on alert.*

Jaydra sent back her own worries to me and circled overhead.

The meadow path led into the center of the settlement. Seen up close, I saw the huts were made of round, gray stones with straw-thatched roofs. In front of each house a banner flew marked with what seemed to be the symbol of the clan, three blue lines under a red flame.

Bower slowed his stride enough to walk closer to me and said, "Judging by the moss on those stone walls, on the north side, this settlement's been here a goodly time, for a couple of decades at the least."

"How is that useful?" I muttered.

He lifted a hand and said, "It means they've evaded Enric's notice for a good time."

I shook my head. "Evading is not enough—and I do not see enough fighters here." Which was true. Children, old men, old women and then a few women and men who looked able to pull a bow watched us as we came into the settlement. People came out of the huts with wary but curious expressions. It seemed to me that this clan had only a dozen fighters. The people seemed thin, as well, as if they had little to eat. The children all offered up clean, round faces, but everyone wore what looked like patchwork clothing—leather and cloth stitched and mended so many times it was now a mix of colors and materials. Women and men all wore their hair long and braided.

A horn blast echoed from the mountains that sheltered the rivers and the meadows on two sides. Nerys raised her head and let out an ululating cry that seemed to be a reply to the horn. Stopping in the center of the settlement, she said, "Ryland comes."

"Is he your chief?" I asked.

Nerys didn't bother to answer. I gave Bower a sour look—I liked this Nerys less and less. But I thought the feeling mutual, for she seemed to dislike me as well.

The sound of galloping hoof beats came to me, and I looked around, trying to find the source. A group of five riders headed to the settlement, riding what looked to be tough little mountain ponies. They wore the same patchwork clothing as everyone here, but with leather jerkins studded with metal, and sunlight flashed off the metal tips of long spears.

Turning to Bower, Nerys told him, "Ryland is our war chief." The ponies slowed as they came into the settlement, their hides steaming. A young man in his twenties led the group. He pulled his pony to a halt and vaulted off, landing on his feet in a graceful and practiced move. His braided hair gleamed in the light like burnished copper. Deep green eyes regarded us with a steady gaze. Strong cheekbones gave him a rough look, and his beard had been braided with bands of silver and gold. He looked first at Bower, seemed to dismiss and turned to face me.

His gaze seemed to hold a challenge, but I recognized a similar soul to myself for there was a touch of the wild in his eyes, as if he was someone who would never do well in a city or even in the confines of a building.

"I am Ryland," he said, looking straight at me. His eyes seemed to warm, and a wave of heat swept through me.

134

From above, Jaydra sent me a puzzled alarm, asking with her thoughts, *Saffron well?*

Not now. I cannot explain. And I couldn't. What was wrong with me? Why did I suddenly feel both hot and cold and as stupid as if a rock had struck my chest?

Glancing up, Ryland shielded his eyes with one hand against the sun's glare and said, "Ah, she is a magnificent beast. With her size, I'll wager she could take down a Grim Bear."

The heat vanished from my body. Annoyed, I crossed my arms over my chest. "Jaydra is no beast. You speak of my den-sister."

His hand falling to his side, Ryland looked at me as if I had sprouted dragon horns and wings. "You are close to your companion animal."

Jaydra not just an animal! Jaydra gave a roar and swooped down over the settlement. Cows bellowed and goats bleated and even a few children started to cry.

"War Chief," Nerys said her voice tense. "That beast overhead is frightening the flocks."

Glancing up, I saw Jaydra swoop down again and then angle up and fly over the meadow settlement in a huge loop. Jaydra seemed delighted by the frightened animals. Even one of the mountain ponies shied and gave a low whinny.

Ryland frowned, and I told him, "Jaydra is just playing. If she meant harm, she could have snatched up her choice of cow or goat, one in each claw."

That earned me even more frowns, so I thought to Jaydra, *Calm now, den-sister. We hope to make these people our friends. Please stop chasing their livestock.*

What good are friends if they will not share food? Jaydra gave another roar, but she circled down to where we stood and hovered over the settlement. That left the mountain ponies pulling to get away.

Ryland waved a hand out to the north, to the mountains. "There are wild pastures on the other side of the ridge, and lakes that have small, but very tasty fish."

Fish? Jaydra's delight bled into me and I had to smile.

Nothing more could be to Jaydra's liking. I told her to go find dinner, and I nodded my thanks to Ryland. Jaydra flew north, disappearing over the mountain ridge. Ryland let out what sounded like a relieved sigh.

Studying him, I didn't think Ryland was as nice as Bower, but he was taller and he didn't strike me as an enemy. He had made no move to search us for weapons and he had at least treated Jaydra with some respect in terms of offering her dinner.

Ryland stepped back and waved for us to follow him. "Come, you must be tired from your travels. Dine with us in our great hall."

I glanced at Bower to see what he thought of this suggestion. But Bower was already strolling after Ryland, looking around as if he wanted to see everything at once, gawking like he'd never seen so much as a building.

Ryland led the way deeper into the settlement, leading his pony and pointing out various parts of their settlement. They grew oats in one field, had a watermill to grind their own flour, and bred cows and goats for both hides and milk.

The huts grew a little larger, and several seemed to be barns for the animals. Chickens scratched in the dirt for insects or bits of grain, and we came at last to a larger, open space in the middle of the settlement. Here, large boulders sheltered some of the buildings while tall trees with wide trunks and protective canopies of branches stood between the huts. It seemed that Ryland's acceptance of us had calmed everyone, for those who had watched us earlier turned away to return to their daily life. Even Nerys had departed, taking her two friends with the bows away.

Many of those who lived here wore strange patterns that seemed to be drawn onto their arms or legs. I glimpsed blue whirls and dots. I also noticed quite a few of the men and women had weapons close to their hut doors.

Ryland paused outside a barn to unsaddle his pony, take off his bridle and toss it some hay and make sure it had a bucket of water. I respected the fact that he chose to look after his steed himself and not hand her over to another as I had seen in some of the villages of the Middle Kingdom during my time there.

Ryland led us to one of the larger buildings, a round structure with an arched lintel of wood over double doors. Bower pointed to the arch which boasted images of dragons and tall stone towers carved into the dark wood. "That's just like the pictures of the old academy that I've seen. This Three-Rivers clan must have been founded by some of the Dragon Riders of old."

Ryland turned around to look directly at Bower for what seemed to be the first time. "You come from the Dragon Academy?"

Bower frowned and shook his head. "Yes. No. I mean…. I come from the city that once housed the Dragon Academy. From Torvald. But it's…well, the old ruins are considered haunted and the king's laws forbid anyone from ever going there. But I've seen the towers from afar."

Ryland stopped in the doorway just outside the large building. He tipped his head to one side and seemed to be studying Bower as if searching for something. In turn, Bower stared back at

Ryland and I was reminded of the way young dragons sometimes square up against each other as if to test each other's strength and skills.

At last, Ryland gave a nod and turned to go inside the building, saying, "Our stories tell us the old academy was destroyed…"

Bower followed Ryland into the large building and I followed Bower. The building looked far grander inside than out—from the outside it seemed only round, river rock stacked high with the wooden doors and carved lintel. Inside the ceiling soared high, all the way up to the roof in an arch. Long tables lined either side of the room, with carved chairs and benches. Two stone hearths boasted huge fires that warmed the room. I was almost too hot in my leather tunic and I pulled at the neck. The floors looked to be made of planks of wood, polished smooth over the ages. Shields and banners decorated the walls with splashes of colors, and I thought these must be the shields for each family.

Bower glanced around, then let out a long breath and stared down at the wooden floor. "By Hacon Maddox when he took the throne, and now Enric rules the kingdom with his Iron Guard to enforce obedience to every law, no matter how harsh or unfair."

"Metal men!" Ryland grimaced and spat on the floor. I was shocked he would treat a good floor so poorly. But Ryland said, "Too well do we know them. We know what they do to our

139

dragons if they ever manage to catch one, and we know what they do to us if they ever come upon our scouts or hunters." He pulled a face and waved to the doorway. "That is why we have the bridge. We built it so it would fail under their weight. But one day, we will find a way to defeat them."

Bower looked up, his eyes bright now and I knew he was about to talk about our quest to find an army to battle Enric. But I did not yet want to reveal why we were here. Nudging Bower with an elbow, I stepped forward and said, "War Chief Ryland, we are parched and hungry from our journey. Why do we not share our stories after we sit and drink and eat?"

Bower's mouth snapped closed. He frowned almost as if I had taken a toy from him, but when I stared at him, he seemed to understand that I didn't quite trust these people of the Three-Rivers clan.

Smiling, Ryland swept me a bow. "But of course. Come and let me find you seats and then we will dine.

Edging closer to me, Bower asked, "Why did you interrupt?"

I lowered my voice and told him, "Because I want to find out first why these people seem to hide their dragons—or if they are hiding other dangerous secrets from us."

Chapter 10

The Boy-King

Saffron seemed to dislike the Three-River clan people, but I found nothing to dislike. They seated us in the hall, brought food and drink, and the hall soon filled until it was noisy and bustling. It seemed as if the entire Three-Rivers clan wanted to come see the travelers who had arrived with a dragon. Inside the building, the hearth fire and wall torches were lit. Meat was brought in to roast in the two huge hearths, and barrels of honey mead were uncorked. Toasts had to be made, bread and meat were served on wooden planks and soon laughter and shouts started to shake the rafters.

Saffron wouldn't let me talk to Ryland about why we had come, but instead kept asking him questions—but she couldn't get him to talk about the clan's dragons.

For my part, I drank only as much as I knew I could handle, sipping from a wooden cup given to me. I was happy, however, to fill my belly with cuts of the rich, dark meat and roasted vegetables offered. I also kept studying the shields pinned to the walls and looking at the dragons carved into the posts that held up the vaulted roof. Everywhere I looked I seemed to see carving of dragons, but Saffron was right. We'd yet to see a live dragon.

How could these people be descended from Dragon Riders if they had no dragons? It was a puzzle.

When Ryland turned away to call for more food and drink, I nudged Saffron and pointed to the carvings. "They at least know what dragons look like. They got the images they carved right."

She frowned, her sandy eyebrows pulling tight. She pointed to the carving nearest us. "But what is going on there?"

Glancing over, I saw a long, slim dragon being held down by what looked like chains and smaller humans. "I am sure that it is just one of their legends."

She parted her lips to tell me what she thought of such a legend, but the banging of a wooden cup on the table cut off her words. Ryland stood and raised his mug. The hall fell quiet, and a pang of jealousy twisted in my stomach. How could he so easily command everyone's attention?

This was what I had to learn to do if I was to be a king. But, glancing around at the packed hall, I didn't know how I was to start being a king to these people. The faces around me seemed hardened by the elements, they almost looked as strong as if they'd been hewn from the very rocks of the mountains. How was I to convince them to let me lead them to a war that might mean the death of every man, woman and child?

I was almost relieved now that Saffron had stopped me earlier from talking to Ryland about our quest here.

Voice raised, Ryland called out, "Three-Rivers clan, we have two new friends with us today. They have travelled from afar and come to us with a dragon!"

A rousing chorus of roars and thumps of booted feet on the floor burst from the crowd.

Ryland held up his hand and the hall grew quiet again. "They have come to us at a time when the metal men from the south are pressing ever northward into our lands. The king and his metal men seek to destroy our way of life and steal away our heritage. But these two new friends will help us, I am sure, with our liberation of the Middle Kingdom from the tyrant of the Maddox clan!"

More cheers rose up. I glanced around. So these people wanted to liberate the Middle Kingdom. I knew now they must be descended from the Dragon Riders of Torvald.

Lifting his cup, Ryland shouted, "The hour is near when we will be able to strike back for all of the wrongs done to us. We will take back the dragon city once entrusted to us."

As others shouted, I wanted to pull Ryland aside and ask him how his people came to the three rivers. Had they flown here?

What stories might he have about the original Dragon Riders who fled Torvald so many generations ago?

Before I could ask him, Saffron shouted over the noise of the crowd. "You may have come from the dragon city, but the throne is not yours to claim, war chief." Saffron stood up and faced Ryland, almost seeming to pit her slender frame and small stature against his immense height and broad shoulders.

She faced the others in the hall and lifted her voice. "I am Saffron of the Western Isles and I flew here on the back of my den-sister, the dragon Jaydra, daughter of Zenema." She waved at me. "I have come with my companion Bower of Torvald."

"Why are you bringing this up now?" I muttered.

Waving a hand at me to keep silent, Saffron addressed the others in the hall. "The Hermit of the Western Isles named this place a sanctuary for the enemies of King Enric. He thought we would find allies in our fight to free the Middle Kingdom and the world from Enric's tyranny."

Around us, heads nodded, but Saffron scowled at the crowd. "But I am not so certain you are dragon-friends. You do not share your homes with dragons. I do not see dragon dens nearby. You do not give out the names of your dragons. Well, I tell you now—Bower is a true dragon-friend. The great den-mother Zenema calls him the True King of Torvald. It is to him the dragons will respond and fight against King Enric!"

A moment of stunned silence held the room. I curled my fists tight on the table and muttered to Saffron, "This was not yet the time to tell them."

She glanced down at me. "I won't sit here and let them talk of a dragon city when they will not even speak of their dragons."

Pressing my lips tight, I knew I should have told Saffron to keep her silence. Her cheeks had reddened and not just from wine, but from the anger pulsing inside her. Even I could feel the spark of her magic starting to stir and it left me uneasy. I did not want her doing anything rash—but she had already done that.

Ryland stared at me, the look in his eyes not so much considering as it was doubtful. I decided he must be wondering how could I be a king. I had not arrived with an army of nobles, nor did I come with rich clothes or a crown.

My face burned and a knot tightened in my chest.

Around us the low hum of talk started and then titters of laughter rose. My face burned hot and my guts twisted. I looked over to see Saffron's eyes starting to get a dangerous glint. I stood and put a hand on her shoulder, but she shook off my touch.

Someone shouted, "Dragons will come to him? Ha! Dragons don't answer to nobody."

The comment stirred more jeering laughs and more rude comments.

Hand falling to her knife hilt, Saffron shouted, "What do any of you know of dragons?"

She was right—these people did not seem to be at all close to their dragons.

Had all the stories I'd ever read of the Dragon Riders been wrong? The tales written down had spoken of how humans and dragons lived in glorious harmony. They were companions, close friends even, who shared everything. But the Three-Rives clan seemed to view dragons as beasts, they kept their ponies and mountain goats closer than they did their dragons.

Ryland put down his drinking mug and lifted both hands as if to call for quiet in the hall. Slowly, the chatter and laughter subsided, but I could still hear people shifting uneasily in their seats and mutters of how no one would follow a boy-king.

Ryland spoke up. "These two strangers do have special gifts, for they did come to us with a dragon that appears to answer their every whim."

"Jaydra doesn't take orders!" Saffron retorted, her words sharp and angry.

Ryland put a hint of steel behind his voice. "Whatever anyone believes of dragons or of you, one thing is clear to anyone with eyes. You are no more than a young woman and this Bower who travels with you is no more than a boy."

A flash of rage curled inside me and I stood. "How dare you name me a boy? I might not be as strong as you, or as tall as of yet. However, I have already battled Enric himself. And I helped defend an entire island. I have proven myself ready to fight for justice and for the Middle Kingdom. Can you claim the same?"

Ryland waved off my words as if they were of no real importance. "You bring a dragon with you, for which we are all deeply thankful. But you must understand, the Three-Rivers clan has been working with dragons for longer than you have walked the land. We were given this sacred mission from the last of the Dragon Riders after they fled their Dragon Academy. This is our holy war."

Murmurs of agreement rose from the crowd.

Their war.

I gritted my teeth. I thought of how my father had been taken by the Iron Guard, and how I had been driven from my house by them, held captive by Enric in the king's dungeons. I thought of those I knew killed by Enric—and how he had almost torched his own city to drive out the rebel Salamanders.

"The people of Torvald would not agree with you," I told Ryland. "But I understand that you must take the heritage given to you by the noble Dragon Riders of old. I, too, take my heritage seriously, for I have the blood of the Flamma-Torvalds in me. Yes, Saffron and I look to be no more than two vagabond youths, flying in from the wild, but I tell you now, what of the stories of Agathea of House Flamma? Was she not a youth when she had to face dark times and learn to be more than just a girl who rode dragons?"

A few heads nodded, but Ryland was frowning as were others.

Shaking his head, Ryland said, "The hour is getting late and we have had too much excitement for one day. Let us take to our beds. Our visitors are welcome to sleep here in our hall, and tomorrow we meet again with clear heads." Ryland looked me over as if measuring my words against the sight of me. I knew myself to be tall and lanky—and dressed more in rags. But while I might not look a king, I hoped I at least had sounded like one. Whispers filled the hall, but Ryland held up a hand and they quieted and Ryland said, "If Bower really is a true dragon king, the test will prove such a thing. If he proves himself, we must follow for long have we sworn such a thing." Ryland looked directly at me. "If you fail, your dragon and Saffron are still welcome additions to the power of ours as we plan our next move against the usurper king and his metal men."

More tests.

My heart sank. Would anyone ever be able to just look at me or hear my words and believe me? Dragons wanted me to prove myself, and now the Three-Rivers clan needed me to do something before they would recognize me as a king. Would this be another test to broker a peace? Or would the test be worse? From the way Ryland had spoken, it sounded as if this test might well end with me dead.

Saffron tugged at my sleeve and turned to the entrance. "Come, Bower. I'll not eat a scrap more with these people."

She strode for the door, and I followed her outside.

Arms crossed against the chill of the night air, she seemed to be seething as she paused by the double doors, waiting for me.

Ryland had followed us out. As voices and shouts rose up in the hall again, Ryland called to us, "Friends, please!"

Saffron turned on him. "How dare you call us friends after mocking us?"

Ryland raised his hands in a placating gesture. It was too dark outside to see his expression, but I thought from his wide-legged stance that he was only trying to calm Saffron. He must feel the energy pouring from her as I could.

Hunching a shoulder against the night, I wondered if we should leave this clan to their own war and try searching for others who might help us.

But Ryland lowered his hands and looked from Saffron to me and back again. "I ask you to understand. Our clan is very different from the people of the city. We have been at war for a long time, since before even the mad King Enric came to the throne. Once long ago, our clan lived in terror of the wild dragons that roamed our mountains. The dragon riders came and showed us how to tame them. But…of late, it is as if a dark spell has been thrown over the land. Our dragons started to turn on us, and we have had to be sterner and stronger with our dragons if they were going to obey us."

Saffron frowned and turned away, but I asked, "What do you mean stern and strong?"

Ryland glanced at me and shook his head. "I do not know how you got your island dragon to perform its tricks. Our dragons would as soon tear one of us apart as it would to smash one of the metal men!" Ryland waved a hand at me. "So you see, it appears a joke to us when you say that this mere…slip of a youth boy here could make our dragons seem tame. Our dragons are fighters—and they will fight him."

It was my turn to shake my head. "Why is it you do not have any of the Salamanders with you? You knew their symbol—the flame within. If they've been here, I don't understand how the noble link between human and dragon could go so wrong. Dragons are not merely beasts, but should be your allies and friends."

My words earned me the flash of a smile from Saffron, but Ryland pulled at his beard and said, "People from the city once traveled to our settlement with dusty, old books, talking of the old days. But our people were dying, and these travelers spoke of ways to hide and only of how to work from within. That did us no good. We told them to stick to the cities and sent them away while we struggled to train our dragons."

My heart leapt. Maybe their test wouldn't be so difficult. If they were trying to train dragons with chains, and I had at least learned from Saffron and Jaydra better ways to work with dragons, this test might be as simple as getting a dragon to behave.

But hadn't I read something once about the wild, black dragons being very different from all others? That thought worried me, so I asked, "Why do you think your dragons and the land is under a spell?"

Saffron asked, "Why do you hide your dragons?"

Ryland snorted as if we both asked stupid questions. "We bring out our dragons only when they are needed. It is too dangerous otherwise."

Dropping her arms to her side, Saffron asked, "What do you mean dangerous? Don't you offer them enough food to keep them happy?"

Ryland thrust an accusing hand up toward the mountains that towered over the settlement. "We drive a muddle of sheep up to them every night! But in the morning you will see and understand." He turned and headed back into the hall, leaving us in the cold and bright moonlight. Saffron sighed. "At least we can sleep next to Jaydra tonight. She'll be warm enough to keep us comfortable." She turned and headed out of the settlement, walking toward the wide, mountain meadow to the west.

Leaving the light of the settlement behind left me feeling more than a little disappointed in these people. They were even more cynical than the people of Torvald. These people knew dragons existed—how was it they did they not love their dragons?

And what kind of test was I to face tomorrow?

My boots seemed to grow even heavier as we trudged toward Jaydra, who lay snoring happily on what I judged to be a bellyful of lake fish. I curled up under her leathery wing, not far from Saffron. But I lay there, eyes open, staring at the stars.

And I kept thinking about the coming day and all I must do.

How was I going to prove I was a dragon king?

CHAPTER 11

CURIOUS

I woke long before Bower, my eyes seeming to pop open and magic stirring inside me. Like always, I shut it down before it could come fully to life. Anger always stirred the magic, and I was still angry with these people for how they seemed to think dragons were just stupid beasts, and angry with the Hermit for sending us here. But all of that seemed useless. The Hermit was dead and I still wanted to see these wild dragons of the Three-Rivers clan to see what they were like. Slipping out from under Jaydra's wing, I stretched, yawned and glanced around.

Dawn seemed a gray light in the east, the settlement sat quiet without so much as a morning fire sending smoke into the air and even Jaydra slept.

Jaydra's mind brushed against mine as some part of her sensed I was awake, but she couldn't rouse herself from her own dreams.

Silver fishes, jumping fishes, tasty fishes.

I patted her neck. "Dream sweet dreams while you may, and keep our boy-king safe," I muttered.

I'd grown fond of Bower, but a need to protect him sat heavy inside me. I had never felt close to anyone other than Jaydra. Even Zenema had been more a mother to me, but Jaydra was almost a part of me. Of course, dragons didn't need a lot of protecting, and it was an unwritten rule that everyone in the clutch had to be able to look after themselves, which Jaydra could do. So it was strange to feel this way.

Is this what friendship is?

From where he was sprawled under Jaydra's wing, Bower's boot twitched as if he too was still caught up in dreams. He was going to need new boots soon, for his looked to be losing their soles and seemed over-large on his feet.

Remembering Ryland's score of Bower as any kind of dragon-kin I wondered if Bower really was ready to control armies. At times it seemed to me that he was as bad at being a king as I was at dealing with magic. I stared at my hands, wondering why it was that sometimes the magic seemed so simple to me—it just happened and was perfect. Other times the power frightened me and left me worried it would twist into something dark—it was Maddox magic after all.

But Zenema's words kept echoing in my mind—the truth of who I was lay in my blood. I had to trust in who I really was inside—that I was not like Enric.

I also had to trust in the truth in Bower's blood.

He had risen to the challenge of organizing the escape of the villagers. He had come up with a good plan to defeat Enric's ships and save the dragons from a terrible battle. I had to trust that when the time came the qualities of a strong and wise leader would be there for him and for all dragons as well.

None of that, however, helped us with getting through whatever tests the Three-Rivers clan would put before Bower— and I was not certain I would be allowed to help him. And I was certain whatever test Ryland planned for Bower, it would involve their dragons. After all, how can a dragon-king be tested if not with dragons?

I had best go and try to find these wild dragons before Bower had to face them.

Using some of our water, I washed quickly, pulled out a thick cloak to keep me warm against the chill of the morning—for mist clung to the air, stirred up by the rivers—and glanced around.

This far north any dragon would need warm dens, and dragons always preferred dens in high places. So the mountains that surrounded the place where the three rivers met must be where these wild dragons lived. The rivers would be too wet, so I set off for the closer mountains, for as the sun rose it showed what seemed to be some large caverns near the peaks.

Thinking of dragons and dens left me wondering how Zenema and the other dragons fared. Had more ships from Enric arrived to lay siege to the island? Or was my dragon-kin now safe on another island, hidden from harm?

My dragon family was tough, strong and quick. I had to trust in that, too. So I put my mind to the task I'd set for myself—climbing up to the caverns I had seen to find the wild dragons.

Used as I was to climbing, I still wished I could fly Jaydra here. However, it was best to meet these dragons without the intrusion of a strange dragon into their territory. Just my appearing in their den might alarm them.

My boots crunched on a layer of frost, but soon grass gave way to shale and iron rock. The mountain side grew steeper, but I could still walk and found goat trails that led me higher.

By the time the morning mists had lifted and the first birds started to sing, I had neared the top.

But somebody else was here as well.

A low male voice said, "Steady you go, steady."

Peering around a large boulder that blocked my path, I saw a man of middle years, prodding a small trio of sheep forward. The animals seemed too frightened to even bleat. The man looked to be from the Three-Rivers clan for he wore their distinctive mix of leather and cloth leggings and tunic and leather boots, and markings dotted his arms with odd designs. He used a staff to urge the sheep forward, herding up the narrow path I had been following.

Looking beyond him, I saw the path led to the cavern mouth I had glimpsed from afar. At this close range I saw it was actually fenced with an iron gate.

The bars seemed too thin to ever pose a real barrier to a dragon of Jaydra's size, but a metal net seemed to be threaded into the bars and over it and that would make it stronger.

They'll never get their dragons to respect them.

I thought of the pure rage Jaydra would inflict on any who tried to imprison her in such a fashion as this. Did these people know nothing of dragons? Why did anyone think that a rider of dragons had ever taught the Three-Rivers clan anything?

The sheep stopped on the path and refused to go any further, despite the man's prodding. I didn't blame them. It is a wise animal that knows to avoid a dragon's den. But the man herding them pulled out a length of rope, tied the sheep together and then tied them to the metal bars.

Reaching down to the belt at his waist, he fumbled with something that clattered. I realized he must have a key and the bars were not a fence, but were a gate. After fitting the key in place, the man jerked back a section of the fence. It gave with a groan of metal on metal. The sheep struggled now to break free of the rope and sympathy for the poor beasts stirred in me.

These dragons had to be very different not to want to fly and hunt their prey. The dragons of the Western Isles not only enjoyed the thrill of a hunt, but they killed fast and their prey hardly had time to even realize it was about to be a dragon meal.

At least my prey can run, Jaydra said in the back of my mind. She was awake now and keeping part of her senses on what I was doing in case I needed her help.

The man shoved the sheep into the cavern, one at a time before hurriedly locking it.

The man turned and started down the path again. I ducked off the trail and hid behind a boulder, but the man was intent on hurrying away. He didn't notice me, and anger surged in me that he wasn't even going to stay and witness the final moments of these poor sheep. The least he could have done was be witness to their fate.

Jaydra thoughts reached me again. *Jaydra does not think Saffron wants to see what happens next, either. Come back. Bower wakes and wants food. So does Jaydra.*

Just keep him busy. Hunt fish for him and yourself, I thought to her.

Jaydra was happy enough to put her mind on hunting fish for breakfast, but I could still sense her senses. She worried over what was about to happen up here behind these iron bars—and she could smell dragons.

A low rumbling echoed from within the cavern, and then a hissing rose. It sounded to me like a dozen or more large, scaly bodies moving in the darkness, shifting and flowing over one another.

The sheep panicked and threw themselves against the metal bars, seeking escape. The sound grew so loud it seemed about to burst from the darkness like a volcano, but it suddenly stopped.

The wind whistled through the rocks, but otherwise all was silent. Not so much as a bird stirred, nor any small creature. Even the sheep held still, seemingly frozen in fear. The sun peaked over the eastern mountains, starting to warm the day and stretching light into the cavern, but I saw nothing.

Was this just some bizarre ritual of the Three-Rivers clan to leave sheep here? But Jaydra could still smell dragon and I could feel part of her senses trained on this spot. She was waiting.

And then I saw something move in the dark cavern.

Eyes appeared first, seeming more red lights. Two sets of eyes blinked and smoke curled into the air. In an instant, two long snouts burst forward, snapping up two of the sheep so quickly the animals had not even a moment to bleat. The third also vanished with a snap and a spatter of blood. I glimpsed scales dark as midnight with the sheen of blue and purple flashing in the light. These dragons seemed much thinner and smaller than Jaydra, with wicked sharp spines along their heads and backs.

And then they were gone, retreating back into the darkness.

My heart was beating fast and sweat cooled on my back and forehead. I stared into the cavern, trying to see if there were more dragons, or just the two I had glimpsed.

I could feel no hint of a dragon mind in the darkness. These dragons seemed as wild as the Grim Bears I had once encountered.

Jaydra, do you sense anything? I asked.

But Jaydra seemed busy hunting the rivers for fish.

I reached out again with my mind, searching the cavern for even a flicker of awareness or sensation. I had always had a strong bond with Jaydra, but even with the other dragons of the Western Isles, I had always been able to reach any dragon mind.

Pulling my cloak tighter about me, I wondered if these dragons simply did not want to open their mind to others. Perhaps having been locked up behind bars like this had left them unable or unwilling to trust any human. Or perhaps the rock here, which seemed to be solid iron, would not allow me to reach these dragons.

I was about to give up and turn away when I felt something.

It at once seemed to me a sense of two dragon minds in the cavern. Their thoughts seemed far different from any other dragons I had ever sensed. Instead of clear thoughts, a wild savagery slipped into my mind, and I wondered if these dragons were all emotion.

Perhaps they had never talked to any human before this. Given how the Three-Rivers clan kept them locked up, unable to fly, I could well believe that no human had even tried to speak to them.

Easing forward on the path, I strode to the metal bars and put my hand through it—perhaps it was just the metal blocking our connection.

My name is Saffron. I have a den-sister named Jaydra, daughter of Zenema of the Western Isles.

Emotions and garbled thoughts hit me, making me tremble. A sense of hatred as strong as my magic battered at me. From the darkness, one eye opened, this one white and swirling and very much a dragon eye. The dragon glared at me and its thoughts struck like a gale force wind.

Hate humans. Eat humans. Hate you!

I staggered back. Never before had any dragon regarded me with such contempt. Never had I sensed such loathing and such a powerful hatred. Pulling back, I wondered if I should try again to reach these two dragons, but in my mind Jaydra was warning me to take care. And she was right.

These weren't just wild dragons, these were dragons that had been abused and imprisoned. It was possible they might never trust any human. Turning away, I could see now why Ryland had said these dragons were dangerous—they were. They were almost as mindless as Enric's Iron Guard, and they were fit only to be machines that killed. These were not the dragons that might be the basis for an army.

I had learned to dislike the Three-Rivers clan last night when they'd seemed so uncaring of their dragons. But now I could hate these people almost as much as their dragons did. For these people had turned dragons into the very nightmare that Bower had always said was how the people of Torvald viewed dragons.

CHAPTER 12

CHALLENGED

Saffron strode back to where I waited with Jaydra, fish roasting on campfire, looking as though she hadn't slept at all. I could see every freckle on her pale cheeks and purple stains smudged her eyes, leaving them looking huge. Her leather jerkin seemed dusty as did her boots, and she strode toward me, coming from the western mountains.

"What happened to you?" I asked and stood. Next to me the fire crackled happily. Jaydra sat not far away, watching Saffron and saying nothing that I could hear.

The sun had warmed the meadow where we had spent the night, but rivers seemed to leave a chill in the air. Saffron's breath puffed in the air like a dragon's.

Saffron stopped in front of me, her cloak thrown back from her shoulders. She fixed a hard stare on me and said, her voice urgent, "We should leave. Now."

"What's wrong? Is this about last night and Ryland not believing I could be king?" I could almost hear a sullenness in my own voice. Even I didn't believe I really would make a great king, so why should I expect anyone else to?

"No, Bower. Please." She reached out and touched my arm. "We can fly back to Den Mountain and then follow the island dragons to a new home. Zenema will know of other dragons who may help us, or we can fly south. Far away from Enric."

"What are you talking ab—?"

A long, echoing call cut off my words. It sounded to me like what I had always imagined the great Dragon Horn sounding like. The call echoed again, and I traced it back to the center of the Three-Rivers clan settlement. It had to be coming from the hall where we had dined last night. From within the settlement, excited whoops rose up. It sounded to me as if this was the call to summon me to my test.

My stomach tightened. The fish Jaydra had brought back for breakfast no longer seemed so appetizing. My mouth dried.

I'm not ready for this.

Panic shook my chest and my fingers, but then I remembered I had not been ready for Ysix's test, either. I pulled in a breath and glanced at Saffron. She was staring at the settlement, her mouth set in a hard line and her blue eyes suddenly dark and fierce.

Before she could ask again for us to leave, I told her, "I can't turn away from this. My father died to keep my bloodline secret, to give me a chance at the throne that is rightfully mine. I can't turn away from my duties—I have to think of all those who suffer

164

under Enric right now. Enric won't stop trying to kill every last person who is part of the rebels, the Salamanders. He won't stop persecuting those who only want to know the true history of their kingdom. And he won't stop chasing us no matter where we go. That means we have to fight—and if we want a hope of winning, then I have to prove to these people I am their king. If I don't...I won't just lose their respect, I'll lose my self-respect."

Saffron shook her head. My words had done nothing to erase the doubt in her eyes or ease the creases lining her forehead. "You don't understand. These dragons are not what we need."

"Yes, but they're what we have," I said.

Ryland and a group of five men marched toward us from the settlement. Each man held a long spear and the men had dressed in heavy leather jerkins, breeches and boots.

I turned from Saffron to face them, glad now I hadn't eaten any breakfast. My stomach seemed to be knotted tight.

Glancing from man to man, I wondered if I was going to have to best one or more of them in combat. If so, I would surely lose. Like every noble son of Torvald, I'd been trained to use a sword, but these men were taller and thicker than I was.

But I noticed with a shock that these men were the ones who looked frightened. They swapped nervous stares, licked their lips and shifted their spears from hand to hand as if they were the ones facing a test.

I bet father never expected my inheritance to have to come to me like this.

Studying the men's fear-filled faces, doubts rose up in me. Were these people with their marks upon their skins and their wild ways the ones my father would have wanted me to lead against our home city?

But I could almost hear him in the back of my mind, repeating the words from some restricted and prohibited book that he had entrusted to my care.

The old kings ruled for all of the people, not just a few whom they liked.

At the time, I'd been a boy and he had been talking about how the Maddox kings had relentlessly favored their friends at court, ignoring the common people and the older noble families who kept away from court. But I knew my father would have included the Three-Rivers clan and the island villagers and every dragon as those to whom a just rule must extend.

Glancing at Saffron, I told her, "A king rules for all, not a few."

I stepped forward to meet Ryland and the others. I didn't turn around to see if Saffron and Jaydra were staying or going. If

Saffron felt strongly enough, she could go. And I knew Jaydra would go with her. But I was hoping both would stay. Saffron might be worried about something, but I wanted their support.

Behind me, Saffron muttered, "Bower, you don't have to do this."

I kept on walking. Of course I did.

*　　*　　*

The sun was well up in the sky by the time all seemed ready for whatever test I had to pass.

I stood on a patch of barren and blasted rock that had been cleared from the mountain side. Fifty spearmen from the settlement created a circle—an arena it seemed—standing alert and in their heavy leathers with their long spears. I stood at the center of the circle, tugging at the breastplate of stiffened leather strips they had given me. It formed a hard shell around my chest and back, but it made any movement difficult. Hardened leather wrapped my forearms and legs, and I thought this seemed a crude imitation of the drawings of Dragon Rider armor that I had seen in books.

Opposite me, Ryland stood just inside the circle, similarly dressed. I had thought that perhaps we were to fight, but neither of us had so much as a knife in hand, and I could not see how we could possibly wrestle or grapple with each other. It was hard enough just to walk.

Saffron and Jaydra had followed the crowd—it seemed the entire settlement, everyone except the youngest children, had turned out to see this test. Just now Saffron hung back, arms crossed over her chest, her expression sullen, as if she could somehow will me to end this. Jaydra hung back with her, almost as if she could hide herself. And it seemed almost as if everyone had forgotten them, for everyone seemed to be staring at me, eyes bright but also nervous.

Stepping forward, Ryland turned and lifted his voice. "We have a challenge called. Bower who comes from the city of metal men says he can lead us in battle." A few laughs rose up, but they sounded nervous to me.

I could see Jaydra peering over the heads of those gathered. Saffron climbed up onto Jaydra's back for a better view—and a better way to glare at me. I licked my lips. A part of me almost wanted Jaydra to swoop down and rescue me from this, but I squared my shoulders.

I wanted both Saffron and Jaydra to be proud of what I had to do—I wanted to be proud of myself. And running would never give me that.

Ryland held up his hand and the crowd fell silent. "This boy-king thinks to become our king—and I say we test him!"

Shouts rose up from the crowd, but the men with the spears remained silent.

Ryland held up his hands again. "We will see if he can hold his own against our wild mountain dragons. Let us see if he can sit atop one as I, your war chief, will!"

The crowd shouted again.

Heart thudding against my ribs, I stared at Ryland. Sit atop a wild dragon? That was the test? Well, I had managed with Jaydra, so perhaps this would not be so difficult a challenge after all.

Ryland called out to the crowd, "If he can do this, if he can show to all that he is worthy to fight with us and really to rain fire and terror down on the metal men, then I will gladly fly at his side and so will we all!"

This time the cheers seemed fewer and mixed with unhappy mutters. Perhaps some did not agree with Ryland's offer for me to lead the Three-Rivers clan alongside him? Or maybe they were making bets about how long it might take me to fail?

Turning, Ryland shouted, "Bring the dragons!"

The crowd suddenly hushed and fear seemed to thicken the air around me. I didn't have much time to wonder why everyone suddenly seemed so afraid of my being tested, for a roar broke from the mountain above me.

A low hiss like a huge kettle boiling over followed the roar. The clatter of chains followed and the sounds grew louder. Gasps came from the crowd and some began to back away.

Dragons. I heard the voice in my mind. It was almost like a voice you might hear in a dream, soft and sibilant. I had heard Jaydra like this a few times before, but this time her voice seemed stronger. Turning, I glanced at her.

Jaydra very deliberately nodded, before flicking her tongue to one side of the circle where I stood. Her thoughts flowed freely into my mind. *Do not show fear, Bower. Stand fast.*

Easy for you to say, I thought to her, but I had no idea if she heard.

I turned to face the approaching hiss.

The men with spears who circled me and Ryland parted and thirty or so more strong men now dragged two dragons into the circle. The dragons snapped at the men and at the chains holding them, but the men seemed to know when to duck back.

I was riveted, aware of only the boiling dark blue and black shapes as they surged forward. I let out an involuntary gasp.

Show no fear! Jaydra bellowed in my mind.

These dragons were nothing like Jaydra and nothing like any of the dragons I had seen in books. Long and sinuous bodies and necks struggled against the chains. They were not as long as

Jaydra and certainly nowhere near the size of Zenema, but they pulled the men holding them off their feet anyway. The black scales looked odd, seeming far more like studs than plates. Barbed spikes stood out from their faces and necks, extending down the sinuous backs. Their wings looked small and leathery. Long tails slashed out and men jumped to get out of the way.

But the worst thing wasn't just the dragon's seeming savagery, it was the way they moved, curling their bodies around each other, using claws and wings for attacks. They worked almost as a pair and I could see immediately how it was going to make it almost impossible to try and mount either of them.

Not that I wanted to.

These wild dragons seemed to me deadly and now I knew why Saffron had wanted to go. She had gone up into these mountains and had seen the dragons. She had figured out these were not like the dragons of the Western Isles.

I had no time to glance at Saffron, or shout to her that she had been right. Two men pounded stakes deep into the ground and the others left off holding down the chains of the dragons and all the men jumped back.

"Guards!" Ryland shouted. The spearmen making up the circle around us snapped to an offensive position, spears lowered and facing inward. We were now surrounded by a glittering circle of points, and with two wild dragons chained to the ground, tails lashing and jaws snapping.

The only parts of the dragons kept relatively still were their heads. Each dragon had about its neck a heavy, iron collar and from it chains thicker than my forearm extended to the ground.

Sun! Jaydra's thought hissed into my mind, but I had no idea what she meant. Perhaps it was some bizarre dragon-to-dragon greeting, but I sensed none of the nobility or the intelligence from these dragons that I had from Jaydra and her island kin.

And now I was supposed to climb onto the back of one of these dragons? How?

Spines, talons and teeth flashed as the dragons faced Ryland and me. I had never been much good at wrestling or any sort of sport—and now I had to jump onto a wild dragon. Shoulders slumping I wanted to give up.

But then Ryland laughed.

The sound had me stiffening my back and turning to stare at the man.

"I'll go first, shall I?" Ryland said, loud enough so that the crowd could hear over the hissing dragons. He took a deep breath, rolled his shoulders and threw himself into a run.

Had he decided one dragon was slower than the other? That one dragon might be easier to climb than the other? Did he know some trick I didn't?

As Ryland neared the dragons, one black head shot toward him, teeth glinting in the sunlight. The chain holding the attacking dragon's neck pulled taut. Ryland threw himself into a roll to avoid being crushed by the dragon's bite. Long teeth snapped together just inches from Ryland's head. He jumped up, and darted away, breathing hard now with sweat pouring down his face. He had failed in his first attempt, but judging by his lack of frustration I had the impression this was to be expected.

With another grunt, Ryland tried another charge at the other dragon. This dragon also snapped at Ryland, but Ryland did not throw himself to the ground this time. Instead, he leapt up. The dragon pulled on the chain, but could not raise its head high enough to snap at Ryland. Reaching out, Ryland caught one of dragon's horns. The dragon reared up, almost dragging its chain from the ground.

The move actually helped Ryland swing up and onto the dragon's neck. He rested there, wedged between the dragon's spines. The second wild dragon, seeing Ryland seated upon its companion, tried to snap at Ryland's head, but it could not get between the spines, and the chain holding it down would not allow it to stand and claw at Ryland.

The dragon whipped its head back and forth twice, then seemed to give up in near exhaustion. Cheers erupted from the crowd, but this seemed nothing like true dragon riding. I glanced at Saffron and saw her scowling at Ryland, looking ready to come at him with her knife. I knew what she must be thinking—there had been no respect in his approach to this dragon, no communication and no friendship existed between Ryland and the dragon.

I did not even think Ryland could control this dragon—all he could do would be to hang on while the dragon flew where he wished. How could these dragons be useful in combat? They seemed to want to fight their riders more than anything else.

Ryland waved a hand and shouted, "I will wait here and give you a chance."

I wasn't proud. I would take any help offered, but Ryland's approach of throwing himself at a dragon seemed a poor idea to me.

The cheers subsided and an uneasy silence seemed to hold everyone. I was left staring at the second wild dragon, which looked from Ryland to me, its eyes glinting as if it wanted one or both of us dead.

How could I do this?

But how could I not?

There might be other wild dragons to face. And I needed to show it would not be mere strength that defeated Enric. No—we needed to be far more clever than Enric could be. Meaning I needed to figure out a way to do this that proved just that.

I clenched my teeth. Sweat dripped down my back under the leather the Three-Rivers clan had put on me. I glanced down at it and then tugged loose the straps and pulled it off. I didn't need a turtle shell on me. I needed agility and brains. I needed to somehow talk to this dragon.

Ryland, for all his muscle and skill—had just shown he couldn't call any dragon to him. Zenema and Ysix had promised they would answer my call, but I needed to show the Three-Rivers clan that dragons were not here to be chained and abused.

Remembering the pictures I had seen in so many books of dragon riders sitting atop dragons, soaring across the sky, I knew this was how it must have started. With someone facing a dragon—and becoming a friend.

I took a step forward, and the black dragon lunged at me, faster this time. It obviously expected me to use moves similar to what Ryland had.

I threw myself to one side. The dragon's mouth snapped closed on the air above me. The dragon pulled at its chain, and I knew the restraints were simply making it even more angry.

Sun, Bower. Sun! Jaydra's thoughts echoed in my mind, but I didn't know what she meant.

The crowd shouted out calls, obviously not thinking I'd been brave enough. I rolled to my feet and blinking as I squinted up at the midday sun.

Was that what Jaydra meant? That these dragons could not see so well in such glare?

Taking a closer look at the wild dragons, I wondered if why this smaller, fiercer breed hadn't been trained by the Dragon Riders of old—or at least I had never read of black dragons being trained. Any feral creature would respond to training, given enough time. Was there also a reason why these dragons were black as a night without moon or stars?

Just as sea dragons are green and blue, like their environment.

That was it! The colors of the dragons had to be directly related to where they lived. That meant these wild dragons preferred to be out at night. The sun might even hurt their eyes, which would only anger them even more.

I studied the dragon in front of me the same way that I would study a new text. I saw what Jaydra had been trying to tell me.

The two wild dragons were actually trying to shield each other from the bright sun. They must be used to darks caverns and moonlit nights.

I had a clue now, but how to use it?

Moving as fast as I could, I jogged around the circle until the sun was directly behind me. With the warmth of the sun on the top and back of my head, I turned to face the dragon that watched me.

The dragon turned its head left and right, as if trying to see me better. My heart thudded hard and my fingers chilled. Could I manage to catch hold before it grabbed me?

Having lived with dragons even for a short time I knew better than to do anything with a dragon without first asking and so I closed my eyes and tried to reach out to it, as I might to Jaydra.

I promise you no harm. And I promise to remove that iron collar from your neck.

When I opened my eyes again, it seemed to me that the dragon's glittering eyes were now puzzled. I didn't know if it had not heard me or perhaps did not really understand, but I knew I had one chance..

A shiver of fear ran through me, but I pushed into a run.

I covered half the distance between me and the black dragon before it had seen that I'd moved. But I had no intention of vaulting onto the dragon's back. What had Jaydra said?

Stand firm. Don't back down.

I saw my chance and jumped up, grabbing the chain that held the dragon pinned to the ground. It snapped taut, but I reached up and grabbed the pin that held its iron collar in place. From somewhere behind me, I heard Saffron yell. In the next instant, I'd pulled loose the pin and the iron color fell from the dragon's neck.

I fell to the ground and stared up at a wild, black dragon now free to do as it pleased. And it pleased to roar up on its hind legs clawing at the air with its front legs and spreading it's wing wide. With one stroke of an arm, it knocked Ryland from his perch on the other dragon's back, and then it turned to me.

CHAPTER 13

SAFFRON AND THE KING

"Bower!" The scream burst out of me as Bower fell to the ground in front of the wild dragon. Somehow Bower had freed the dragon, but the hate within the dragon's mind washed through me, leaving me in no doubt of its intent to kill Bower.

The dragon reared up over Bower and I knew it intended to snap Bower in two with one bite.

I flung out my hands, reacting as I had when I had caught him in mid-air over the ocean. Power burst from me, tingling on my fingertips and in my chest. But this time the magic went wild. Instead of flinging Bower away from the dragon and to safety, my power flew out in a burst around me. Raw energy flew from my hands, sparking green and golden in bright bolts that struck outward. It was as if my scorn of these people was fueling the magic, striking out at everyone and everything.

A boom like that of a cannon shook the earth.

People flew backwards, knocked to the ground. My magic struck the two wild dragons as well, sending them flying, but also tearing their chains to pieces.

The wild dragons roared. Free of their constraints, they leapt into their air and took flight, spiraling up into the clouds until they had disappeared.

I had no time to follow their departure with my thoughts for I feared I had killed Bower. He lay still on the ground. I jumped from Jaydra's back and ran toward his side, leaping over the bodies of those I had knocked off their feet. Around me, those who had gathered were groaning, holding their heads and struggling to regain their feet.

The horn that had sounded earlier was echoing again from the settlement, but I gave it no heed. I reached Bower, skidded to a stop and dropped down in the dirt next to him. He gave a moan and I put a hand on his shoulder. "Bower, can you hear me?"

Checking him for injuries, I saw he had badly grazed his right hand and arm—the sleeve of his tunic had torn open. Thankfully, the stiffened leather wrapped around his arms and legs seemed to have prevented any broken bones.

His eyes fluttered open and he asked, "Did I do it?"

Jaydra landed with a thump next to Bower, spreading out her wings over us to keep us safe. She scanned the skies and thought to me, *Wild dragons gone.*

I was glad of that, but just now we had other concerns.

Glancing around, I saw the crowd was slowly getting to their feet. The men with spears seemed to have recovered first. The blare of their horn sounded again and again with an odd urgency. However, instead of anyone looking at me or Bower, everyone seemed to be staggering toward the settlement.

Ryland ran past us, a gash on his head bleeding from his own fall from the dragon I had freed. "Get him up," he shouted.

"What happened?" Bower sat up and put a hand to his head.

I didn't want to tell him just yet that I had caused this mayhem, so I simply shook my head.

However, Ryland paused not far from us and pointed to the eastern mountains where three black flags now fluttered, stark against the blue sky. "We're under attack!"

Pushing himself to his feet, Bower shouted at Ryland, "The flags—what do they mean? Who is attacking?"

Ryland waved us to keep up with him. Bower broke into a limping run and I followed after, with a quick thought to Jaydra to take to the air and see what she could see.

Talking as he ran, Ryland said, "The Salamanders taught us to use flags. With it we can pass message for many, many leagues. What that shows is that someone has attacked our scouts to the south and west." He ran into the settlement. Everyone seemed to be hurrying past, but a man stopped to hand Ryland a sword belt.

Ryland whistled for his steed, and turned to Bower. "You are certainly lucky. I don't know what happened back there, but I know you were about to be dragon-food. Bravely done...but dragon-food nonetheless."

I opened my mouth to confess, but Bower interrupted. "Where are your other dragons? We'll need them."

We? Bower really did think of these people as his responsibility, even if no one had declared him king.

Someone brought Ryland his saddled pony. He took the reins and told Bower, "It's the metal men coming. Their king and his vile magic tricks have caused us to lose two of our dragons. They were the only rideable ones we had, for the others are all far too wild. Without those two dragons we haven't got a hope of countering the metal men."

I did not like to think of more dragons caught in catches, but even less did I like thinking of the Iron Guard. I'd seen those metal soldiers in Torvald and had even managed to destroy one during my magical battle with Enric, but that hadn't been anything I'd planned. I'd sent my magic out and it had torn one of the Iron Guard almost in two. I still had no idea how I had done it.

Must I always lose control to be able to use my magic to defeat Enric?

I shuddered. The Iron Guard was an army created by magic—horrible magic. I wanted nothing to do with it.

Magic isn't something Saffron does. Magic is Saffron and Saffron is magic. Jaydra thought to me from far above.

I knew Jaydra's thought magic was as natural as breathing, for that was how dragon magic could be.

And look what Saffron did—Saffron saved Bower and freed two dragons.

That was one way of looking at it. But I still did not have great faith I could use my magic exactly as I wanted. After all, I hadn't intended to knock everyone flat just a few moments ago.

My cheeks burned, but I was still not sorry I had freed those two dragons. I didn't think Bower would be sorry, either, for he had been trying to free one of them. Glancing at Bower, I said, "If the best anyone could do was sit on a dragon, how would those wild dragons be any use against King Enric?" I looked at Ryland. "What was your plan? Just to goad the dragons into a fury and point them toward the enemy line, hoping they decided to attack the enemy rather than you?"

Ryland shot me a hard look, but Bower said, his tone grim, "The Iron Guard. That's what they're called in Torvald. They are unstoppable. Unbeatable."

"They're Maddox magic," I muttered.

Ryland shook his head, threw his pony's reins over the animal's head and swung up onto the pony's back. He nodded to where his riders were approaching with their tough mountain ponies. "We have to try."

"We can help," Bower said.

I didn't want to hear that. If Enric was coming, it might be best if we left. But Bower looked determined, so I looked up to where Jaydra circled overhead and asked, *Jaydra, will you fight with us?*

Jaydra's voice sounded joyful and fierce in my head. *Jaydra will always fly with Saffron.*

"We have a dragon. One who will fight with us and who can scout," I said.

Ryland's mouth flattened, but Bower nodded at my words, and then said, "But we don't have any weapons other than a knife or two."

"Three-Rivers clan can provide." Ryland called out to a youth who was running past. "Bring them swords, bows and signal flags and quick!"

The boy nodded and hurried away. Around us it seemed as if the entire settlement was taking up arms, including women, children and the old. People came out of their huts strapping on leather armor or sword belts or carrying long spears.

Wheeling his pony, Ryland called out to the other mounted riders to follow him. They rode off in a cloud of dust. A few moments later, the boy Ryland had sent to get us weapons came back with one short sword, three scraps of what seemed to be red cloth and a bow and a quiver of arrows. Bower took the sword and the red cloth. I grabbed the bow and arrows.

"All I could find," the boy said and sprinted away.

Bower strapped on the belt and tucked the red cloth into the belt, telling me. "We can signal Ryland with these flags." Bending down, he picked up one of the fist-sized rocks from around an extinguished fire pit. "I'll fill a pack with these. We can throw these from above if nothing else and keep the king's forces distracted."

We were going to fly out on our first direct battle with Enric and somehow rocks did not seem to me to be a powerful weapon. But I had arrows and perhaps all Ryland needed were eyes in the sky.

Calling to Jaydra, I asked her to land in the settlement so we might mount. We had no time to secure our blanket saddles to her back, so we simply swung up on and secured ourselves as best we could between the ridges of her spine. Jaydra launched herself into the air, and I leaned forward as we sailed up into the clouds.

At first, I could see nothing of any army, but Jaydra's dragon senses picked up on smoke in the air, and she thought to me, *Look to the mountain slope.*

Smoke curled up from what seemed to be a small village with what was now no more than smoldering ruins. I glimpsed blackened walls and figures moving through the wreckage, smashing anything still standing.

"The Iron Guard," Bower shouted from behind me.

Pulling out one of the scraps of red cloth, he held it out so it flapped in his hands. Below us, red fluttered on the ground and I knew it must be Ryland or someone from the Three-Rivers clan signaling back to Bower—or that was what I hoped. I did not want to think we had alerted the Iron Guard that we flew overhead.

Ryland and his mounted warriors seemed to have found a path across the river bridge and over the mountain. I could see now why they used small, sure-footed ponies. No horse could have crossed that bridge.

Shouting to me, Bower said, "By what I've read, Dragon Riders of old used to harry their opponents. They always had two riders, and one carried a bow or a spear and would fire down on their enemies."

I glanced back at Bower. "Did you fall too hard on your head? What are arrows and rocks going to do against soldiers made of metal and powered by magic?"

Bower shrugged. "We want them looking at us—not at Ryland's force."

I shook my head, but thought to Jaydra, *Take us closer. Bower seems to want more excitement than is good for any of us.*

Jaydra dipped one wing and we circled downward. The air stank of smoke—and of burning flesh. I could now see this wasn't so much a battle as it had been a slaughter.

Below us, sunlight glinted off the Iron Guard as if these were huge men in armored suits, but I had seen these Iron Guards up close. I knew these were not men, but mechanical things powered by Enric's dark magic. Each guard seemed almost as tall as a good-sized tree, with iron plates sculpted to represent an almost human figure and a faceless war helmet.

Each guard seemed to carry a longsword made of the same dull iron. Around them, scattered like dolls, lay the Three-Rivers clan scouts who had obviously lived in these now burning huts. I counted ten bodies, but I wondered if any had been able to flee, or had the attack come too suddenly.

I had no idea how many Iron Guards we faced, but I could see at least a dozen moving in and out of the trees and forest.

"Hey!" Bower shouted and hurled a rock. The stone struck the blackened wall beside one of the guards. But Bower's next stone struck Iron Guard's helmet and the guard seemed to stagger a step.

"You might just be making it angry," I told Bower.

From below a human voice rose up, shouting, "Dragon!"

Soldiers in armor and the king's colors of deep purple stepped from the woods, some raising bows and notching arrows to fire up at us.

Jaydra roared and turned, using her scales to shield us and herself from the arrows. It would take far worse to harm her, but I could feel her annoyance as the arrows poked her side. We could beat any humans, but more and more soldiers seemed to be pouring from the forest. Had Enric sent his entire army here?

Jaydra roared again, turned and plummeted down. I could only cling to her spines and hope Bower knew enough to lean close to Jaydra and hang on.

She tore over the army, making men duck away, pulling bows from hands with her claws, tearing and grabbing at anything that moved. Screams and shouts rose up. Jaydra wheeled around and came at the archers once more, scattering the soldiers before she rose up into the air.

Concentrating on showing Jaydra where she should fly, how low and how fast, I tried to be an extra set of eyes for her.

Behind me, Bower shouted, "I know this is working, but we have more trouble coming."

I spared him a glance and saw Bower was pointing out beyond the woods to another clearing.

More of the Iron Guard marched up the mountainside along with more human soldiers. We did seem to be facing an army.

"How many?" I asked Bower.

He shook his head. "Too many for the Three-Rivers clan. More arrows flew up at us.

Jaydra roared, turned to block the arrows with her scales and then tensed, ready to swoop down on her attackers.

No, sister! There are too many, I thought, willing her to be cautious.

Never too many for a dragon! Jaydra sent to me an image of scattering the army again. I feared she was going to try to attack an army on her own, so I sent to her an image of needing to warn the Three-Rivers clan of what they faced.

Reluctantly, she ascended into the air, out of range of the archers below.

189

Suddenly Jaydra croaked and started to fall out of the air, plummeting toward the ground, and at the same instant Bower gasped in pain. I had just enough time to register that no part of any of our bodies had blood on them. Neither Jaydra nor Bower had been hit by the arrows below.

And that was when it hit.

I gasped. Pain washed over me, spreading through me as if I'd been struck by lightning. But I knew what it was.

I'd felt this before when Enric's magic had gripped me.

Is the king here?

Suddenly, Jaydra croaked. Her wings folded. Bower cried out as well, and I knew he must be feeling the grip of the king's magic, like some horrible hand wrapped around us.

We tumbled through the sky, and I knew I had to block this cursed magic.

Reaching out with my mind, I tried to sense Enric. I could find no trace of him, but still his magic seemed to be wrapped around us. Jaydra could not control her wings—they seemed to be torn off by his magic.

We were racing toward the ground.

Clasping Jaydra's neck with my hands, I closed my eyes and let the power surge from me. The feeling of my dragon-magic was entirely different from Enric's. It was different, too, from when I tried to use magic on my own. With Jaydra, the magic felt right and natural. It was as if this was who we were always meant to be.

My hands warmed and Jaydra spread her wings wide, but it was almost too late.

Opening my eyes, I saw the dark green canopy of trees, and then we hit.

For a moment, I could do nothing. My entire body seemed to ache. I knew I had fallen from Jaydra, but I didn't know where. Forcing myself, I opened my eyes and blinked back the pain.

We had fallen into a wide tree, and I lay sprawled over the branches that had caught me. With a moan, I managed to sit up. I almost fell from the tree, but I reached out to Jaydra, searching for her.

Jaydra well. Bad magic, but well. Glancing down, I saw she had crashed through the branches entirely and now sprawled on the ground. She stood and shook her wings as if to right them again.

"Bower?" I called out.

A groan from the tree branches above me told me he was alive. The limbs shook and Bower managed to pull himself from the leaves. Face pale, he stared down at me. "What was that?"

I started to climb down the tree, my arms and legs hurting and my chest still sore as if I really had been held too tight by a giant hand. "I think…I think it was Maddox magic. A curse of some kind thrown at us—but I don't know how. I don't think Enric is here."

Bower started to climb down. His foot slipped and he started to fall, but Jaydra caught him with a claw and set him on the ground. I slid down the tree and leaned against the trunk, patting it to thank it for saving our lives.

Bower looked from me to Jaydra. "Iron Guard, archers and magic being thrown around. Ryland and the Three-Rivers clan will be slaughtered. We have to warn them."

I nodded. I had thought the same.

Brushing the leaves from his jerkin, Bower started to walk and then stopped. "Which way should we head?" he asked.

I pointed to Jaydra. "Back up on our dragon. We'll never reach Ryland in time on foot."

Bower nodded and turned, but his head came up and his hand fell to the swords at his side.

For a moment I didn't know why, but then I saw what he must have seen.

Three Iron Guards stepped from the woods, swords drawn and all three facing us. They made no move toward us, but an eerie sound like that of a rising wind seemed to echo from their helmets and then became a voice.

"Saffron."

The single word pulled a shiver from me for it seemed filled with malevolence.

It was Enric's voice, horribly distorted by however he was using these Iron Guards to speak to me.

"Saffron Maddox...return to me.".

How could this be Enric's voice?

Trembling, I stared at the Iron Guards that were speaking with Enric's voice. More magic at work, I knew.

Balling my hands into fists, I stepped forward to face them.

"Why would I want to do that?" I shouted at the Iron Guards, wondering if the king, wherever he was, could even hear me.

He could.

"'You belong with me....'"

Each of the Iron Guards raised their swords. I didn't know if the gesture was meant to beckon me or appear threatening.

"I am my own person" I shouted. Jaydra gave a rumble that seemed to me that she agreed. "I belong with my dragon-kin."

"Dragons? What need do we have for dragons?"

Each of the Iron Guards took a step forward. I could not mistake the threat this time.

Bower stepped closer to me and took my hand. "We should be ready to run," he whispered.

I shook my head. How could we outrun these Iron Guards? I was not even certain we could mount Jaydra in time to fly away.

Magic tingled in my fingers. I had torn apart one Iron Guard, but could I fight three at once?

Suddenly, a shout echoed, along with the clang of swords and the neighing of horses.

"Ryland," Bower muttered. "They must have met up with the king's army."

The sound of thundering hooves and the clash of battle drifted to us on the wind.

The three Iron Guards facing us seemed to take no notice of the nearby battle. But why should they? What weapon, other than magic, could harm them?

"Saffron…return to me…"

This time the words carried a prickling that started in my chest and spread to my skin. Enric was trying to use his magic to pull power from me. He was going to do something terrible, I knew, and I had no idea how to counter it.

"Bower?" The word came out choked and I had no idea what I was even asking him to do. My hands were shaking, and I knew Bower had to feel that.

He let go of my hand and I glanced at him. Eyes narrowed, he pulled back his arm and threw something—a rock.

It hit with a resounding crack and ricocheted off the helmet of the center Iron Guard, leaving a small dent.

Enric's magic faded from around me. I felt it fall away like a dark, heavy cloak.

Turning to me, Bower said, "I think the Iron Guards are acting like some kind of watchtower beacon, letting Enric reach out to us here through them."

Of course. The king couldn't cast his magic this far. No one was that powerful! He was using these Iron Guards, but this must be costing him a great deal.

I knew what it cost me to pull on my power. Could I make Enric use all his power? Deplete him for short time?

"Jaydra, help me!" I shouted, and sent her an image of what I needed her to do. She sprang into action. With a swipe of her tail she lashed out, knocking over the Iron Guards. I didn't think this would stop any of them, but I knew that now Enric would have to struggle to reach them again with his magic.

We had a chance.

I yelled at Bower to leap onto Jaydra. From our right, I could hear the battle coming closer to us. I didn't know if Ryland and his warriors were winning or losing, but I had to do something. Power surged into my hands. I had to unleash it if we were to survive. I started forward.

The odd echoing voice of the king sounded again, booming through the forest. "Saffron...return to me..."

This time, however, the words came from fifty Iron Guards who stepped from the forest around us.

"I'll return you something right enough," I muttered. Lifting my hands with power glowing a bright green and gold on my fingertips, I stretched out my arms.

CHAPTER 14

BOWER AND THE DRAGONS

The voices of the Iron Guard filled the air like an unnatural thunder, rolling toward the village and echoing over it. It made my knees shake, but Saffron was walking toward the Iron Guards.

What was Saffron doing?

A line of Iron Guards had stepped from the tall trees and filled the air with an unnatural, echoing voice that seemed to be calling to her. That voice left my insides shaking, but Saffron was walking toward the Iron Guards, her hands raised and magic sparking from her fingers. However, I didn't know if she could really handle so many guards.

Sounds of battle neared—the clash of swords, shouts and screams, the frightened whinnies of the horses. I could smell it as well in blood spilled and fires that still burned. Ash floated on the breeze. We had to get to Ryland.

Even as I thought that, Ryland appeared to the right, still mounted on his pony, his sword now blood-stained and his face dirty with smoke. He pulled his mount to a halt and looked from the Iron Guards to Saffron. I didn't know if he thought Saffron was responding to Enric's magic commands, voiced by the guards. But I had no time to worry about him.

I had seen Saffron's magic before—had even felt it. It was becoming clear to me that when Saffron used it on her own, it always seemed to come out too strong and too wild. It was as if, on her own, her power controlled her rather than the other way around. But with Jaydra just now, Saffron had been in better control.

Just a few moments ago, Saffron had called on Jaydra for help. I hadn't been certain what Saffron meant, but when Saffron and Jaydra eased the magic that seemed to crush us, I knew they had been working together. It was dragon magic and Saffron's magic that had saved us. Now Saffron wanted me to call to Jaydra and run, but I was certain Saffron needed Jaydra here. She needed help.

Even as I thought that, Jaydra landed between Saffron and where Ryland sat on his pony. Ryland struggled to control his mount—the pony wanted nothing to do with any dragon. Ryland's expression tightened, but I glanced at Jaydra. "Help her again," I shouted. I could only hope Jaydra understood.

Shouting and battle yells grew louder as Ryland's men neared. Arrows began to skim the air, landing in the ground from shots gone wild. I feared Saffron was about to get herself killed— so many Iron Guards faced her, and they were backed by Enric's magic.

I started to wonder if Enric's magic had gone dark because he had no dragons. Could magic only stay pure if aided by dragons—was that really all Saffron needed to help her? But I stared at the Iron Guards, with sunlight glinting off their metal armor—what we needed were more dragons. That might sway the balance of power here.

I had no innate magic as Saffron did, and I was no mighty warrior like Ryland, but I had been born with royal blood in my veins.

The blood of a Dragon King.

Zenema had spoken to me and I had mentally communicated with Jaydra a few times. Saffron had always told me as well that when the time came I would know how to reach out to a dragon and ask for their help. During our training on the island, she had said it was the one thing she could not teach me—I must know it or not. But it was my birthright, or so I thought, to command dragons. Or maybe not so much as command, as beg for their help.

Letting my worry for Saffron, my fear for her rise up, I looked to the skies and shouted, "Dragons, we need your aid. Now is the time to come to us!"

Nothing happened.

The sky overhead remained nothing more than drifting smoke and high clouds. The sun was starting to sink into the west and I knew we could not afford to be out here in the woods with these Iron Guards—they would have no difficulty seeing in the dark, but we would.

Anger and frustration leaked in to replace my fear. Maybe I was doing this wrong. Saffron always just sent thoughts to Jaydra. Maybe Jaydra could hear me and would call the other dragons. But Jaydra was needed by Saffron, so I closed my eyes and poured my emotions into one thought and plea. *Dragons of the Western Isles—dragons of old, you once listened to my forebears, now listen to me. The rightful Dragon King of Torvald calls upon our ancient bond.*

I wasn't even sure if the words were really mine. Maybe I had read them in an old book, but they felt right to me and seemed to well from my heart.

For a moment, the world seem to hold still. Then it was as if the wind brushed my face and I rode the currents and the world spread out below me as if I was upon Jaydra's back. My senses did not seem to be my own, and then a voice rumbled through my mind.

Hail, Bower, True King and dragon-friend!

Opening my eyes, I called out, "Zenema!" But I could still see nothing more than smoke and clouds in the sky.

Dragons come. Ysix flies to you with her brood. As soon as we had a new den safe, she left to join you, drawn by Jaydra's thoughts. Resist and be safe. Dragons will be with you by tomorrow nightfall.

Suddenly my mind was empty of Zenema's voice, but something had changed within me. It was as if some part of my mind's long asleep had woken. I had a sense of warmth inside me, an awareness now not just of Jaydra but of dragons approaching from far to the southwest. I could sense their senses, feel their wings beating almost as if they were my own.

And that wasn't all.

It seemed as if I could sense all dragons near to us.

In the peaks of the mountains around us, three minds touched mine. These were not island dragons, and neither were they the wild, angry black dragons I had faced earlier. I caught a sense of power and minds that were both old and wise. Looking up, I spotted three dots of red growing larger and larger. These dragons appeared far larger than Jaydra, with huge wing spans, thick bodies and powerful necks. Three of them flew in a V-formation. With roars, they swooped down on the Iron Guard.

The dragons released jets of flames down into the trees, setting the tops ablaze. Ryland's pony tried to bolt, but he held it in place with a tight rein and a force of will. Saffron was still walking toward the Iron Guard, and they stood in a line now, facing her.

The air seemed to boil with arrows from the king's army, but the red dragons swatted them away or flamed them to dust. The red dragons turned and rose into the sky, starting to climb and turn again for another attack. But could they reach the Iron Guards this time?

The weird voice from the Iron Guard boomed once more, calling out their frightening message, "Saffron Maddox...return to me."

Saffron's magic—green and gold—spilled from her hands, shot out to tangle with a darker magic that lurked within the Iron Guard. Something like thunder seemed to rise from the ground with a deep rumbling. The ground shook as if the trees were trying to tear their roots from the earth. I staggered, trying to keep to my feet. Jaydra let out a roar and rose up in the air slightly, hovering just over Saffron. The green and gold of Saffron's magic wrapped around the dragon, and the entire world seemed to shake.

Boulders larger than any Iron Guard bounced down from the mountain. I threw myself to the side as a boulder rolled past me and I feared for Saffron, but Jaydra was swatting the boulders with her tail, knocking them into the Iron Guards as if they were nine-pins to be flattened.

The first row of Iron Guard raised their arms as if to ward off the huge rocks crashing into them. Boulders smashed into the guards. I saw several shattered into parts that lay twitching on the ground. Boulders smashed into the line, knocking into trees, trapping guards in clouds of rock and dust. I could hear Ryland's pony neighing as if it wanted to be anywhere but here.

More boulders rolled past me, and I got up and ran, seeking to get out of the way, dodging the rocks. The red dragons overhead wheeled and tore down, parting company with each other, now reaching down with claws to pluck up any enemy and then drop him from a great height. I heard screams and the clatter of the Iron Guard as rocks stuck them down, or as they fell and came apart in a horrible smash that almost sounded like a scream of fury and pain. Dust and smoke swirled in the air, along with stray arrows that now fell with their fletching on fire.

Choking on the smoke, I tried to look for Saffron. I could no longer see the sparks of her magic. Had one of the boulders she had shifted loose struck her? Had she fallen to one of the Iron Guard? Seeing no other choice, I ran for the spot where I'd last seen Saffron, knowing that if I could not find Saffron's slight body I could at least find a huge dragon such as Jaydra.

Bower! To me!

Jaydra's call sounded in my mind. The smoke cleared, pushed away by a sudden breeze. Jaydra stood guard over Saffron's slumped form. She lay still on the ground. Both had been surrounded by the remaining Iron Guard, who were cautiously closing in.

Jaydra lashed out with her tail, knocking back the Iron Guard. But they rose and came at her again. She snapped at them, and any she caught she dashed to the ground, smashing them with her powerful claws. Some of the Iron Guard were now missing arms or legs, but still they struggled to come at Jaydra and Saffron. I knew they must be trying to get Saffron away from Jaydra—and take her alive. That was why they did not use their swords.

From the side, I could hear Ryland's war cry, and the clash of sword on metal. He, too, was hacking at the Iron Guard. But his sword would do little. Overhead, the red dragons roared, and the sounds of battle in other parts of the woods carried to me. But I kept my focus on Saffron. I had to get her away from here.

And Jaydra knew this.

Waiting until Jaydra cleared a gap in the circle of Iron Guard, I ran past and dove under Jaydra's swooping tail. Running to Saffron's side, I grabbed her, my heart hammering. Every muscle in my body screamed at me. I was still aching from my battle with the wild dragon, but I could not think of that now. Lifting Saffron's limp body, I threw her slight form over my shoulders, then reached up to grab onto Jaydra scales. My grip slipped, but Jaydra slapped my back side with her tail, boosting me onto her broad back.

Clinging to the spines on Jaydra's neck, I urged her to fly with my thoughts.

She needed no more encouragement. Leaping forward, Jaydra slashed at two of the Iron Guards with her claws, knocking them flat. She vaulted into the air, her wings stirring the smoke and dust into a mix that left me coughing and my eyes stinging.

When I glanced down again, I saw we had gone high above the forest. The three red dragons circled around us, continuing to attack the king's army and the Iron Guard with fire and claw, knocking trees down on the army and Iron Guard, striking out with deafening roars. Far below us, I saw Ryland turn his pony to head up the mountain. A horn echoed and I hoped Ryland was calling the Three-Rivers clan to retreat—escape was the best we could hope for now.

Clutching Saffron close to me, I put my cheek against hers. She seemed cold, but she was breathing and I could feel her heart still beating against mine.

Saffron's fingers twitched and a spark of gold jumped at me. I hoped she would not use her magic just now. I had had enough of magic for this day.

With nowhere else to go, I urged Jaydra to return to the Three-Rivers clan's settlement. And I just hoped we would be safe there for long enough to regroup and figure out what to do next. Saffron gave a groan and muttered something as if a fevered sleep held her. But I really wasn't sure if it was that, exhaustion, or dark magic that had struck her down.

Pulling her closer, I muttered, "You have to be well again. You must be." I did not think I could continue this fight without her.

PART 3

LEARNING TO LEAD

CHAPTER 15

UNWELCOME

The eerie voice that had called to me echoed again in my mind. It seemed to be trying to pull on my power. The voice shifted and seemed to fade into the sound of wind through the trees.

Cracking my eyes open a fraction, the voice faded into nothing. I thought that somehow I must still be stuck in that mountain forest with the Iron Guard marching toward me.

Instead, clean mountain air brushed my face. Jaydra's wing beats carried to me. I tried to talk but it seemed too much effort so I let myself slip away again.

When I woke next I heard voices and footsteps and could smell cooking fires. But the steps seemed hurried, and the voices rose like the sharp cries of the seabirds as they argued over fish. Dragging my eyes open, I stared up at a rough wooden roof. Under my hands I could feel a wool blanket that covered me. Another seemed to be underneath me. The clanging of metal and hurried footsteps carried to me from outside.

Sitting up, my head spun. Fatigue dragged at my arms and legs and left me wanting to lie down again, but I forced myself upright.

I lay in a small hut, on a rough, brown woolen blanket on the floor. A small table and two roughly-crafted wooden stools shared the room with me.

Where am I?

Saffron? Jaydra breathed warm thoughts against my mind. The wooden walls creaked and I realized Jaydra had curled almost completely around the hut.

"Jaydra?" I asked and put a hand to my throbbing head. It felt as if my skull had been pounded between two rocks. Flashes of what happened came back to me—the Iron Guard, Enric speaking through them, my magic rippling out and pulling at the mountain rocks, sending them tumbling as I poured my anger and hatred of Enric.

Something had held me back from destroying everything.

It seemed to me that Jaydra had been working with me somehow.

Den-sister slept deep and long. Saffron went where even Jaydra could not follow, Jaydra thought to me, and I sensed her sorrow at the idea that we could be separated like that.

It was the magic, I knew. It had almost killed me. But had it stopped King Enric's dark army?

I felt drained, as if all of the strength had left me. What would this magic do to me if I kept using it like this? Would it turn me into a walking skeleton like Enric had become—was that why he had to use illusions to make people believe he was still young? Was he really old or just aged by magic?

My skin chilled and I rubbed my arms.

What if magic makes me become someone like him?

Saffron can never be Enric, Jaydra thought to me, her tone firm and final.

The poles supporting one side of the hut creaked again as she leaned closer. Suddenly, I wanted to be outside with her in fresh air and free from these confining blankets. I fought to stand, staggering to the hut's canvas door.

The canvas seemed almost too difficult to part, meaning I was weaker than I knew. I staggered outside and stopped.

A circle of long spears had been driven into the ground, set so they pointed at the hut and where Jaydra lay curled. Jaydra butted her head against my shoulder, but I stared at the spears. While Jaydra could easily hop over them, the message was clear.

Jaydra and I were now regarded not as guests, but as potential enemies.

*　　*　　*

"What do you mean, I'm being held under suspicion?" I said once again to Bower.

211

We sat outside the hut where I had woken, looking at the wall of spear points. Clouds dotted the sky, driven on a cold wind. Bower, it seemed, was still a guest, and some of the warriors had moved the spears to allow him to come in. He had also acquired a coat and had brought me and Jaydra water and fish.

He looked as if he was still a little shaky on his feet—he had been glad to sit down on a blanket I had pulled from the hut. A bruise was swelling on his cheek and a bandage of a strip of white linen wrapped his head. He was also moving a little slowly, I thought.

I wasn't surprised at all, given the battering we had both recently taken.

But why was he a guest while I'd been stuck behind a wall of spears?

"It was what the Iron Guard said. Or rather what King Enric said through the guards. It seemed like you responded to that call." Bower shook his head and stared at the hard-packed dirt within our spear circle. Just beyond the spears, I could see people hurrying past. It was as if everyone had something to do except us. Were they getting ready to pack up and run? Or were they getting ready to defend their settlement?

"You said Enric was using those guards the way that the Three-Rivers clan uses horns or flags—to send a message from afar."

Bower looked up. "It may be because they're metal. The Iron Guards acted like lightning rods—or like magical relays."

"Is that some other bit of magic? I've never heard of a lightning rod. Does it create lightning?"

"It's a thing you put up on a building, a metal pole to draw a storm's lightning to the pole and not any part of the structure. I think somehow Enric can reach his Iron Guard with his magic, and I'll bet he has them stationed between here and Torvald, so Enric's magic can jump from one guard to the next, covering vast distances."

I frowned. "That's still got to take a lot of energy from him. Did we at least beat back his guard and army?"

Bower frowned and let out a sigh. "It's as I said, the Iron Guard is unstoppable. You managed to destroy a lot of them. So did the red dragons that helped us. But the Three-Rivers clan fears they will regroup and head here next."

Peering past the spears to the settlement, I watched the Three-Rivers clan bustle about. Women hurried past, carrying baskets of what I guessed would be food to take with them or store. I could see a blacksmith sharpening a sword. Boys were fitting leather armor to each other. "These people....nowhere will be safe. If all it takes for Enric to reach out with his magic is one Iron Guard, he'll be able to spread his power from one end of the world to the other."

"I know," Bower said. He sounded depressed at the idea. "I think that is partly why this." He waved at the spears. "I think Ryland is more than a little afraid of what could happen to his people."

"Meaning I could happen to them. He thinks I will betray him, his clan and everyone else, too."

Picking up a rock, Bower tossed it at the spears. "I'll keep talking to Ryland."

I shook my head. "He can't really listen to you, now can he? Not while still looking like a leader to his people. And he keeps me and Jaydra here. I could ask Jaydra to tear down half of the village and she would do so. Or we could just fly away, right over the top of those spears."

Bower shifted, winced and glanced at me. "I can't go."

"I know." I sighed. "If we're to fight Enric's army we need Ryland and the Three-Rivers clan. Just what happened back in the woods? I only remember bits and pieces."

Picking up a straw, Bower drew a line in the dirt. "Ysix and her brood are coming. They'll be here by nightfall."

"What?" I stared at him. "How do you know such a thing? Did Jaydra tell you?"

He shrugged and tossed the straw away. "No, Zenema spoke to me. After you started with your magic, I called for help from the dragons. You were right—I called the dragons and they came." He waved to the mountains tops.

Looking up, I saw three dragons perched on the rocks. They were larger than any dragon I had ever seen, with shimmering red scales. Even from this distance, I could see how they were grooming each other. They also looked to be keeping an eye on the settlement.

"They came to help you?" I asked.

"Us," Bower said. "They helped us."

Glancing to where Jaydra snoozed with one eye half open, I asked her, *What do you think of the reds? Are they like the wild dragons—mindless and angry?*

They hear Jaydra but do not always understand. They have forgotten much. She opened one lazy eye wide. *Jaydra senses reds are suspicious—they wonder why Jaydra is here with you when Jaydra could be with them instead.*

It had never occurred to me that Jaydra might want to go off to visit other dragons. Even on the island, we had always been together. I suddenly wondered if I was holding her back.

Jaydra huffed out a breath as if I was being stupid, closed her eyes and settled back into a doze, refusing to listen to my thoughts. Tired as I was, I was also frightened of what had happened—and what might come next. But I felt better knowing it was Jaydra's choice to stay beside me.

I also had Bower, and I proceeded to drag from him everything that had happened. It seemed that I had slept a night and almost a full day as well.

I still had no real recollection of why I had walked toward the Iron Guard. Blood called to blood, Enric had told me once. Maybe his commands through the Iron Guard had drawn me, but I had also struck out with my magic. I remembered that—but not the boulders rolling loose.

Staring at me, Bower said, "Jaydra watched out for you. She helped you channel your magic. And then I called out for the aid of any and all dragons. Zenema said Ysix and her brood were on their way, and then those three reds—Crimson Reds, they were once called—came from the mountains and rained fire and destruction down on the army. It at least gave us a few days of time—Enric's army is going to need to regroup before they can attack again."

Glancing up at the red dragons on the mountain top, I watched them stretch their wings and asked, "So they heard you call?"

Bower nodded. "I think they must be refugees from Mount Hammal, the home of the dragons of Torvald. They must have escaped, much like some dragons did when they fled to the Western Isles."

"We are not refugees," I protested, echoing Jaydra's annoyance over such an idea.

A small smile lifted Bower's mouth. "You are not. And you said Jaydra was born onthe islands. But once upon a time, the dragons of the Middle Kingdom lived near Torvald and the Dragon Academy. And I think that these Crimson Reds came from Mount Hammal. They fled Torvald after the old king was overthrown by Hacon Maddox, and they hid themselves here in the far north. I don't think any human even knew of their existence before now." Bower stared up at the mountain and the huge dragons. "I wish I could hear their story—learn if they even remember anything of what was once a great dragon academy."

"That would make them as old as Zenema or even older."

"Not if they are the children of the dragons who fled—much as Jaydra is a child of Zenema."

I nodded—he had a point there. "But I thought you said you called them. How can you do that and not hear them the same way I hear Jaydra's thoughts?"

Bower's cheeks reddened, and not from the wind that had risen. "I can't even talk to Jaydra all the time. And Zenema only talks to me when she wants to. When the battle was ended and before you woke, I tried reach out to the Crimson Reds, but all I got was a buzzing in my head and then a headache. I kept hearing clicks and mutters that didn't make sense."

Bower spent too long in his city and in his paper books, Jaydra thought at me.

I had to laugh—for Bower had once carried a bag of books with him.

"Did I say something funny?" Bower asked.

"No, it's just…nothing. Just Jaydra making a joke."

Jaydra sent me a surge of affection and I sent it back to her. Then I turned to Bower and waved at the spears. "Ysix is not going to be happy if she gets here and finds the Three-Rivers clan tried to imprison me and Jaydra."

He nodded and frowned. "That is just what is worrying me. It seems to me that Ysix is not much like Zenema. What if she burns the settlement when she gets here? Maybe you could talk to her first?"

I shrugged. "Ysix may not want to listen."

Bower sighed. "Ryland said he and the elders will meet in council tonight to decide whether to release you or not. They also want to figure out how to get the Crimson Red dragons to help them."

I sat up straighter. "And just how does Ryland expect to lead red dragons if he is not a dragon-friend? He treated his black dragons like they were prisoners. If he has no connection with the red dragons, what's he going to do? Try to chain them, too?" I shook my head. "Ryland will have to ask us to help him with these dragons, and then we can ask the reds if they will help. It's starting to sound like the Three-Rivers clan needs us more than we need them."

"That's how we view it, but Ryland saw your magic. While you slept, the entire clan could talk of nothing other than the stories of how you moved boulders to smash the Iron Guard."

"That should impress them."

Bower shook his head. "Ryland is suspicious of such power—it's magic that is too much like Enric's power. Add in the distrust between the dragons here and the Three-Rivers clan, and I'm not sure Ryland is wrong to be cautious." Bower looked at his hands for a long moment, and then glanced up at me. His face seemed even paler, what with the bruise on his cheek. He asked, "Why do I feel like I should be happy, but I'm not? I managed to call the dragons, I managed to fight by your side, and yet it feels like we already lost everything?"

"We haven't lost." I put a hand over his. I tried to make my words firm, but I had my doubts. Even with Ysix and her brood, and those three red dragons, even with Jaydra on our side and even if the Three-Rivers clan fought with us, would it be enough?

We had met the Iron Guards and the king's army—or at least part of his army—and his magic and his forces had been stronger.

We had to find a way to defeat Enric, but I wasn't sure how we could do that.

Forcing a bravado I didn't quite feel, I squeezed Bowers hand and told him, "We just haven't won yet."

And I hoped those words were true.

*   *   *

Shortly after I spoke to Bower, the Three-Rivers clan horn sounded. It was either a warning or a call to assemble. Judging by how people walked past the spear circle, their steps slow and deliberate, I judged the council was about to start.

Bower told me he would tell me everything that happened and left. Again someone parted the spears for him and he stepped outside. I hated the idea of sitting here, doing nothing, but Bower could talk better than I could.

But I was not going to spend another night in this hut, trapped behind spears.

We can go? Hunt...fish? Jaydra opened her eyes but didn't raise her head.

Standing, I pulled the blanket from the ground and wrapped it around my shoulders. I thought to her, *Yes, we will. I won't let them treat us as if we are sheep to be penned, but first we must give Bower time to see if his talking will work his own kind of magic with words.*

While we waited to hear from Bower, I began to stretch my muscles, doing what I could to make myself ready for whatever came. I was stronger now than when I had woken—the food Bower brought me helped. But I still felt weak—magic would not even spark from my fingertips, and my chest seemed hollow and empty.

The evening darkened. I wondered if Ysix was near. Stretching my thoughts out, I sensed she and her brood were near but had stopped at the lake to feed and drink so they might arrive rested. I sent to her my approval of such a plan, and got back from her faint impatience, as if she wondered why she would ever need my approval.

So I sat down again to wait, resting my back now against Jaydra's side. Even from where my hut sat near the edges of the settlement, I could tell the council wasn't going quite how anyone had planned. Angry shouts lifted into the air, the words indistinct, but nothing happened. And Bower did not return.

A few fires were lit in the settlement, but I noted that every flame seemed shielded, as if the Three-Rivers clan was worried the king's army might spot them. I heard the flap of wings and looked up to see three dragons circling the settlement. Waves of curiosity came from those dragons, and I thought the reds must be wondering what had happened to the Dragon King who had called them.

I sent thoughts out to the red dragons, but it was as Jaydra had said—they either didn't really understand my thoughts or did not want to let me know they had heard me. The three reds landed not far from my hut, and Jaydra lifted her head to speak to the reds in dragon, with whistles, clicks and hisses.

Evening was starting to fade when I heard bootsteps outside the spear circle. I stood and watched as what seemed to be a half-dozen men and women strode to where the red dragons sat in the meadow. The moon was rising, turning the red dragons into huge, dark silhouettes that blocked the stars.

I couldn't quite see who was headed to face the red dragons, but I assumed Ryland would be there and Bower, too. Or could the Three-Rivers clan be so unwise as to try to negotiate with these dragons without Bower? They certainly had not been wise in how they had treated their black dragons.

Leaning against Jaydra, I watched the small group stop a good distance from the red dragons—however, they were still close enough that the reds could have flamed everyone with one breath.

I thought I recognized Ryland's voice but I couldn't hear what was being said—the wind carried the words way. But Jaydra thought to me, *Jaydra hears humans.*

Her dragon senses were sharper than any other creatures in the land.

"Please repeat to me what they say!" I asked, my eyes fixed on shadowy figures that faced the three dragons.

In my mind, Jaydra repeated Ryland's words.

Oh, mighty dragons, we humbly beseech your aid. We ask you to remember who we were, and who you were of old... The dragons and their riders.

Suddenly, Jaydra was snorting soot and fire as the lead crimson dragon lifted its head and roared a gout of flame into the sky. Even from this distance I could hear the panicked cries from the delegation as they ran backwards a little way, before realizing that the Crimson Reds really had no intention of killing them all—yet.

"What was that about?" I demanded of Jaydra.

Their clutch-queen called them liars. Jaydra snorted as if that was the best joke ever.

"Why would she do that?"

She can smell their blood and knows none are true dragon-friends. She smells on them the scent of the black dragons—she smells the hate the black dragons had for these people.

"Those are strong words." Didn't Ryland know better than to lie to a dragon? To lie was to insult them, for it was treating them as if they could not sense the truth.

But what worried me more was that all the dragons I'd ever known were very straightforward in that they did as they pleased. If a dragon didn't like you, it would either never talk to you again or would kill you. Simple as that. So while dragon minds could be complex and subtle, their emotions were very direct.

The reds hissed and rumbled an answer. The human delegation could not understand the dragons, but two stepped forward and spread out blankets. On this, they unwrapped what seemed to be gifts for the dragons.

Gold trinkets glittered in the light of a lantern held aloft. From how one woman put her hands over her mouth, as if grieving, I guessed this was everything precious held by the Three-Rivers clan.

They're attempting to bribe the dragons? I thought to Jaydra.

Jaydra's amusement drifted to my thoughts. *Shiny metal? What dragon has need of such a thing when we have shiny scales and the skies?*

I would have laughed if not for the fear spreading up through my belly. How would these large red dragons, each the size of a house, take being insulted twice now? Jaydra would probably sweep her tail at them, casting them aside and fly away, never to be seen again, but these dragons might not be so polite.

Not worth killing, Jaydra informed me, and I hoped she was conveying the thoughts of the red dragon.

She was not.

The biggest dragon let out a roar and smoking flames.

The half-dozen people started to back away. I knew now that Bower could not be with them—even he knew better than to treat dragons with such poor manners. But more men hurried out from the settlement, the tips of their spears glinting.

This was far too much like how the villagers had faced Jaydra, myself and Bower.

Watching the warriors start to advance on the dragons, I told Jaydra, "Bower is not there and this is all going wrong. It's time for us to do something before someone is hurt."

I no longer cared about what the Three-Rivers clan would think of me if I broke from their ridiculous cage of spears, and I was done with waiting for Bower to fix things with his words.

Jaydra sprang to her feet, unfolded her wings and casually flattened the hut by sitting on it. I dragged myself up her neck and settled onto her back. With a leap, we were flying free.

CHAPTER 16

DANGEROUS ALLIANCES

I'd tried to go with Ryland to see the dragons—Saffron would expect me to be there—but two of the elders held me back, refusing to let me leave the central hall where the council had been held. From there I watched Ryland and the other five approach the dragons. I had told him to be stand fast, echoing what Jaydra had told me when I had faced the wild dragons. He seemed to manage that part, but now I could feel the anger of the Crimson Reds. Ryland had done something very wrong and I had to fix this.

Breaking free of the two old men who kept trying to hold me back, I slipped past the other warriors and ran after the dozen men now headed toward the Crimson Reds. I had to dodge hands that kept reaching out to grab me.

Ryland and his council had decided to approach the dragons to judge where their loyalty lay. I feared now that they'd said the wrong thing, had perhaps treated these Crimson Reds as they had the wild black dragons. In truth, I thought the Three-Rivers clan seemed a little afraid of the Crimson Reds—they were huge dragons and needed to be respected.

I had tried to offer what little advice I could to Ryland, telling him not what I had read but what Saffron, Jaydra and even Zenema had taught me.

Running now toward the Crimson Reds, I saw that Ryland and the others had spread out bits of gold. A cup, a belt, some chains and silver plate glittered in the lanterns' light. I sprinted past two more men who tried to catch me, slipping out of their reach. There were advantages to being slight.

Yelling, I called out to Ryland, "What are you doing? These dragons fled Torvald because humans turned against them. This is about offering them a return to their home in Mount Hammal!"

Turning from the Crimson Reds—and backing up more than a few steps—Ryland looked at me, his mouth pulled down and his hand resting on the hilt of his sword. He did not look a man ready to listen to reasonable arguments.

The warriors now assembling at the edge of the settlement as if they could protect their huts with spears, grabbed me. I struggled to break free, but a roar from above had everyone stopping and looking up.

A flash brightened the sky as Jaydra let out a dazzling breath of flame and swept toward the Crimson Reds. The red dragons called back to Jaydra with a roar. I had no idea what they were saying, but I worried it did not bode well for the Three-Rivers clan.

"Saffron! Jaydra!" I called, pulling an arm free to wave at them, unsure if they could hear me over the noise of the Crimson Reds as they roared, or over the shouting villagers.

Jaydra landed with a heavy thud between the warriors and the Crimson Reds. Saffron climbed down from Jaydra, but without her usual agility. She was as worn out by events as was I, but we had to prevent this from becoming a disaster.

Instead of addressing Ryland and his people, Saffron turned to face the Crimson Reds. She swept a deep bow, her arms spread wide and then straightened to start at the huge dragons. "Great dragons, I am Saffron of the Maddox clan, and kin to the kings who stole the throne of Torvald and who have tormented us all. But I'm also Saffron, den-sister to Jaydra and den-daughter to Zenema, of the Western Isles. I beg you to forgive these humans. They do not know how to speak or behave, but I believe they can learn."

The largest of the Crimson Reds stepped forward and thumped her tail against the ground. I had a sense of distrust from her. Jaydra edged a little closer to Saffron and hissed as if warning the other dragon not to take out any insult on Saffron.

Things didn't seem to be going well, and Saffron confirmed my fears when she turned to glare at Ryland. "How dare you insult these noble dragons in such a manner as this. Do you think dragons can be bought with worthless trinkets? You have no business talking to dragons."

Ryland's mustache twitched and I thought I saw a spark of anger in his eyes. He lifted his chin and told Saffron, "We know how a dragon should be treated."

One of the burly warriors next to me let go of my arm and shouted, "All these beasts know is pain and blood anyway!"

Glancing around, I took in the glinting spears and the torches that had been carried from the settlement by some of the clan. I wondered if I had been deluding myself. The alliance I had wanted to build with dragons and the Three-Rivers clan seemed utterly impossible just now.

Jaydra curled her tail around Saffron as if to protect her. The red dragons had fixed their stares on the warriors and I thought it looked as if these Crimson Reds were ready to destroy this settlement.

But more dragon roars sounded from the sky.

Looking up, I saw a half-dozen dark shapes outlined against moonlit clouds. A dragon mind touched mine and I knew that Ysix and her brood had arrived. They swooped over the settlement, stirring up a wind with their leathery wings. Turning, I called out to the Three-Rivers clan, "The dragons have come to join our fight against Enric."

"Join our fight or finish us all," Ryland muttered.

Ryland unsheathed his sword, which glinted in the light of the torches and candles.

I waved at him to put away his weapon. "Ysix comes. I know this dragon. She is kin to Saffron's Jaydra."

Warriors and the rest of the Three-Rivers clan started to fall back, leaving only Ryland standing his ground. Ysix, and the dragons with her, landed a short distance from the Crimson Reds, who turned to watch the sea-green and blue island dragons. They seemed to be speaking with clicks and whistles and I wondered what they were saying.

"Den-mother Ysix, welcome," Saffron called out.

Queen Ysix, I thought, wondering if she would hear me. *You come just in time.*

I glanced around me. Saffron, Ryland and myself were the only ones left facing the dragons. All the others had retreated back to the settlement, taking their torches and lanterns with them. The last of the daylight lit the scene, leaving more shadows than anything. Ryland spread his legs wide, as if into a battle stance, his sword ready. He was not a man, I judged, to be dismayed by greater numbers, but now I wondered if he would ever be able to treat a dragon as an equal in battle?

The dragons were still exchanging some kind of greeting that Saffron seemed to be able to understand, judging by how she was looking from Ysix to the red dragons.

And then, to my astonishment, Ysix pushed her voice into my mind—but she seemed to address everyone at once. *Saffron and Jaydra, Ysix recognizes you both. And Bower of Torvald, Ysix is come as promised. But what is the meaning of weapons lifted against dragons?*

Ryland's mouth fell open and he glanced from Saffron to me and finally stared at Ysix as though he could not believe what he had just heard.

I stepped closer to Ryland and said, "Best be respectful and listen to Ysix. She is wise beyond your years."

Ysix hissed, and then sent out her thoughts again. *I am Ysix of the Western Isles. Who dares draw a sword against Ysix and Ysix's brood?*

Ryland opened and closed his mouth uselessly. He dropped his sword. I kicked it aside so it might not be easily retrieved and told Ysix, "Queen Ysix, before you is Ryland of the Three-Rivers clan, who oppose the false king. Thank you, Queen Ysix, for hearing my call and coming to our aid. And please forgive Ryland. It has been too long since the Three-River clan had a dragon to instruct them. They have forgotten much as have the black dragons of the north, and even the Crimson Reds seem to no longer know how to share their thoughts with humans."

Ysix seemed to be enjoying this scene, or that was the feeling I got from her. The emotion came to me just underneath her thoughts. She bowed her head and something like a rattle or purr of pleasure rumbled in the air. *Well met, Bower of Torvald. As Bower vouches for this Ryland, Ysix will recognize Ryland. After all, the blood of the true Dragon King flows through Bower.*

"You honor me, Ysix." I bowed and when I looked up again, Saffron smiled and winked at me. I was going to take that for her approving of my words.

Now formalities are done, what is there to hunt? Dragons cannot survive on gold alone.

Ysix let out a roar that seemed laced with laughter. It was a little unfair of her to rub Ryland's mistakes in his face, but when I glanced at Ryland I saw him staring at the ground as if ashamed.

He looked up again and went down on one knee. "I...Queen Ysix," Ryland said his voice thick and awkward. "I beg your pardon for greeting you with sword drawn. And noble dragons, forgive our mistakes. Bower is right—it was long ago that Dragon Riders came to us and much has been lost over the years."

Ysix inclined her head. *Ryland has fought beside my family? Ryland is enemy of the dark king?*

"Aye, aye—queen." Ryland nodded and stood. "And it would be an honor to fight alongside a dragon such as you."

I started to grin. At least Ryland could recognize strength when it landed in front of him. He had spoken as eloquent as any dragon-friend. Turning to me, Ryland again went down on one knee, leaving me shocked and speechless.

"Bower of Torvald," Ryland said, his voice not quite as strong as it had when he had spoken to Ysix. "If a queen dragon recognizes you as descended from dragon kings, then I must as well." He stood and called out to the other warriors. "People of the Three-Rivers clan. We have guests to feed and oaths to pledge. From this day forward, we must seek to be friends to all dragons."

Glancing at the settlement, I saw the warriors had moved forward, their spears drooping much as had the island villagers. I knew then that they must have heard Ysix's thoughts—she had spoken to everyone here. They all now knew that a dragon could not just speak to other dragons, but could speak to them as well—dragons would never again be regarded as dumb beasts.

I looked to Saffron and she nodded back at me, then patted Jaydra's neck. Pride swelled in my chest. We had done it. We had brought the Three-Rivers clan and the dragons together. For the first time, it seemed possible that we might have a chance to fight Enric's dark rule and his foul magic.

CHAPTER 17

HOW TO BEFRIEND A DRAGON

Ryland really is taking this well, I confided to Jaydra from where we stood at the edge of the meadow.

Most of the Three-River clan had gathered in the meadow near the settlement. Scouts had been sent out to keep an eye on the king's army and the Iron Guard, but so far there was no sign of a threat to the settlement. It was possible the king's army was still in disarray after the battle on the other side of the mountain. But Ryland did not want to be caught unaware. And then Bower had insisted that the Three-Rivers clan must become better acquainted with the dragons. So here we were.

I stood with my arms crossed, tired of waiting already, and even more tired of Bower's pacing back and forth. Jaydra crouched next to me, warming herself. The sun had just peaked over the eastern mountains and the air held a cold bite.

Just above the lush, green meadow, dragons either perched on the lower part of the mountainside or sat on the higher rocks, watchful and still. They all now had full bellies, I knew, both from the meats roasted and presented to them last night and from river fish they had hunted this morning.

The red dragons seemed to keep mostly to themselves and perched higher than any other dragon. I wondered if the reds were by nature arrogant or shy. I would have to ask Ysix or Zenema when I had the chance.

Jaydra huffed out a warm breath and thought to me, *Reds cautious. They think Ryland too like a dragonet making foolish mistakes. But Ryland learns.*

I had to suppress a smile. Jaydra's thoughts seemed to have a newfound maturity, and I wondered if now that Ysix was here was she perhaps trying to impress the den-mother?

"If he doesn't get his arm bitten off, that is," I told her.

Ryland was out near the red dragons with some of his warriors, offering them more platters of roasted pig. The reds didn't seem all that interested, not with full bellies, and seemed to be enjoying ignoring Ryland and his men.

Ysix had already told Ryland she would not fly with slavers, which was what she thought of the anyone who would imprison dragons behind bars in caves. When Ryland told his warriors they would have to free the rest of the black dragons they held, that had caused an uproar and a council meeting that had gone on long into the night.

"It's true," I'd told Ryland. "You have to befriend them if you want them to fight for you. Either that or let them go." Ryland

236

had at least argued the rest of his clan into freeing the dragons. Half the settlement had gone to get the black dragons and bring them here.

Coming up to me, Bower stopped, the stiff leathers of the Three-Rivers clan squeaking as he moved. "This is going to work, isn't it?"

"At least the black dragons will all be free. That's something."

From the mountainside, Ysix gave a roar.

Looking up to where she sat on her haunches, her long neck stretched up into the sky. I thought that she already had decided she was in charge. That might prove to be a problem if things did not go to as she wanted them.

"Here they come," Bower said.

I looked to the west where two of the burlier warriors stood on either side of an iron gate that barred one of the cavern openings.

Ryland waved, positioning his warriors along a path that led from the cavern down to the meadows. All the men seemed to be white-faced and while I couldn't see if they were shaking in their boots, I knew I would be if I had to face angry wild dragons that had been imprisoned since they'd come out of their eggs.

A nervous silence seemed to settled on those gathered in the meadow. Everyone had to be expecting the worst—the dragons would attack. Or they would fly away.

To be honest, I wasn't sure what would happen, but I told Bower, "They need to stop seeing dragons as a threat."

He just shook his head and kept staring up at the iron gates and the cavern.

The horn of the Three-Rivers clan sounded. Ryland lifted a hand and let it fall.

The metal gates screeched and banged open.

Ryland waved a green flag now, and several of his warriors took up packs and then started to spread something out of those packs, leaving a trail of something silver-looking from the cavern down to the meadows.

"Do you really think the black dragons will stay for fish?" Bower asked and glanced at me.

Fish! Jaydra lifted her head.

I shrugged "It's hard for a dragon to resist fish. But they may decide to feed on Ryland or at least take a bit out of his men."

Bower's frown deepened.

The warriors left the fish on the rocks in front of the cavern opening and all the way down to the meadow, hurrying away from the cavern as fast as they could.

Bower shook his head and started to pace again. "Those dragons have had years of only seeing humans when they were dragged out and goaded into battle or into that ridiculous challenge of Ryland's."

Leaning against Jaydra's side, I told him, "The dragons need to see these people not as their captors but as friends. Fish is a good start."

Jaydra was snuffling the air and wondering why this silly human was wasting all his good fish.

I kept my attention on the cavern where I could now see a writhing mass of four wild dragons. Four more came out, and then another four, and after that I almost lost count. It had to be almost twenty dragons now.

The black dragons' loud hissing was answered by the red dragons that hissed back and spread their wings. I could feel the black dragons setting every other dragon on edge—it was like having unruly children around.

As the black dragons stepped into the sunlight and hesitated I could see they were thinner than any other island dragons. They looked to be a quarter of the size of the gigantic red dragons.

A dozen of them sniffed the fish, their wings folded tight. Their heads were not the most graceful I'd seen, and spikes jutted out, looking vicious and mean.

One dragon glanced around, one eye a milky white from an old injury. Others had cracked scales. They stepped over and around each other, weaving around as if sharing their body warmth.

Blacks are frightened, Jaydra thought to me.

I straightened, turned and hugged her neck. "Of course. Thank you, Jaydra."

Bower glanced at me. "What? Did you spot something terrible?"

Waving at the blacks, I told him, "The dragons are scared. They're moving like dragonets in a clutch. Young dragons rely on their clutch-brothers and sisters for reassurance. As feral and savage as these dragons might be, they are really like children."

"They need trust," Bower said, tapping his fingers on his leather breeches.

One of the black dragons lunged forward to seize another fish on the path. A gasp rose up from the crowd. Another dragon came over to steal the fish from the first dragon, and then noticed the fish further along on the path.

The black dragons spilled down the mountain path, hissing and gulping down fish. The largest one with a white eye was the only one to be cautious. She held back and kept looking over to where Ysix and her brood perched.

Ysix called out a hooting challenge to White-eye, who halted. I could see her trembling.

"What are they saying?" Bower asked.

I shook my head. "I think Ysix is wondering whether White-eye is a threat or not."

"White-eye?" Bower asked, and then said, "That's a good name, but I thought a dragon always told you its name."

Before I could explain that the black dragons weren't much for names or talking, the dragons swarmed into the meadow. I could count them now and nineteen black dragons sniffed the air. So far they had not tried to fly away, but a few of them started to spread their wings as if testing them.

I nodded at Bower. "Now it's up to us." A shiver of apprehension trickled down my back, but I strode toward Ryland and his men, keeping the black dragons in front of me. Bower a few paces behind me, his boots rustling in the tall grass. Ryland might be the war chief of his people, and Bower might be the future king, but I was the only one who really knew what I was doing. But my fingers twitched and my heart raced as I approached these dragons—there were so many of them.

And they are not of your den, Jaydra said, her mind close to mine.

I glanced at her. She had taken flight and hovered not far overhead. I nodded to her, thankful she would be near to me both physically and mentally. I might have need of her very soon.

The black dragons had stopped in the meadow and were now spread out in smaller groups of four or five. They seemed to be all claw, spikes, dark scales and wary eyes. On the mountainside, Ysix was now ignoring them, opening her long wings to show off her belly scales as she preened as if she had nothing better to do.

It was a show of strength by Ysix. She wanted to prove she thought of this as her territory and was at home here.

White-eye hissed and lifted her head. The other dragons seemed younger than her, for they all looked to her.

Walking up to Ryland, I told him, "The dragon there with the white eye—she is the den mother. The queen. If you manage to get her on your side, the rest will follow her guidance."

Ryland looked tense, as if he had braced every muscle in his back and shoulders for action. He didn't even look at me or Bower, but asked, "And how, by the three rivers, do I do that?"

Bower gestured to a pack of fish that lay on the ground, which was now starting to stink. "That seems a good way to start."

Ryland reached into the pack and pulled out a large mountain-lake fish.

I nodded to him and said, "Hold it up to White-eye. She can smell it from where she is. Make certain you have White-eye's full attention."

Jaydra sent me reassurance that the black dragons were interested, but cautious.

White-eye's glance flickered to Ryland, but she turned to stare up at Ysix almost immediately. White-eye wasn't going to be wooed that easily.

I told Ryland, "Now throw the fish to White-eye."

Ryland did as I asked, but two of the other black dragons rose up and snapped the fish from the air.

White-eye turned and hissed at them and they jumped back from her.

"That didn't go so well," Ryland said.

"White-eye is testing you—well, testing all of us, I think."

"I've got an idea," Bower said and walked toward the black dragons.

Fear for him flared in me and I snagged the hem of his tunic to stop him. "What are you doing?"

He glanced at me and lifted a hand. "During the battle with Enric's Iron Guard I managed to summon the Crimson Reds. And I talked to Zenema. You said that was because of the power within my blood, that I am the rightful Dragon King. So maybe I can talk to them?"

243

"All of them? At once? Will you look at just how wild these black dragons are."

Ryland glanced at the dragons and then at Bower. "If you can get these beasts to listen to you, you really are the Dragon King, and all will acclaim you as such."

I glared at Ryland. "They're not beasts. Did you learn nothing last night?"

Ryland shook his head and smoothed his beard. "I learned your island dragons are different. But I speak now of the black dragons. No one has ever heard a thought from any black dragon."

With a low growl, I fought down the urge to thump him. Keeping my voice low and to the point, I said, "The sooner you realize, Ryland, that all dragons have as much sense and even more brains than *you*, the sooner we will have a true army."

A sort of prickling behind my eyes swept through me and I sensed a mind reaching out to mine. The hairs on the back of my neck stood up as a wave of awareness stirred—an awareness of Bower.

He stood staring at the black dragons, his fingertips pressed to his temples. It felt something like what Zenema could do, when she turned the force of her attention on you—waves of a bright mind, dazzling as the sun. I had not known Bower had such power.

I could almost sense Bower's thoughts.

Glancing up at Jaydra, I thought to her, *Can you hear Bower's thoughts?*

Sweat trickled down Bower's face. His forehead bunched tight. The black dragons started to turn and look at him, their expressions startled and suspicious.

Wait, let Jaydra share minds with Saffron.

Jaydra rarely shared her full mind and senses with me. But suddenly I could feel what it was like to be her—to have a body as long as a house, as strong as the mountains and as quick as a dancing bird. Scales like liquid metal contained a fire within that was always burning. And the world changed.

I sensed the red dragons on the mountainside, breathing in their scents—the sea breeze of Ysix and her brood, the sulfur tang of the reds, and the earthy scent of the blacks. Their shapes seemed to glow, hot for the reds like a bonfire, warm for Ysix and her brood, and warm coals for the blacks. The minds of the other dragons touched mine—but the black dragons' emotions seemed hot as a savage forest fire.

Another voice grew louder in my mind—it spun soft colors of an almost orange-golden hue. It was Bower's thoughts.

No one is going to hurt you. We are your friends.

Does his voice seem to be colors to all dragons now? I asked Jaydra.

Jaydra's voice wrapped me in waves of her own unique blue-green energy. *Bower is becoming a king.*

And the dragons can all hear him? They will listen to him?

Was it really that easy? As easy as a trick of the magic in the blood?

Of course not. Each dragon must decide to listen or not to queen, king or mouse.

Bower's thoughts seemed reassuring to me, calming almost. *This is Ryland. Ryland brought you fish. He sets you free to choose your own path now.*

A shadow rose up inside Jaydra's mind—there was something she wasn't telling me, something she hid with what seemed a cloud, but she thought to me, *Dragons sense something different about Bower—just as Saffron is different, too. Dragons can smell the magic you have within you.* Jaydra started to push my thoughts away, detaching her mind from mine.

Am I not your sister in words and heart and mind? I asked her, feeling a little hurt. The realization that Jaydra, my closest confidant, might be keeping secrets from me left me feeling isolated in a way that I had never felt before.

All dragons have their secrets, even Jaydra There is something Jaydra does not understand about magic and humans...and what Bower is and what we are. Give Jaydra time to think.

With that, Jaydra pushed me firmly back into my body. With a gasp, I staggered a step. I was left small and inconsequential once more, dizzy from the sudden shift from being dragon-sized down to Saffron-sized.

Ryland grasped my elbow. "Are you well?"

I pulled away from him and simply waved a hand.

Bower stepped even closer to the black dragons, his face creased in concentration. Something dark spilled from his nose. Blood. What would forcing his innate blood-magic do to him? He seemed to be having some sort of effect on the younger dragons—they stared at Bower as if they could not look away. However, Bower's nose started to bleed. Even this seemed to interest the dragons, for one came close enough to sniff Bower.

Nudging Ryland, I whispered, "Feed them, now while they are interested and not terrified."

Ryland seemed to snap out of his own haze of wonder. He bent and pulled a fish from the pack at his feet. The closest dragon snapped it from the air. White-eyes came closer to snag a fish. Another fish, another throw and another snap of dragon jaws.

Of the twenty or so wild dragons, about twelve began to crowd forward, wanting fish or to examine Bower. A few of those gathered gave gasps, but many edged closer to see the young, black dragons, their eyes wide and their expressions ones of awe. Some even muttered, "Why did we keep them locked up for so long?"

"I'm running out of fish," Ryland told me.

Glancing down, I saw Ryland's pack was almost empty. However, I was starting to worry about Bower. Blood still trickled from his nose—he kept wiping it away—and he began to sway on his feet.

"Bower." Stepping to his side, I shook his arm. "What is wrong?"

Bower's sending of his thoughts blinked out at once. The wild dragons all fell back, but their hunger was overriding the anxiety now filtering out from them. They had not yet flown away.

White-Eye thumped the ground with her tail and whatever that meant it wasn't anything good.

Jaydra? I asked.

The black chides her children for listening to the king-human. She calls them back to her, Jaydra's thoughts didn't have any worry in them, but then Ysix rose up on her hind legs and let out a long roar.

I did not need Jaydra to translate as White-eye turned to confront Ysix and exchange hisses and angry whistles with her. They were arguing about whether humans could be trusted.

The argument was decided when White-eye let out a sudden jet of flame—a rare feat for any dragon. Spreading her wings, she launched herself into the air and circled the Three-Rivers clan's settlement. The other black dragons crouched in the meadow, looking from White-eye to Bower and then to Ysix. From their hisses and grumbling, they sounded as if they, too, were arguing about what to do.

Ysix gave another roar. White-eye answered with a hiss and another flame. Wings spread out and with a flurry of movement, roughly half the black dragons took to the air, joining White-eye. The dark cloud of dragons circled once before heading north, into the snow-capped mountains.

Sounding distressed, Bower shouted, "We have to stop them. We need every dragon we can get."

"We don't need those dragons," I told him.

Ryland smiled and spread out his arms to indicate the twelve dragons who had remained and who now were nosing Ryland's fish pack, looking for more. "Saffron is right. We should be proud of what we have here." Turning to his warriors, he ordered, "Bring them more food!"

I held up a hand and stepped closer to the black dragons. "No. Leave them to Ysix for now. They have just lost their den-mother and need another strong dragon to reassure them."

That is true Saffron. Ysix's thoughts reached out to me, and from the way Ryland's face paled I knew her thoughts had touched his mind, too.

Spreading her wings, Ysix glided down into the meadow. She called the black dragons to her with whistles and soft purrs. The black dragons cautiously approached her.

Leave us, Bower, Saffron and *Ryland of Three-Rivers,* Ysix thought to us. I knew it for a command, not a request. *These young ones have suffered enough and they need to learn to hunt for themselves. Ysix will teach them.*

Ryland headed back to the settlement with his people. I stayed close to Bower in case he needed help. His nose had stopped bleeding at last—meaning it had something to do with his trying to communicate with the dragons. Just now, he seemed dazed, but he smiled at me and said, "We still have to work with the dragons—feeding them is a long way still from flying with them."

I glanced at the eastern mountains. "It is. And I worry we will not have time. The Iron Guard is still out there, and the king's army. We might have a few days, maybe a week at most to train before they get here."

Bower nodded. "I've been thinking on that. And I think we need to ask Ysix and the Crimson Reds if they could keep an eye on the king's army—but also maybe they can divert them away from this settlement."

*   *   *

It took most of the night to work out a plan that Ysix—and the Three-Rivers clan—would both approve. Ysix had been busy with the black dragons, teaching them how to fish in the rivers and integrating them into her brood. The red dragons still kept to themselves, but Ysix spoke to them in dragon, and seemed to get some agreement—they hated the Iron Guard it seemed and approved of any plan to harass them. The Three-River clan also finally agreed to set scouts out to watch any path that allowed approach to their settlement—they feared losing the lives of more scouts, but with orders to be alert and to leave if any of the king's men were spotted, that seemed to reassure everyone.

The red dragons flew off that night to scout out the king's army—they would be able to spot them in the darkness or the daylight, for they could smell the army and the Iron Guard as well. Ysix told them not to attack, just to draw the army away from the settlement—lure them into heading north instead of west. The Three-River clan scouts left at first light. It was a good plan and would gain us a little time to train.

I used some of that time for a bath and a hot meal, and to clean my green leather tunic and polish my boots. Bower spent his time—after being forced into at least some clean clothes by the women of the settlement—with the Three-Rivers clan working to make dragon saddles. I had never seen such a thing, but Bower insisted he had seen detailed drawings in books of the harness once used by the Dragon Riders of Torvald.

The saddles at least made sense to me in that no one here had grown up riding dragons. I knew how to cling to scales or spines or horns, but these riders knew nothing. The saddle would help them not fall to their deaths. It took hours for Bower to finally approve all the harness straps, for he worked hard to make certain the leather would be wide enough to hold but would not alarm the dragons or harm them.

Over the morning meal in the great hall—warm bread and slabs of roasted goat—Ryland announced to the Three-Rivers clan that it was time to begin training their dragons.

Bower, for all of his wise words yesterday, looked only too bright-eyed and eager to follow Ryland now, but I stood, pushing back my plate and told them all, "That is not how it is done. There is no training of a dragon as you would a horse or a mountain pony. A dragon is a partner—a friend. A dragon will choose who to respect and who to ignore. That means not every dragon and every person will fit together, just as not every person will be your friend."

Bower frowned, Ryland tugged at the braids in his beard, but other heads began to nod as if I must know everything about dragons. Of course, all I had known was what I'd learned growing up with the dragons of the Western Isles. Jaydra and I had simply bonded with each other. I could still recall that she had made the first move to become my friend. None of the other dragons in her clutch chose to be with me.

Jaydra sent me warm thoughts of approval of my words, and Bower stood and said, "Saffron is right. Everything written about the Dragon Riders of old speaks of how the dragon must choose its riders. In the old days, a dragon might choose two riders, but if your dragons will choose at least one of you that is the first step to a deep bond between the Three-Rivers clan and your dragons."

Ryland stood now, too, and said, "I will be the first. Let whichever dragon thinks they can handle me choose me!"

Since only humans were here, I decided he was speaking more for the benefit of his clan. But his words were good, and he spread his hands wide and said, "Remember, we do this to heal an ancient wound between our species. And we do this to put an end to the evil of Torvald!"

I noticed Bower wince at those words and I nudged him with my elbow. "It is the evil of my family they are being asked to battle, not your city."

He nodded and shrugged.

Ryland picked up his dragon saddle, fashioned last night, and strode from the building. Bower and I followed, as did most of the Three-Rivers clan. A few hung back—some of the old men and the warriors who were shaking their heads and muttering about the folly of trusting dragons. Women with young children stayed in the settlement, but many of the boys and girls followed us, along with other warriors and women who now wore the leather strips of armor of the Three-Rivers clan. We had with us perhaps thirty people, half of them carrying dragon harness, and I wondered who would be chosen by the dragons and who would be left behind.

Ysix had taken all the dragons—except the reds that were out hunting the king's army—to the lake to feed this morning. The black dragons' bellies stuck out, full from their feasting. But they all became alert as the people of the settlement stepped into the meadow.

At first the black dragons hung back, staying near Ysix, but she nudged them forward and slowly they approached, a few tasting the air with their long, forked tongues. Their eyes seemed to change color and a few of them gave snuffling breaths of smoke.

It is like a call you cannot ignore, Jaydra whispered in my mind.

One black dragon pushed the others out of its way.

It eased hesitantly toward Ryland, and then stopped, lowering its snub nose to sniff the man's red hair and beard. It didn't move, but held its face beside his, gazing directly into his eyes with its own. To his credit, Ryland stood stock still and stared back into the dragon's eyes. A deep, rattling hiss rose from the black dragon.

It was purring.

Ryland raised a broad, battle scarred hand and patted the dragon's nose. "You are...uh... a good boy." The dragon butted at Ryland's hand as if to ask for more attention. A grin spread over Ryland's face.

"Girl," I corrected. "She is a good girl."

Ryland beamed ever wider. "Ah, then a beautiful dragon. A strong, fearless beauty!"

In answer to these compliments, the dragon gave another rattling purr and lowered its head still further. Ryland's chest puffed out at the sight of a dragon actually enjoying his touch.

"Ryland, the saddle," Bower said and nodded to where Ryland had left his dragon harness of leather and cloth.

Ryland held up the saddle to the dragon so she could see and inspect it. Ryland had also wisely pocketed some of the roast goat, and he slipped a little to the dragon now, leaving her pleased enough with him that she sat waiting patiently.

Together, Ryland and Bower slowly put the saddle on the black dragon. She hissed at Bower, but Ysix gave a sharp, warning whistle and the black dragon lowered her head and huffed out a breath.

Bower, his voice low and soft, showed Ryland and the others how to fasten the saddle, adjusting it to allow for the dragon's size, and any spines. To fasten the harness straps, Ryland had to crawl under the dragon. I saw his face pale, but he took a breath and managed to accomplish the task. Glancing around, I saw that Ryland was gaining new respect from his people.

So was Bower.

While Ryland seemed aware of his dragon and her moods, Bower did not. He kept talking, explaining things, as if he was lecturing Jaydra.

"And then these tie here and here, leaving space for lances, bows and spears. That was how it was done in every drawing I've ever seen of the harness of the Dragon Riders of old. Really, we should have a helmet as well and armor, and another saddle and harness a little further back, for a second rider to act as your Protector."

"Protector?" Ryland almost laughed. "Why would I need a protector? I am on a dragon."

Bower straightened and blinked twice. "That is a very good point. But there always used to be two riders on every dragon. One was called a Protector, who used the weapons, and the other a Navigator, who could read maps and communicate with other riders. Maybe that was just a tradition of the academy, but I wonder if there was a need for it that evolved such a system?" He tapped his chin and I could see he was getting lost in ideas.

Jumping in, I asked Ryland, "Is there any other rider your dragon wishes to choose?"

Ryland slapped a thick hand on the dragon's neck and spoke to her, which I took as a good sign. "You can if you want, you know." His dragon stared at him and would not even look at anyone else. Ryland's grin widened. "We have chosen each other. That is enough for us, I think."

Bower nodded and glanced at those gathered. "Who wants to go next?"

A forest of hands rose as everyone clamored for the opportunity to have a dragon as a friend. We faced a busy morning of dragons choosing their riders and their friends.

Stepping closer to me, Bower watched the scene as dragons either snubbed someone trying to touch them or turned and singled a person from the crowed. A few dragons were happy to pick out two riders, but most would take one only. Bower let out a breath. "Well, we have harnessed dragons—now we just have to see if any of these riders can stay in the saddle."

CHAPTER 18

RIDING DRAGONS

"Bank right! Right!" Saffron screamed the words from her perch just ahead of me on Jaydra.

We had allowed some of the recruits to fly ahead of us so Saffron could keep an eye on them, but she seemed to be spending all of her time yelling at the Three-Rivers clan riders.

Ahead of us, three black dragons and their riders wove in and out of the clouds, narrowly avoiding each other. They were, quite frankly, all over the sky. We hadn't had any collisions yet, thanks to Saffron yelling at the riders and Ysix roaring at the black dragons. I rather thought it looked as if we were herding a flock of starlings, if starlings were clumsy, prone to sudden changes of direction and about the size of small houses.

The choosing had gone smoothly. Only one person had gotten tangled in their dragon's harness and no one had been bitten. But when it came time to mount and fly, four riders had fallen off at once, before the dragon was barely in the air. And with a dozen dragons and riders to train, we split the new riders and their dragons into groups of three. Two of the dragons narrowly missed each other again and I winced.

Saffron covered her eyes and then shouted to me, "And you want them to be able to scout out the enemy? To even attack and fight and somehow stay in the sky?"

"Well…" I started to say when one of the black dragons came hurtling toward us. I shouted out Saffron's name, but Jaydra was already turning and diving low.

The black dragon coming at us gave an alarmed squawk and turned as well. We missed a collision by little more than an arm's reach. Jaydra dove down into the forest below.

She skimmed the surface of the river and its white water and rocks, then rose again into the air. Wind tore at my hair and cut into my skin, but I couldn't help grinning.

Ysix roared, and I looked back to see her trying to keep the three black dragons following her and not copying Jaydra's reckless dive.

We'd lose half the riders to the water!

I had to smile as Jaydra lazily soared back to the others, but my grin faded as I wondered if Saffron was right. We had so little time to train—the king's army was far too close, the Iron Guard far too fierce and we hadn't even started on how to fight from the back of a dragon.

Morosely, I watched the black dragons as they flew, falling, then bouncing back up, drunkenly sliding to one side and then the other, stalling and falling again, and almost flipping upside down.

Where is the graceful, deadly dragon of old?

I tried to remember the old stories about Dragon Riders flying across the sky and bringing order to the land and terror to the enemy, perfectly in time with each other. Were these dragons trying to do too many things at once? Was it the riders who were throwing the dragons off balance?

Mountain dragons can't fly straight, Jaydra thought to me, and I knew Saffron had heard as well for her shoulders shook as if she was laughing at what Jaydra had thought.

She was right.

The black dragons I had seen flying on their own looked more like serpents weaving through the air, and nothing like birds. The dragons of the Western Isles and the huge Crimson Reds flew steady and level—more like a bird. But these blacks jerked and flinched this way and like they had bugs under their scales. And then I realized the truth of that.

"Of course!" I shouted. "Mountain dragons can't fly straight!"

Saffron glanced back at me. "The dragons will hear you and lose heart. I know it's funny, but it's not their fault their riders are—"

"No, no… they literally cannot fly straight. They have to twist in the air like a leaf on the wind." I wiggled a hand in the air. "We're trying to teach them how to fly like Jaydra…like Ysix. But these dragons are built different. They're smaller. Thinner."

Saffron's mouth went wide and her eyes glittered. "Of course! That's why the reds swoop and glide. They have much larger wing size."

"And why the Western Isle dragons like Jaydra must beat their wings to move faster. Every dragon species is different. The old books of the Dragon Riders of Torvald that my father managed to save for me were from a time when the Dragon Academy really only had Middle Kingdom dragons. They didn't have these black dragons—or the Western Isle dragons."

Saffron urged Jaydra closer to the black dragons. "Ryland! Riders! We're going to try something new!" She shouted and waved at them. "We want you to hold on tight and let your dragons fly as they wish."

Ryland frowned and shouted back, "Are we not supposed to control our dragons? Fly them as we wish?"

Saffron shook her head.

From the stiff set of Ryland's shoulders and the dark expression on his face, I could tell he thought Saffron was being stupid, so I called out, "Your dragons want to twist and turn in the air. They have to." A lump rose in my throat, but I swallowed it back and shouted, "I had it wrong. We can't bring the old academy back. But we can do something new. We're going to fly like we fly—not the way that Dragon Riders once did!"

Ryland nodded as if this made sense to him.

"When you're ready," Saffron called out. "I'm going to tell Ysix to tell your dragons to just fly naturally." She bowed her head.

Ysix gave an answering roar, followed by clicks and whirrs as she spoke to all the black dragons, even the ones in the meadow still. I glanced down and sat the riders there jumping into their saddles. Their dragons spread their wings.

With a final shriek, Ysix gave the command.

The black dragons on the ground rose up into the air, and the three flying with us broke away from the tight formation we had been trying to corral them into. In just moments, they became a cloud, twisting together, spinning and tumbling. I watched in amazement as they lost almost all their ungainliness and became an undulating wave.

Of course, the question was could their riders stay put and not become ill from all this turmoil.

In answer, one rider shouted as the black dragons spiraled past, all the dragons from the ground now joining the others. The dragons were moving too fast for me to tell whether it was a scream of joy or a shout of terror.

"At least none of them have fainted yet," Saffron called.

Leaning forward, she urged Jaydra to chase after the black dragons, indulging in the natural dragon sport of chasing each other raucously across the sky.

The black dragon in the lead was, rather unsurprisingly, Ryland's. At times, Ryland stood up entirely from his saddle, holding onto his dragon's horns as she whirled across the sky.

"Ryland, would you be able to fight?" The wind whipped my words away, for now we were flying almost as fast as the black dragons.

Grinning manically as he held on, Ryland began to shift his way, as if to get the dragon beneath him to change direction. For the most part, it did.

Saffron laughed and shouted, "It looks like how they try to ride them on the ground—hang on for dear life!"

That was true. It looked almost exactly like how Ryland had tried to ride the chained dragon in their sport, only this time the human and the dragon were working together.

With a sudden snarl, Jaydra powered herself forward on strong wing beats, almost catching up to the Ryland's mountain dragon.

I could feel Jaydra's excitement, thrumming up through her body and into mine.

"You'll never catch us," Ryland shouted, waving one gauntleted hand at us before hunkering down and allowing her to spin even faster.

Saffron gave a harsh yell, and I could feel her encouraging Jaydra with her thoughts to catch up to Ryland. Jaydra pushed herself faster, and Ryland pushed his dragon faster still. I couldn't believe how fast these mountain dragons were—I had thought that Jaydra was the fastest thing in the sky.

Jaydra let out a rumble of delight as she caught up with Ryland's dragon.

Behind us, Ysix crowed with pleasure. Everywhere I looked, I saw dragons. Ysix, her brood now in the sky, the dark mountain dragons—it looked a monumental game of chase-tail, scorching the sky with smoke and calls.

For a moment, everything felt right. I had never known such perfect joy as that moment, with the sky covered with the sound and sight of playing dragons.

And I knew this was how the world was meant to be.

This was what I had to bring back to the Middle Kingdom—or die trying to do so.

*　　*　　*

Saffron was acting strangely. She had complained of a headache and sought her bed early this night, telling me it had been a long, hard day. But Saffron never before had complained and the only time I had seen her take to her bed was when she was more than half dead from an injury. So what was wrong?

I didn't actually have that much experience when it came to girls—well, when it came to anyone my age, apart from Vic Cassus who I'd thought a friend and who had betrayed me to the king. Which meant I didn't know him quite so well either. But I was certain something was bothering Saffron. This just wasn't like her.

And Jaydra wasn't talking to me about Saffron.

Sitting on the ledge of rock that held the settlement's main hall, I listened to the songs being sung inside. It seemed the Three-Rivers clan was having to come up with entirely new songs about riding dragons and taming dragons.

Although we were not really taming them.

If anything, it was more the other way around, with Ysix and the dragons teaching us how to treat them and work with them. It was all about equal respect.

The Three-Rivers clan still had a long way to go, but at least we had finally mastered some basics. There was no time to waste if Ryland's scouts and the Crimson Reds were to be believed.

I watched the shadowed forms of the dragons who had settled on the mountainside above the settlement. Ysix gave a few rumbles. The reds had returned and Ysix had learned from them that the king's army and the Iron Guard had camped on the far side of the mountains and seemed to be waiting—for orders perhaps. No one knew.

There was still no sign of White-eye and the other dragons that had flown away with her. From what little I had gleaned from the inscrutable Ysix, we were very unlikely to see her again.

The black dragons who had stayed shunned their old cavern, but they did like to den inside the caves on the mountain. I was a little surprised, though, that Ryland had not brought his dragon into the settlement—the two seemed as attached as were Jaydra and Saffron.

It was also surprising that Saffron wasn't out here with me and with Jaydra, who lounged in the meadow just outside the settlement. Like the other Western Isle dragons, Jaydra would have little to do with the Crimson Red dragons, which perched far from all other dragons.

Staring up at the dark hillsides and the black sky, I found myself wondering why the reds had responded to my innate abilities.

Of which I know nothing about!

Not that long ago, I'd been an outcast from my own city, hunted by the king, accused of harboring knowledge of the old history. I'd been just about the lowest person in all of Torvald, and had thought of becoming a wandering scribe. Now, I really was a traitor to my king, for I had fought against him. Zenema had declared me to be a king—and I had found a letter from my father, telling me I was actually a Flamma-Torvald, and the true heir to the throne.

The changes in my life had come so fast at times I felt I had lost control of everything.

I wished that my father was still alive to guide me. Or even that I had had more time with the Hermit of the Western Isles. Or that I had someone who could tell me what to do next.

Bower needs no one to command him. Kings take counsel, not orders!

The shock of Jaydra's thoughts rocked me, almost knocking me off the rocky ledge. I stared out into the meadow and could just make out her dark shape and the glow of starlight off her scales.

I had heard her before, but we did not have the same natural connection Saffron had with her. I could really only communicate with a dragon with all my attention and willpower.

A few moments later, Jaydra rose and padded across the meadow, slipping into the settlement as silently as a cat. It was amazing how quiet she could be. She settled down next to me and her thoughts tickled my mind almost like a dream voice.

Bower has no real magic. No dragon tricks.

Thanks! I thought a little huffily. But I knew what she meant.

I was not like Saffron. She could wield the Maddox magic, the same power Enric used. I had seen her do incredible things, even thwarting Enric's terrible plan to try and burn the city of Torvald just to eliminate the rebels he saw as a threat.

We had stopped that plan and left Torvald unable to be walled in again. If Enric tried his plan again, the people could at least escape. But Enric still had his Iron Guard.

Saffron cannot control magic, Jaydra thought to me.

Surprised to hear these words from Jaydra's mind, I turned to face her and asked, "But why are you telling me that? And isn't this a lot of effort for you to communicate with me? I'm not bound to you."

Bower is bound, Jaydra replied. I thought she sounded a little smug about it, as well. *King magic holds all dragons as does the queen's magic. All are part of dragons and part of humans. All are one.*

Frowning, I tried to understand what Jaydra was trying to tell me. "You mean the Torvald magic is the same as what a queen dragon has? The ability to communicate mentally with everything?"

Jaydra cocked her head to one side, a curiously bird-like gesture as if she were asking me to tell her the answer.

I didn't know what she wanted me to say. What might be right before my eyes that I could not see? Tired as I was from the day, worried about how we were going to win against Enric, as well as worried about Saffron, I gave a sigh and then asked Jaydra, "Do you know what's wrong with Saffron—other than that we have to face Enric, and it was a hard day, and tomorrow is another hard day. I mean, I know it's a lot—but Saffron's never flinched from anything difficult."

Saffron is sad that Jaydra keeps a secret. But not really a secret, it is a riddle, Jaydra thought to me.

"I'm good with puzzles. Maybe I can help work it out?"

Hooting calls drifted down from where the dragons perched. Looking over, I could see dark shapes moving against the purpling sky. What were the dragons saying to each other? Why could I only understand them sometimes?

I wanted to curse my past. I slumped down and rubbed my arms, wishing I had thought to wear a heavy cloak outside. If knowledge in Torvald hadn't been so hard to come by, I might have already mastered the powers of the Flamma-Torvalds and be able to communicate with all dragons by now.

Jaydra moved closer as if to warm me with her body. *That is the riddle, Bower. If it is magic for human and dragon to share a mind, is it magic that also breaks our ties? Or is it a lack of magic? And if there is a place where Jaydra and Saffron are one thing in our hearts and minds, is there also a place where Saffron and Enric are one?*

Her thoughts chilled my heart. I shivered, feeling a buzz in the air between us as Jaydra huffed out a sooty breath. *Jaydra saw Enric speak to Saffron through his metal men. Jaydra cannot protect Saffron from such magic. And now Jaydra feels a shadow looming over Saffron—Jaydra does not know how to defeat shadows.*

It was starting to make sense. "You're sensing Enric. Maybe that's what his troops are waiting for—him to come. He must be using…what, a blood connection with Saffron to…to do what? Enchant her? Curse her? But Jaydra, Saffron's magic works better when you help her."

Jaydra does not know how to help now.

Now. The word echoed in my mind. Suddenly worried about Saffron, I stood and headed for the hut given to her for sleeping.

Saffron's hut stood next to mine. Technically, it was the same one where Saffron had been held behind a wall of spears. But the spears were gone and the ground had been smoothed.

Even so, I kept trying to shake off a dark feeling that squeezed my heart as I approached the hut.

The canvas door glowed softly from the fire inside the small metal box the Three-River clan used for heating. The tang of wood smoke hung in the air.

I knocked on the wooden frame of the door and then pushed the canvas open. The room wasn't that big, with only a bed made of wool blankets stacked on the floor, a couple of stools and a small table.

Saffron lay wrapped up in the blankets, her back to the door. She seemed asleep, her breaths even and deep. I sat down on one of the wooden stools and watched her, warming my hands against the small metal box that sat in the center of the room.

Had I started to worry about Saffron just because Jaydra was worried? Were we seeing too much in Saffron's connection to the Maddox clan?

Surely what she does has to be more important than her blood ties?

But wasn't it my blood ties that had led me to think myself king? And Saffron's connection to Enric had led him to want to keep her with him—and he seemed to want her back, enough so that he had not sent his Iron Guard to destroy this settlement.

Not yet at least.

He wants her—but why?

Was it simply a family thing?

I rejected the idea almost as soon as I thought it. Enric Maddox didn't know anything about family, despite some of the pretty speeches that he'd given over the decades about the Middle Kingdom being one happy family. The king knew only one thing—how to rule with fear.

Maybe he doesn't want her, but needs her for something?

That seemed to make more sense to me.

Enric must need Saffron in order to do something—to reach the dragons maybe? No, that didn't fit with what I knew of Enric, a man who hated dragons and did his best to make them seem a dangerous creature of myth. Enric would destroy any dragon as powerful as Ysix or Zenema.

Saffron murmured something.

Standing, I moved to her side and touched her shoulder. "Saffron?" I whispered.

She turned from me, flinging herself onto her back. She shoved the blankets down and then clutched at them. I touched her shoulder again. "Saffron, it's only a dream."

Sweat slicked her face and she turned her head from one side to the next. I started to fear she was in the grip of some terrible fever.

I put a hand to her forehead to see if her skin was hot or cold. As soon I touched my skin to hers, a charge sizzled up my hand and through me. I pulled back but my heart thudded and my hair stood on end as if a thunderstorm was approaching.

"Get away from me," she muttered, her words slurred. She lifted her hands as if trying to fight off someone or something.

I couldn't let her struggle like this—I had to wake her.

Putting both my hands on her shoulders, I started to shake her, but as soon as I took hold of her, pain shot up my arms and into my chest. I tried to gulp down a breath but couldn't. I couldn't move. It was as if I was being ripped from my body and taken elsewhere.

For a moment, I managed to close my eyes.

When I opened them again, I could see nothing but darkness. However, I was still holding onto Saffron's shoulders. But instead of lying on her blankets, she was standing, as was I. Hadn't I just been leaning over her?

She put her hand on my wrist and asked, her voice taut and anxious, "How is it that you are here, Bower?"

"Where are we?" I tightened my grip on her shoulders, afraid if I let go I would lose her in the darkness around us.

"I don't know! I think maybe I'm still asleep. This...I feel as if I've been here before in dreams. Bad dreams." She pulled away, but she kept her hand wrapped tightly around my wrist. She was glancing around, looking left and right as I had seen her move as she lay on her blankets in the hut.

"But I didn't fall asleep. I just touched you."

Saffron's hand gripped my wrist even tighter. "Somehow I pulled you into this. Or maybe the darkness did."

It was dark—darker than the deepest part of a night without moon or stars.

Saffron turned and looked at me. "Am I dreaming you, or are you dreaming I'm here?"

I shook my head. "You were sleeping. But I think this...it's because we're somehow connected through your magic and through Jaydra and the other dragons."

Saffron turned suddenly and said, "Something else is here."

I felt it as well. The darkness itself seemed to changed temperature, with a chill that crept into it. I could see nothing, but a feeling swept through me as if something had gone terribly wrong in Saffron's dream.

"Wh-what is it?" Saffron said, her teeth chattering and her hands shaking now.

I moved closer to her, chilled as well, wishing I had a fire. Wasn't wishing supposed to change a dream?

A sound like the hissing of boiling lifted and seemed to be getting closer to us.

"Bower?" Saffron stepped closer to me. She seemed as unable as I was to control this dream. Or had we been swept somewhere by a dark magic? Closing my eyes, I tried to will us back to reality, but when I opened my eyes again I still stood next to Saffron in the darkness. I wondered if letting go of her would free me, but I could not leave her here.

The hissing seemed to surround us. Something like a wind or like invisible hands seemed to be pulling on my clothes. My hair whipped about as if a storm was riding.

And then a mocking voice lifted from the darkness, so loud I winced and covered my ears with one hand. "Saffron, child."

Even though the voice seemed to have no body, I recognized Enric's harsh tones. In the darkness, a light started to glow and slowly spread out into the king's face, huge and distorted. He looked as he always had to me—or almost always—his skin smooth, his dark hair long and shining. But his eyes seemed unfocused and his glance darted about as if he could not quite see us.

"Saffron, come home." His stare kept searching the room.

Leaning close to Saffron, I whispered, "He can't see us."

But as soon as I spoke, his stare flickered toward us. "Ah, but I can hear you. And I know you reach for me. Saffron, I can give you so much more than you have ever dreamed of."

Beside me, Saffron tried to pull away from me as she turned to flee from that distorted, huge face.

"Saffron, don't let go!" I whispered to her.

Enric's face expanded, growing so large it seemed to fill the space around us. "Reach out, Saffron. Join your mind to mine."

"No!" Saffron wailed, wrenching her hand free and turning to flee Enric.

In an instant, I felt the presence in the darkness seem to focus on us.

"Ah, there you are, Saffron. And the boy who would steal my throne."

The king's stare focused on us, and waves of malevolent hate poured over me, as hot as any furnace. I thought it to be more like the fires of Torvald when they had burned so many books, and

277

nothing like the clean warmth that came from the belly of a dragon against your back.

Saffron kept shouting at the king that she would never join him. I grabbed her hand and held tight. When we had been together, we had always been stronger.

Enric's face wavered but his voice swept over us, booming and painfully loud. "You must, Saffron. You will be queen. You will rule Torvald at my side. All you need to do is throw aside this false king. What does he know of family, Saffron? You are a Maddox and meant to rule."

"Saffron!" I shouted, my voice small compared to Enric's.

The king's voice rose like a wave that would throw us all away. "Look at him. Do you think he can rule? Admit it. You know he is weak. He is a fool. He is not fit to wear the crown."

Saffron fell to her knees. "I can't fight it. I'm sorry, Bower, I can't hold him out for much longer."

I clung to her hand. I didn't want to lose her to the darkness, to Enric's magic. I feared she might end up trapped in this darkness forever while in the mountain hut her body starved away to nothing. I knew Enric was trying to bend her to his will. But Enric hadn't been able to see her—or us—at first.

That meant he hadn't created this darkness—he was just using it. It had to be some part of Saffron's mind—for it was her dream.

Her nightmare. And that meant Jaydra should be able to reach into this place.

I knelt down next to Saffron. "Find Jaydra! Find your sister."

Saffron glanced at me, her tear-streaked face lighting with a glimmer of hope.

I held her hand even tighter. "You are connected with Jaydra. Reach out for her.".

"You are Saffron of the ancient clan of Maddox, born of storm and fury. You have no other kin than me." Enric's voice boomed and his anger battered at me like an invisible hand.

"Jaydra," Saffron whispered, her voice breaking.

Enric's stare turned to me. "You cannot come between me and what is mine!"

"She's not yours," I called out, but I could feel Saffron being tugged from my grip. I clung to her..

Looking up, Saffron at last faced Enric. Her hands began to glow and I could see she was pushing back at Enric with her magic. Turning to me, Saffron said, "Bower, I need your help. Help me call Jaydra."

Lifting my head, holding tight to Saffron's hand, I closed my eyes and threw the entire weight of his mind against him.

Jaydra!

I thought the word, but it seemed to echo as if I had spoken it.

Enric roared, "Mine! The girl is mine."

Wind and shards that felt like ice battered me. My hand started to slip from Saffron's.

But something inside me sparked bright.

It was what had happened when we had battled the Iron Guard. A knot of emotions like joy and hunger and excitement surged through me. I felt as if I were a dragon.

Suddenly, I knew the shape of Jaydra's mind, of every dragon's mind. They hovered so close I felt I could just reach out to touch them, to pull them close.

But my grip slipped away from Saffron's hand.

Eyes opening, I cried out for her. I could see her—almost. But it seemed as if we were spiraling into an eternity of darkness.

And then a red flame blossomed into the dark.

CHAPTER 19

OF RIDERS AND FRIENDS

The moment our hands broke apart, I felt Bower reach out with his mind to call Jaydra. She roared into the darkness, or a dream version of her did, dragon fire blazing and pushing back the blackness.

I didn't know how Bower had done it.

She blasted the wavering image of Enric with fiery breaths, and I wondered if he too would writhe in his bed as this terrible nightmare rolled through his mind.

Enric's huge face lost its youthfulness. His hair receded, becoming mere wisps, his cheeks became sunken and his corpse-like face dwindled, shrinking under the onslaught of Jaydra's cleaning fire. As his image faded, his wavering voice called out, "Too late, Saffron. I have seen where you are. My armies are coming!"

With a flash of flame, Enric vanished. Jaydra swept me up in her claws, but where was Bower? I called out his name.

He answered at once, his voice weak, "Here...here." He was locked in Jaydra's other front claw. Now the challenge was to break free of this vision.

Jaydra spoke aloud to me as if she could always speak, "Now. Both of you. Too dark place for human or dragon."

In the next moment, I was staring up at the ceiling of my hut. Bower sat next to me. I pulled in a shaking breath. My blankets had been tumbled and sweat slicked my back and face. Glancing around, I couldn't see Jaydra, but the hut creaked and I knew she had wrapped herself around the structure. She sent me warm but exhausted thoughts, as if bursting into my dream—that horrible dream—had taken a great deal from her.

Bower ran a hand over his face. "That was...terrible."

I agreed. My head was pounding with the most vicious headache I had ever experienced. Rubbing my temples, I struggled to sit up. I noticed Bower did not try to help me and I didn't blame him. Somehow I had pulled him into that vision, but if I had not I wasn't certain I would have been able to free myself. "I...I didn't know Enric could do that." I rubbed my arms. I was still chilled. "If I had known the king would be able to reach through to me...he knows where we are. He said so. Perhaps I should have flown off with Jaydra. At least then I wouldn't be a danger to anyone."

"Don't apologize." Bower groaned, stretched and rubbed the back of his neck. "I am not even sure Enric knew what he was doing. Remember how at the start he couldn't see us? He might be just learning new magical skills. And we are stronger with you."

"Our enemy is growing stronger as well."

"Well, this might not be such bad tidings." Slowly, Bower stood. He sat down again on one of the two wooden stools, his shoulders slumped.

"Bower, Enric reached into my mind. How can I ever sleep again? And you should see how you look right now, with dark circles under your eyes and your face is…well, it's probably whiter than mine. But…but…well, thank you. For saving me."

Bower gave a tired smile. "It was Jaydra, not me. But think, for a moment—if the king is learning new tricks that means he doesn't know everything. He hasn't ever had to face anyone as powerful as you—and he hasn't had to face dragons. He might be scared."

"Might be? I can't imagine Enric scared of anything. What if this happens again?"

Bower shook his head. "That we cannot allow. I think the answer is to use your connection to Jaydra. She can connect to your waking thoughts and your sleeping ones, too. I don't really know how it works, but I think you need to stay closer to Jaydra than ever before."

The thought of spending more time with Jaydra felt right…it felt comforting to me. Would Jaydra feel that way? "So you think the closer I am to the place where I and Jaydra are one, the further I move away from whatever connection I have with Enric?"

Bower yawned and rubbed his face as if to reassure himself that he was actually really here, or as if to keep himself awake. "It's a guess, but it is all we have. And now, I do not feel much like sleeping, but I'm exhausted."

"I know what you mean." I stood and grabbed two blankets. "I also don't feel much like staying inside." Heading out, I led the way to where Jaydra lay. She cracked one eye open.

I greeted her warmly with my thoughts, weary, but infinitely glad she was here. She pressed her long, graceful snout against mine, and huffed a warm breath into my shoulder.

I was so scared, Jaydra. I didn't know how to reach you.

Jaydra did not know how to reach Saffron either! Enric had you both hidden.

I handed a blanket to Bower and we both curled up under Jaydra's wing. *I'm sorry, sister, for drawing away from you after you told me you had a secret. I should have respected that. It was wrong of me to be upset.*

That matters not. Jaydra sensed something beyond the shadow of the king. Dangerous powers are loose.

I nodded and glanced at Bower, who was clearly too exhausted to stay awake. He lay slumped against Jaydra's the side.

Can you look after him? And me?

Jaydra closed her wing over us. *Jaydra guards. Ysix guards, too, now. For all dragons know now to beware Enric.*

Despite my fears, I pulled my blanket tight and fell asleep listening to Jaydra's even breaths.

But I wondered how she had managed to tell all the dragons to guard us.

*   *   *

I woke to the sound of birdsong and crept out from under Jaydra's wing. She was awake as well, and Bower was already up and heading back with two bowls of something steaming, and a bag of what smelled like fish slung over his shoulder. Jaydra sat up at the smell of fish. Bower handed me a bowl, offered Jaydra the fish and sat down next to her. The air had a chill to it and mists curled over the meadows. Cooking fires wove smoke into the air. Jaydra nosed the bag and soon was dragging fish out for her breakfast.

Staring at the porridge Bower had brought me, I couldn't take my mind off of what had happened last night. Tired as I was, it felt as if we had turned a corner, faced a challenge and had won a small victory.

I still couldn't take my mind off of what had happened.

Glancing at the hut, I told Bower, "I'm not sure I can ever go back in there."

He nodded. "I don't think we should. Enric may only have seen the inside of the hut. That may have been what he meant when he said he knew where you were."

I shook my head. "No. I think he's sending his army."

Bower nodded. He frowned and stirred his porridge with a wooden spoon. "It was like a trap, that darkness. I think Enric had been waiting for a chance to try and catch you."

I hunched a shoulder. "I hate the idea of him just out there, waiting for me to make a mistake."

Bower ate some of his porridge. I couldn't eat a bite. And then Bower said, "I think Enric needs your magic for some reason. Maybe his is running out, or maybe he wants to use your connection with dragons for something."

I thought back to the dream. "Did it seem to you that Enric wasn't really able to hide from us in that dream—that vision? He made himself seem…well, powerful, but I had a sense of something behind his anger. I felt fear coming from him—and it wrapped around me and became my fear."

Looking up from his bowl, Bower frowned and asked, "What would scare an all-powerful sorcerer king who can enter sleeping minds and animate metal golems?"

Tapping my spoon against the porridge bowl, I asked, "What was that prophecy again—the one you told me about? Enric talked about it once, but I forgot some of it. Something about old and young. He thought he could use it to secure even more power."

Bower put down his breakfast, cleared his throat, and began to recite in a clear, steady voice "'Old and young will unite to rule the land from above. From the dragon's breath comes the return of the True King. It will be his to rebuild the glory of Torvald.' It's the Salamander Prophecy—the rebels believe it foretells Enric's downfall."

"Maybe Enric is starting to believe you really are the True King," I said.

Bower frowned. "He didn't seem too convinced of that last night."

"That was a trick, wasn't it? He was acting tougher than he really is. Think about how, at the last battle, when we faced the Iron Guard, you summoned the Crimson Reds and they fought the king's army. Enric must have seen that, or at least sensed it, through his Iron Guard. After all, if he can send his voice out through them, he probably uses them to see what they see. I think he's starting to fear the prophecy is about to come true."

Bower started to nod. "That would explain why he created that dream-trap or whatever it was. He wanted to use his connection to you to find out what you know—to learn how to defeat us." Bower stood up. "We need to tell Ryland and get the Three-Rivers clan moving. The river and that narrow bridge won't protect them from whatever dark magic Enric has planned."

I knew that much. Shaking my head as I stood, I told Bower, "I can't see a settlement being able to pack up in just a few days. And there is so much training needed before our dragons and riders are ready to head into battle."

"We'll just have to train more on the move. And I think we need to throw a few problems in the way of the king's army. We'll see if Ysix and her brood can act as scouts—and they can also set up a few traps for the army. Block paths by felling trees, and even start a few fires that will put the army in trouble. We need time, and that means we have to create it." He turned and headed for the center of the settlement, calling back to me, "Get the warriors on their dragons. It's going to be a busy day."

Glancing at Jaydra, we swapped amused stares. Bower had sounded for once like a true leader.

I put a hand on Jaydra's neck and stared at the hut where I'd had that horrible dream.

You know what, Enric? You were wrong. Bower isn't weak. He may not be the tallest, or the broadest, or the best fighter, but he is strong in a way you will never understand.

And I knew Bower was someone I would follow as my king.

*   *   *

It turned out I was right—it took four days to get the Three-Rivers clan ready to leave. A day was spent with them arguing in council—no one wanted to believe Enric's magic made him powerful enough to get across the rivers that protected the clan. Finally, Ryland simply had the children come in and he asked the elders if they wished to risk these lives. Two days more of packing up supplies and belongings and at last they were ready to depart.

The elders, the youngest, and those who could care for them, would leave for the mountains to the north.

"We have caverns there where the clan will hide," Ryland told me. "And the paths are so steep and hard, the Iron Guard will not be able to reach them."

I hoped he was right.

While the Three-Rivers clan made ready to move to safety, Bower and I worked with their riders, but we soon found out it was best for the riders to simply learn from their dragons. Ysix was able to communicate a little with the Crimson Red dragons, and she got them to agree to go with the Three-Rivers clan to see them to safety. The reds actually knew the mountains even better than the clan.

Everything seemed set.

Ysix had had her brood flying watch, but had seen nothing of the king's army or the Iron Guard. It was as if they had vanished. Some muttered this meant they had been beaten and retreated, but I kept thinking of how dragons could make themselves invisible. I feared the king might be able to do that with his forces.

Bower spoke about this to Ryland and it was agreed that all those able to ride a dragon would head to where the king's army had last been seen. Ysix and her brood would come with us. We hoped we would find nothing—but at the very least this would be more good training for the new dragon riders.

With that in mind, we parted company with the Three-Rivers clan. Ryland's people cried to see him and the other riders take to the sky. A few pressed bread and fish on us to keep us provisioned. Jaydra, wearing a new dragon harness which seemed to please her a great deal, given that it was made of a dark-green leather and decorated with fringe, gave a roar and leapt into the air.

We had been flying most of the day, using the gorges and deep valleys of the mountains to help the new riders become better acquainted with their dragons, and their dragons with their riders.

We needed much more training very quickly. We also searched for sign of the king's army.

That many men had to leave traces—trees hacked down, or fires lit, or some sign upon the land. We had seen nothing, and my eyes were growing tired. The wind and sun had stung my cheeks, and I was about to suggest we land and make camp for the night when one of Ysix's brood made a strange, gargled noise.

"Verkaia?" I shouted, calling to the youngest of Ysix's brood.

Jaydra threw us into a tight turn that made my stomach churn. It churned even more when I saw a black shape like a huge arrow sticking out of the dragon's side.

Saffron called out the dragon's name again.

For a moment, my vision blurred as Verkaia's pain swept into Jaydra's thoughts and into mine. But I didn't need to see in order to feel what we had to do.

Fly to her, Jaydra, fly fast!

My heart was in agony as I held on tightly to Jaydra's new harness. Jaydra gave a roar and sped toward Verkaia's side. Reaching out with her claws, she snagged the huge arrow and pulled it from Verkaia. Verkaia gave a snarl. A smear of blood marred her scales, but she could still fly and soared upward now.

Who did this? Who is attacking us? Jaydra's thoughts swirled with a mixture of panic and fury.

However, she was not as furious as Ysix, who roared spit fire and then sent thundering thoughts that rocked me. *Who dares attack Ysix's brood?*

The sun seemed to darken for a moment as Ysix crossed in front of it, her rage sweeping out as dark as her shadow.

"Saffron?" Bower shouted. "Down there!"

I looked to where he was pointing. For a moment, I saw nothing—but then the ground shimmered. Shapes began to emerge and soon became the forms of soldiers. Enric had indeed been using his magic to hide his troops, but now they were on the move, spilling out from under the cover of magic and trees. I glimpsed immense shapes, much taller and broader than a human, their armor dark with rust. It was the king's Iron Guard. They held huge spears and swords, and carried giant bows of blackened metal with long darts that they aimed skyward.

Only these were not darts.

"Harpoons!" Bower shouted.

He was right. I had seen such metal harpoons used by the island villagers to hunt the huge fish of the ocean.

One of the Iron Guard hefted a metal harpoon and threw it toward one of the black dragons. The dragon turned and spun, but the harpoon hit, and then I saw the chain attached to the end of the harpoon. The dragon thrashed in the air and her rider only barely managed to hang onto her horns as the dragon spun about on the end of the chain.

"Jaydra, the chain," I shouted, pointing her in the direction of the thick iron chain that was attached from the end of the shaft.

The black dragon and the guard were engaged in a deadly tug of war, but more of the Iron Guard were raising their deadly bows.

Jaydra dove underneath Ysix, who was belching fire at the Iron Guard. Seizing the chain between her front claws, Jaydra wrenching it apart. The black dragon whistled her thanks and spun away as another wave of harpoons sped past us.

Don't get hit! Please, den-sister, fly fast!

I sent all of my strength to Jaydra as she dodged and dived, batting away one of the harpoons with her tail.

Cowards! Ysix's anger nearly split my skull. With a snarl and a roar, she tucked her wings close, falling into a dive.

"Ysix, no!" I shouted, but too late.

One harpoon tore through Ysix's wing, another speared her tail. She slammed into the Iron Guard archers, scattering them and smashing two of them, their parts left to flop on the ground.

Ysix lit the forest with her fire, sending every man in the king's arm running.

"Saffron, we have to help her," Bower shouted.

I knew what he meant. We had fought the Iron Guard before but we only barely survived.

Glancing around us, I saw the black dragons had become what seemed an angry, dark cloud. I knew they must be unsure what to do—Ysix their den-mother was on the ground. They both must wish to flee and must want to help her.

Turning, I called out to Bower, "How many Iron Guard do you see?"

Jaydra was already getting ready to launch into a dive that would take her to Ysix's side.

Looking down, I could see the Iron Guard were converging on Ysix and trying to chain her to the ground.

"No more than fifteen," Bower called to me.

Reaching out to Jaydra, I showed her the idea I had in mind for our attack. She agreed with a fierce snarl, flicking her tail to change her direction just slightly.

Jaydra fell into a steep dive. Bower gave a yell, and Jaydra roared.

Release Ysix and fight like hunters!

294

Ysix managed to catch one Iron Guard in a jet of orange dragon fire. The force of the blaze knocked the guard down and it let go of the chain it had been holding. Its metal armor glowed red, but it was not melting. It rose again to its feet.

We would need a hotter fire than what a blue dragon such as Ysix could produce.

Jaydra swooped low to the ground and seized one of the largest boulders on the hilltop. She spread her wings and soared up again.

A harpoon narrowly missed Jaydra, and I glanced back to see it skim past Bower. He ducked closer to Jaydra's spines.

Looking down, I judged us to be high enough and called out to Jaydra, "Now!"

She released the boulder. It fell, smashing onto one of the Iron Guards holding Ysix and pinning the guard to the ground.

But Ysix was still tangled in chains.

Ryland came hurtling past, his dragon roaring. The dragon seized an Iron Guard in a grip that would have crushed any weaker creature. It swept the Iron Guard up into the air and then dropped it from high into the sky, sending it tumbling, its arms and legs flailing even as it crashed onto the sharp rocks below.

Four other Iron Guards swarmed over onto Ysix, trying to hold her while the others raised their bows again.

One harpoon missed and Jaydra batted another aside with her tail, sending it slamming back at the Iron Guard.

"Bower, you've read the stories of the Dragon Riders. How do we fight this?"

He shook his head. "I never read of this happening. This is a new weapon—we need a new attack!"

Before I could ask what he meant, the air around us seemed to darken and chill. It was too much like the dream of the darkness. Cold seemed to seep under my skin and spread through me like a sickness.

Below us the forest seemed to move—but it wasn't the trees moving. No, Enric's army became visible, stepping out from under the trees, a force so vast I had no idea how we could ever defeat them

But there was something else here—I could feel Enric here as one feels the ice of a freezing winter.

CHAPTER 20

COUNTERING THE KING

"It's an ambush!" I shouted to Saffron.

I had thought we had only fifteen Iron Guards and a few troops to deal with, but now I saw mounted horsemen and infantry in such large numbers that this had to be nearly the entire army of Torvald.

How had he hidden them? Or gotten them here so quickly? Or had they been on the march here ever since our first fight against the Iron Guard? He must have thought to crush us early, before we had a chance to prepare.

I glanced around at the few dragons we had in the air, and then called out to Saffron, "We have to pull back!"

She didn't seem to hear me. But I could see from the direction of her gaze that she was staring at the army that was appearing over the land like a dark tide.

Neither of us had ever seen a battle of this size, but at least I had read the accounts in a few books. I also knew what happened when a large force such as this met a small one, such as the one we had. "We aren't ready for this battle. We lack the numbers we need."

She pointed below us. "We have to free Ysix. Call in the other dragons. Any other dragon. *All* the other dragons."

She was right. Our only hope might be the havoc the immense Crimson Reds could cause.

Closing my eyes, I took a deep breath and reached inside to the place where I could feel the tingle of Jaydra's thoughts.

In the next instant, I could feel Ysix's anger and pain. Jaydra's desperation filled my mind. I sensed the black dragons panic and their need to reach Ysix.

And then I stretched out beyond these dragons.

The world suddenly seemed filled with dragons—some curious about me, some insulted that I would disturb them, some excited about my contact. Breathing hard, my heart pounding, I sent my thoughts to all I could touch.

We call for your aid. Come protect your brothers and sisters, your winged family that makes their home in the skies.

A pulse of power seemed to ripple out of me and shimmered on my skin like sunlight. The hairs on the back of my neck and the back of my arms rose. A tingling vibrated in my chest and head. This was like the feeling I'd had when Saffron had called on her magic—but it was also different. For now I could feel a pulse that seemed to extend in every direction, as if I was hearing the heartbeat of every dragon in the word..

The sensation vanished in an instant as a single word floated up from the forest below us.

"Fools."

Eyes flying open, I stared down at the Iron Guard below, which now numbered at least a few hundred. They faced the sky, ominously still now.

And I knew Enric was speaking through them.

But then Saffron turned, slapped my arm and pointed to a single black steed. The rider wore pale, gold armor. Even this far away, I could see the waxy sheen of his skin and the glint of a crown on his head.

Enric.

The contrast between his glittering armor and his soldiers with their dark uniforms and grim, shadowed faces seemed as stark as the contrast between day and night.

An army of mounted knights surrounded Enric. Behind them rumbled stranger contraptions pulled by black horses.

Enric raised one white hand and the world seemed to still. I could not even hear the whisper of the wind. There was only Enric's voice.

"Foolish children, you have disobeyed the rightful king for too long! I gave you, Saffron Maddox, the chance to reign at my side, to learn who and what you are, and all you do is cavort with dragons and traitors. May you all be cursed!"

At the last word, a force seemed to erupt from the Iron Guard, like a wave made of pure air. It spun up, dust marking its path and hit like a gale. The blast left my limbs aching. Pain slammed into my chest. I clutched at it, unable to draw a breath.

Saffron cried out and doubled over, and Jaydra for a moment tumbled free before she could right herself with a rumble. Around me, I saw the other dragons and riders tumbling as if rocked by a sudden wind.

How can we fight against this?

I had no magic like Enric. I had no army of metal soldiers to do my bidding. My eyes stung and I wanted suddenly to turn and run. Enric was right—I was nothing. I had—

Bower has no magic. Bower has Saffron.

Jaydra's thoughts spun into me and seemed to be the slap of warmth I needed. I straightened. Jaydra was right. I had Saffron—she had me. We had beaten back Enric's magic in the dream. Why not do the same here and now.

"Saffron, take my hand!" I reached forward to touch Saffron's shoulder. Despite how my arms ached with the residue of Enric's curse, the connection I had with Saffron and Jaydra thrummed between us. Warmth bled into me, pushing back the chill that had seemed to seize my heart.

I went beyond that—reaching out again to every other dragon in the world.

"What are you doing?" Saffron mumbled. Jaydra began to steady in the air.

"It's our connection. I am connected to every dragon, and to you. And you have your magic. Use that! Use your magic through me—through the dragons. Enric might have an army and his Iron Guard, but we have our dragons.

Saffron stiffened, but then she held out her hands. Her power glittered on her fingertips and spread up to her wrist and then to her arms. It was a like the rising spark of a dragon's fire, growing hotter and building into an explosive power.

The ache left my arms, and the world seemed to warm.

Saffron was doing this—she was pushing back Enric's magic. But Jaydra gave a shriek and wobbled in the sky. I glanced down to see a blackened harpoon jutting from Jaydra's side. It had slipped between her scales and dark blood began to well. It was distraction enough.

"Jaydra!" Saffron screamed the word. The glow of Saffron's power began to fade. I could feel panic pouring out of Saffron and into me through our connection—and then Saffron's power erupted with a flash.

CHAPTER 21

RIDERS ON THE STORM

One instant I seemed to be connected with Bower—and with more dragons than I knew existed. The next, my own side throbbed with an echo of Jaydra's pain. My heart seemed to stutter and then the magic I had been holding within me uncoiled and took over.

"Saffron!"

I heard Bower's yell as if from far away. I knew without looking that he was staring at me, eyes wide, but I had slipped to another place. It was as if I could see everything at once from high up in the clouds and also from very close. Black dragons tumbled and scrambled away. The army below seemed to shrink back. Even Enric's illusion of youth and power faded. Only the Iron Guard stood still and unmoved.

I felt oddly detached from everything, and I watched myself as if it was someone else muttering the ancient, odd sounds that tumbled from my lips. My hands, raised in the air, moved of their own accord, making shapes I knew but did not know. Drawing power I did not recognize, but also knew within my heart would crush those who had harmed me.

For to harm Jaydra was to strike at me.

My magic would not stand for that.

Den-sister, come back to us!

Jaydra's thoughts reached me, but only barely.

For now my head could only heed the power that filled my heart.

Lifting my head, I muttered in a tone of voice that seemed to be someone else's voice. I spoke the words that called down fury, that pulled the storm from the sky. I wanted the world to hurt as I hurt. I wanted the storm to rage as I raged.

A boom split the sky, the answer to my words. Dark clouds boiled up, turning the day to night. Rain began to fall, and wind howled.

And still it was not enough. My anger and rage wanted more. I was fury.

Saffron?

Jaydra once again tugged at my thoughts, but her worry could not sooth the pain in my soul. My power was unleashed—and it would only be satisfied with the storm I was pulling

Jaydra lurched to one side. I could hear Bower shouting as if from miles away. And Ysix screamed in fury and agony that found a home within me.

Rain began to lash my face, fierce as I was. Storm clouds swirled and thickened. But it was still not enough for me.

"Saffron?" Bower shouted.

I couldn't seem to think what he wanted. Power raged through me, and Bower's clumsy attempts to reach me were less even than Enric's futile grabs for my attention.

I was the storm now. I was cleansing rain and wind that would sweep away all who stood in my path.

Jaydra. Use tail. Use chain against the guards. Bower's words made no sense to me, but from miles up in the clouds I saw him unclip himself from his harness and crawl with a dagger in hand to where the black harpoon lodged in my side. Or was that in Jaydra? I could no longer tell.

From far below, Enric bellowed through his Iron Guard, "Surrender! Surrender your dragons!" With a twist of my hand, I turned the rain to hail, sharp and biting. Everything seemed to be happening not to me, but to someone else, someone far away. I caught a hailstone almost as big as my thumb and stared at it, then tossed it to let it fall on its way to the army below.

Spreading my arms wide, I spread myself into the wind—into the storm.

Glancing down, I saw Enric, surrounded by his knights, staring up at us, watching what he thought was our demise.

We'll see who is the fool now.

The hail grew, becoming as large as my fist at my command. They pummeled dragon, rider army, king and Iron Guard—for my magic wanted all to hurt. All to feel my pain.

I raged—and the sky raged back at me.

Lightning streaked down from the black clouds I had called, scorching the ground, striking down one Iron Guard.

I knew suddenly I would blast the world—I was the lightning, I was the storm. I was—

Saffron!

Jaydra's urgent plea shook me from my magic—I was suddenly in my body again and not in the clouds. Glancing around, I saw Jaydra was being pulled down to the ground by the Iron Guard and the chain attached to her side and the harpoon.

She suddenly whipped around in the air, pulling on the chain that held her. She lashed out with her tail, striking the Iron Guard, sending them toppling like dominoes. They released their grip and Jaydra soared back into the air, roaring, the heavy iron chain still dangling from her side. With a slash, Bower cut a gash and the harpoon dropped away, out of Jaydra's hide.

Jaydra's mind brushed against mine, as close as if she had never vanished.

Jaydra, where did you go?

Where did Jaydra go? Saffron's magic took Saffron away. Jaydra couldn't reach Saffron or Bower.

Her fear drifted to me through her thoughts. I could see why, for the heaviest storm I had ever seen had fallen upon us.

Bower climbed back to his harness, his knife bloody, and yelled, "You called the storm—can you send it away?"

I shrugged and waved my hands. "I don't know what I did. I just reacted to Jaydra being hurt. But where is Ysix?"

Pointing down, I waved at the ice and hail now covering where I'd last seen Ysix.

The Iron Guard that had held her now seemed to hold noting but frozen chains. Icicles from frozen rain weighted down their arms from the wind whipping against them, slowing them even more than the ice. Even the dragons were having problems flying in these conditions.

But the ice was one thing the Iron Guard could not defeat. I saw that at once and shouted to Bower, "We have to use the ice and your idea together!"

"The tail whips?" Bower asked.

"Tell the other dragons, Bower. Talk to them as their king!" I gasped, the air biting cold in my lungs. I shivered and glanced around. The mountain dragons were handling the cold better than the island dragons, and I wondered how long even great Ysix of the warm Western Isles could last under this freezing sleet.

Once again the air thrummed as Bower reached out with the affinity he had with all dragons. His voice echoed in my head.

Use the ice against our enemy!

Ysix's brood was the first to respond.

They caught the images Bower sent them with his thoughts and used his plan. Swooping down toward their enemy, they spun at the last moment and used the wind to power their turns as they slapped down the Iron Guards.

The air rang with the clang of metal and screeches of the dragons.

The Iron Guard, left slow by ice and cold, fell and skidded across the thickening ice on the ground. The Iron Guards could no longer find their mark with their harpoons in this storm, which was only growing worse.

We still had to reach Ysix, and I started to tell Bower that when a hard boom break the sky. A flash erupted from the king's strange metal carts, and I saw they had cannons like on the king's ships. Metal balls screamed through the air.

A dragon's scream left me wincing, and I saw a black dragon falter and then plummet from the sky.

Magic tingled in my chest once again and flared from my hands.

Saffron-sister! Jaydra threw her mind toward mine, wrapping me in her awareness, trying to save me seemingly from even myself.

Another cannon boomed. I couldn't stop myself. I threw out my hands, my anger and magic bursting out. Words I didn't know flew out as well.

Wood cracked and splintered and one of the carts jerked into the air and collapsed.

"My magic worked," I gasped, staring at my hands. I'd done something—something intentional for once.

"Do that again," Bower shouted.

I did, striking out as the storm raged around us. Both Enric's army and the dragons were caught in the icy gale, but the storm seemed to seek out those on the ground. The winds seemed fiercer far below, and the king's troops had not come prepared for winter.

With a flash, flames erupted across the sky. The red dragons burst through the dark clouds like vengeance on wings. Lightning crackling along their shoulders. The flicker of electricity made the den mother snarl and roar as she unleashed her fire on the king's soldiers.

And then even more dragons flew out of the clouds.

Bower had not just called a few dragons—he seemed to have called all.

I had never thought I would see the likes of what I saw now.

Flashes of light illuminated storm clouds and floods of dragons falling on the soldiers below. Horses reared and bolted into the forest, bucking and sending their riders flying. Dragons knocked down the Iron Guard with their tails or snatched up any man who tried to stand before them.

And everywhere, the sounds of screaming and shouting and dragon roars echoed.

"Free those chained," Bower shouted, using both his voice and his connection to the dragons.

The other dragon riders and their dragons fell like hunting packs of wolves on the frozen statues of the Iron Guards. Two of the Iron Guard shattered when the dragons hit them.

But where had Enric gone?

Jaydra swooped low over a mound of snow and ice, with two Iron Guards frozen in place and still holding the frozen chains that attached to a harpoon. I forgot about Enric and thought to Jaydra, *Is that Ysix?*

An idea hit me—could I free Ysix with my magic, but I did not want to risk hurting her. I had controlled my magic once, but I might not again. So I asked Jaydra to call up her flames.

Jaydra will try. She growled, landing on the ground and rearing up.

"What is she doing?" Bower yelled.

Jaydra arched her back and her neck.

"Her fire. Not all dragons can summon it, and not all the flames are strong enough." I put both hands on the side of her neck to feel the powerful bellows and muscles there starting to pump.

You can do this, Jaydra. Den-sister, fire-starter, mighty hunter, show them what you are. What you were always meant to be!

A haunting whine rose from within Jaydra, growing fast into a roar. She spread her jaws wide and a whoosh of flame brushed over the mound of ice. Jaydra's fire wasn't as molten orange as Ysix's, but the flames hit the snow, turning it into steam and water.

For a moment, I could see nothing because of the clouds of steam and the smoke from Jaydra's flame.

But then Jaydra gave a trill and I shouted, "Ysix, answer us!"

A bolt of molten orange flame lit the scene and Ysix roared into the sky, shaking off metal chains and ice. She seemed in far too much pain to answer but flew up, screeched for all dragons to get out of her way.

Glancing around, I saw we had freed all the dragons. It was time to fly northwards and to safety.

Enric's voice rose up, soaring above the wind that beat at us. "Traitors! Thieves!"

His power struck me the next instant.

Enric emerged from the stormy battlefield with a half dozen of his knights. His horse I realized was not a real animal but a mechanical beast. Enric's hand glowed with a horrible, sickly purple hue as he spread his magic in front of him. I swayed and caught at Jaydra's spines so I would not fall. Pain struck me as if Enric had plunged a sword into my chest.

With a rumble, Jaydra tried to launch herself into the air, but she only hopped on the ground.

I felt as if I was being wrapped in a thousand burning chains.

Enric pulled his mechanical horse to a halt. "Kneel! Kneel before your king!"

Another wave of pain ripped through me. Jaydra gave a gasp and collapsed to the ground, her legs buckling.

I had escaped from Enric before, but only with Bower's help.

"Bower…need you," I gasped, wondering if my bones were going to fracture. Turning, I grabbed Bower's shaking hand.

We had to combine what was left of our ebbing strength.

"You seek to bring these monsters to my capital? Return them to my kingdom?" Lightning sizzled, flashing white, and for a moment I saw Enric's real face. The illusion of him being young and darkly handsome faded. I saw him as he was, ancient and more skeleton than man. His head bald, his skin wrinkled and sagging, his body thin and hunched. How long had he been using his powers to extend his life? For decades or for many generations?

He slashed his fist in front of him. "Dragons demean us. They befoul human nature. They are nothing more than vermin upon the land."

Rage sparked within Bower. It spread to me, igniting my magic.

From behind me, Bower's voice rose up, strong and clear. "Dragons do not demean us—they remind us of what we can be. And you are no fit king, Enric Maddox. You will fall, I promise!"

I lifted my hand, but my magic seemed only a pale glow—I had used too much of it. I had saved nothing.

Through Bower, I could sense the other dragons fleeing. With Ysix freed, her brood rose above the storm and sped away, the mountain dragons going with her. Bower sent the red dragons as well, and released the others. I knew he was here, buying them time to get away.

We couldn't defeat the king—I was too tired and had spent too much of my power summoning this storm and blasting the king's cannons.

I could see that Enric sensed I was weakening, for his power glowed darker. He stretched out his hand. Pain enveloped me.

A screech cut through the agony lashing me. With a sudden flash, the pain evaporated.

In front of me Ryland and his black dragon now tangled with Enric. The king's knights had scattered, their horses giving terrified whinnies and bolting into the storm. Ryland's dragon took to the sky again, waved away by Ryland.

Bloodied and bare-chested, lifting his sword he shouted, "Fly. Now. Go. The True King must live."

Enric still on his metal horse, but with it fallen and frozen and pinning him to the ground, lifted a glowing fist. Ryland's sword shattered.

"Ryland," I shouted, but Jaydra launched herself into the air.

The last I saw of Ryland was him facing Enric, a knife in Ryland's hand and Enric's magic, dark and fierce.

And then we flew into freezing clouds and at last reached above them to the warmth of the sun again.

EPILOGUE

A BITTER VICTORY

"Saffron?" I didn't want to wake her, but she had slept for hours now.

It had taken a long flight to reach the caverns where the Three-Rivers clan had taken refuge. The Crimson Red dragons led the way. The clan, instead of mourning the loss of Ryland, planned to celebrate his heroic death—a war chief, it seemed, could ask for no better end to his days.

It was cold this deep in the mountains, and the wind was biting and fierce, but it was a natural cold, one that came from Saffron's magic. The caverns smelled of minerals in the rock and even the dragons liked them.

I had glanced back once at the magical blizzard Saffron had called up. I couldn't tell if it was growing larger or fading. I didn't know enough about weather or enough about magic to tell. I did know Saffron felt bad about having called it up, even unknowingly.

She had asked once on our flight if I thought the storm she had created would spread across the Middle Kingdom without end.

For a moment, I had reached my mind toward it as if it was just another dragon. Nothing happened. Storms were not dragons, and so perhaps they could not be spoken to.

Now, Saffron opened her eyes and stared up at me. I touched her shoulder. "Are you well? You've slept for more than a day."

"I think so," she said, her voice so soft I had to strain to hear it.

Liar. Jaydra's thoughts contradicted Saffron's words. Since I had spoken to all dragons, I seemed to be having an easier time talking to Jaydra.

Sitting down on the floor next to Saffron, I leaned my back against the smooth cavern wall. "You know, I think these are dragon caves. They're a lot like the caves back on Den Mountain."

That, at least, had Saffron sitting up and looking around.

Jaydra's thoughts suddenly filled my mind, but I knew she was hiding the words from Saffron. *Maddox magic. Saffron has no control—it is controlling Saffron. When Saffron calls it, it comes between Saffron and Jaydra.*

I realized with a falling heart that Jaydra was right.

Saffron really did need to learn to control not just her magic, but herself. She would be a danger to everyone until then. But how could I help her with that?

"We made it out," I told Saffron. "That has to count for something. And…and while there was time when you seemed to give yourself over to the magic completely, you did that out of love. To protect us all. You also managed some control—you can learn more."

Saffron put a hand on the smooth wall and trailed her fingers over it. "How many came back?"

I let out a long breath. "It's a tattered band of dragons and their riders. We lost three riders. Two dragons. Ryland—"

"Gave his life to save the True King. Do you finally believe you are that, Bower?"

I stood again and put my shoulders back. "To do anything less would be an insult to Ryland—it would diminish his deeds. The Three-Rivers clan plans to sing of his great exploits tonight. I think we should be there."

I held out my hand to Saffron.

We had already paid a heavy price for our escape. But we had learned a few things about Enric's weaknesses. And about our own.

And now I had to start thinking of myself as a king—and stop doubting myself. If there was one thing I'd learned from that battle—and from dragons—it was that a king must inspire those who follow him. Saffron needed me just now. And someday soon I knew I would have need of her powers—powers under control.

She glanced at my hand, at my face, and a small smile quirked her mouth. "King Bower—kind of sounds good, doesn't it?"

END OF 'DRAGONS OF KINGS'

Book 2 of the Upon Dragon's Breath Trilogy

Dragons of Dark, Book Three of Upon

Dragon's Breath Trilogy is out now!

Thank you for purchasing 'Dragons of Kings'

(Upon Dragon's Breath Trilogy Book Two)

If you would like to hear more about what I am up to, or continue to follow the stories set in this world with these characters—then please sign up for my mailing list at

http://www.subscribepage.com/b7o3i0

You can also find me on me on

Facebook: www.facebook.com/AvaRichardsonBooks/

Homepage: www.AvaRichardsonBooks.com

63337783R00182

Made in the USA
Lexington, KY
03 May 2017